FRIEND
HIGH PLA

D1757110

Donna Leon was named by *The Times* as one
Greatest Crime Writers. She is an award-winn
novelist, celebrated for the bestselling Brune
Donna has lived in Venice for thirty years and p
lived in Switzerland, Saudi Arabia, Iran and Chi
she worked as a teacher. Donna's books have b
lated into thirty-five languages and have been p
around the world.

Her previous novels featuring Commissario
have all been highly acclaimed; including *Friend*
Places, which won the CWA Macallan Silver Da
Fiction, *Fatal Remedies*, *Doctored Evidence*, *A Sea o*
and *Beastly Things*.

Praise for *Friends in High Places* and Donna Leon

'Leon is a skilful plotter . . . Brunetti is a nicely shaded
creation, a moral man who is also all too human. *Friends in
High Places* is a splendid read, clever and provoking.'
Observer

'*Friends in High Places* [is an] elegant police procedural set in
beautifully imagined Venice.'
Sunday Times

'Beautifully written and immaculately plotted, *Friends in
High Places* is further proof that Leon can do no wrong.'
Scotsman

'An elegant and cunning writer . . . With her usual skilful
plotting and perfectly judged pace, Leon teases out a tangled
drama of institutional sleaze, loan-sharking and drug abuse
. . . This is Leon's best so far . . . I don't think I could
understand a crime fan who didn't love Donna Leon.'
Scotland on Sunday

Also by Donna Leon

DONNA
LEON

FRIENDS IN
HIGH PLACES

arrow books

Arrow Books
20 Vauxhall Bridge Road
London SW1V 2SA

Arrow Books is part of the Penguin Random House
group of companies whose addresses can be found at
global.penguinrandomhouse.com

Penguin
Random House
UK

First published in Great Britain by William Heinemann in 2000
First published in paperback by Arrow Books in 2001
Reissued by Arrow Books in 2009

www.penguin.co.uk

A CIP catalogue record for this book
is available from the British Library.

ISBN 9780099536581
ISBN 9780099269328 (export)

Typeset by SX Composing DTP, Rayleigh, Essex
Printed and bound in Great Britain by Clays Ltd, St Ives plc.

Penguin Random House is committed to a sustainable future
for our business, our readers and our planet. This book is made
from Forest Stewardship Council® certified paper.

MIX
Paper from
responsible sources
FSC® C018179

for Christine Donougher and
Roderick Conway-Morris

. . . Ah dove
Sconsigliato t'inoltri?
In queste mura
Sai, che non è sicura
La tua vita

Where are you going so rashly?
You know that within these walls
Your life is not safe.

Lucio Silla
Mozart

1

When the doorbell rang, Brunetti lay supine on the sofa in his living room, a book propped open on his stomach. Because he was alone in the apartment, he knew he had to get up and answer it, but before he did, he wanted to finish the last paragraph of the eighth chapter of the *Anabasis*, curious to know what new disasters awaited the retreating Greeks. The bell rang a second time, two insistent, quick buzzes, and he put the book face down, took off his glasses and placed them on the arm of the sofa, and got to his feet. His steps were slow, regardless of the insistence with which the bell had sounded. Saturday morning, off duty, the house to himself, Paola gone to Rialto in search of soft-shelled crabs, and the doorbell had to ring.

He assumed it was one of the children's friends, come in search of either Chiara or Raffi or, worse, one of the bringers of religious truth who delighted in interrupting the rest of the hard-working. He asked of life nothing more than to lie on his back reading Xenophon while he waited for his wife to come home with soft-shelled crabs.

'Yes?' he said into the answerphone, making his voice sound so unwelcoming as to discourage aimless youth and frighten off zeal of any age.

'Guido Brunetti?' a man's voice asked.

'Yes. What is it?'

'I'm from the Ufficio Catasto. About your apartment.' When Brunetti said nothing, the man asked, 'Did you get our letter?'

At the question, Brunetti recalled having received some sort of official document a month or so ago, a paper filled with the catch phrases of bureaucracy, something about the deeds to the apartment or the building permits that were attached to the deeds: he couldn't remember. He had done no more than glance at it and blanch at the formulaic language, before slipping it back into its envelope and dropping it into the large majolica platter that stood on the table to the right of the door.

'Did you get our letter?' the man repeated.

'Ah, yes,' Brunetti answered.

'I've come to talk about it.'

'About what?' Brunetti asked, propping the phone under his left ear and bending to reach toward the pile of papers and envelopes that lay on the platter.

'Your apartment,' the man answered. 'About what we wrote in the letter.'

'Of course, of course,' Brunetti said, leafing through papers and envelopes.

'I'd like to talk to you about it if I might.'

Caught off guard by the request, Brunetti conceded. 'All right,' he said, pushing the buzzer that would open the *portone* four floors below. 'Top floor.'

'I know,' the man answered.

Brunetti replaced the speaker and pulled a few envelopes from the bottom of the pile. There was a bill from ENEL, a postcard from the Maldives he hadn't seen before and which he paused to read. And there was the envelope, the name of the issuing office in blue letters at the top left corner. He removed the paper, unfolded it and held it at arm's length to bring the letters into focus, and read through it quickly.

The same impenetrable phrases caught his eye: 'Pursuant to Statute Number 1684–B of the Commission of Fine Arts'; 'With reference to Section 2784 of Article 127 of the Civil Code of 24 June 1948, subsection 3, paragraph 5'; 'Failure to provide this issuing office with adequate documentation'; 'Value calculated according to sub-paragraph 34–V–28 of the Decree of 21 March 1947.' He ran his eye quickly down the first page and then turned to the second, but still he found only officialese and numbers. Schooled by long experience working in the Venetian bureaucracy, he knew something might be hidden in the last paragraph, and so he turned to that, which did indeed inform him that he could expect further communication from the Ufficio Catasto. He turned back to the first page but whatever meaning might lurk behind the words continued to elude him.

Close as he was to the front door, he could hear the footsteps on the last flight of steps and so opened the door even before the doorbell rang. The man in front of him was still moving up the steps and had already raised a hand to knock, and so the first thing Brunetti saw was the sharp contrast between the raised fist and the perfectly unassuming man who stood behind it. The young man, startled by the sudden opening of the door, had surprise splashed across his face. The face was long, his nose the thin beak so common to Venetians. He had dark brown eyes and brown hair that looked as if it had recently been cut. He wore a suit which might have been blue but might just as easily have been grey. His tie was dark and had a small, indistinguishable pattern. In his right hand he carried a worn brown leather briefcase; it completed the picture of every colourless bureaucrat Brunetti had ever had to deal with, as though part of their job training was the mastery of the art of rendering themselves invisible.

'Franco Rossi,' he said, shifting his briefcase to his other hand and extending the right.

Brunetti took it, shook hands briefly, and

stepped back to allow him to enter.

Politely, Rossi asked permission and then stepped into the apartment. Inside, he stopped and waited for Brunetti to tell him where to go.

'In here, please,' Brunetti said, leading him back toward the room where he had been reading. Brunetti went over to the sofa, slipped the old vaporetto ticket he used as a marker inside his book, and placed it on the table. He gestured to Rossi to take a seat opposite him and himself sat on the sofa.

Rossi sat on the edge of the chair and pulled the briefcase up on to his knees. 'I realize it's Saturday, Signor Brunetti, so I'll try not to take too much of your time.' He looked across at Brunetti and smiled. 'You received our letter, didn't you? I hope you've had time to consider it, Signore,' he said with another small smile, then lowered his head and opened his briefcase. He pulled a thick blue folder from it. He centred it carefully on top of the briefcase and tapped at an errant paper that tried to slip from the bottom until it was safely back inside.

'As a matter of fact,' Brunetti said, taking the letter from his pocket, where he'd stuffed it when he answered the door, 'I was just rereading it, and I must say I find the language a bit impenetrable.'

Rossi looked up, and Brunetti saw a flash of genuine surprise pass across his face. 'Really? I thought it was very clear.'

With an easy smile, Brunetti said, 'I'm sure it is to those of you who deal with these matters every day. But to those of us who aren't familiar with your office's particular language or terminology, well, it's a bit difficult to understand.' When Rossi said nothing, Brunetti added, 'I'm sure all of us know the language of our own bureaucracy; perhaps it's only when we pass into that of another that we find it difficult.' He smiled again.

'What bureaucracy are you familiar with, Signor Brunetti?' Rossi asked.

Because he was not in the habit of broadcasting the fact that he was a policeman, Brunetti answered only, 'I studied law.'

'I see,' replied Rossi. 'I shouldn't think our terminology would be very different from yours.'

'Perhaps it's no more than my unfamiliarity with the civil codes referred to in your letter,' Brunetti said smoothly.

Rossi considered this for a moment and then answered, 'Yes, that's entirely possible. What is it, though, that you don't understand?'

'What it means,' Brunetti answered directly, no longer willing to pretend that he understood.

Again that puzzled look, so frank that it made Rossi look almost boyish. 'I beg your pardon?'

'What it means. I read it, but because I have no idea, as I told you, of the nature of the regulations to which it refers, I don't know what it means, what it all applies to.'

'Your apartment, of course,' Rossi answered quickly.

'Yes, I understood that much,' Brunetti said in

a voice he had to force to sound patient. 'Since it came from your office, I gathered at least that. What I don't understand is what interest your office could take in my apartment.' Nor, for that fact, did he understand why an employee of that office should choose to visit him on a Saturday.

Rossi looked down at the folder on his lap and then up at Brunetti, who was surprised suddenly to notice how long and dark his lashes were, much like a woman's. 'I see, I see,' Rossi said, nodded, and looked back down at the folder. He opened it and pulled out a smaller one, studied the label on its cover for an instant, and handed it across to Brunetti, saying, 'Perhaps this will help to make it clear.' Before he closed the folder that was still on his lap, he carefully aligned the papers that lay inside.

Brunetti opened the folder and removed the papers from it. Seeing how close-set the type was, he leaned to the left and picked up his glasses. At the top of the first page was the address of the building; below it appeared plans of the apartments beneath his own. On the next page was a list of past owners of each of those spaces, beginning with the storerooms on the ground floor. The next two pages contained what appeared to be capsule histories of the restorations done to all of the apartments in the building since 1947, listing the dates when certain permissions were requested and given, the date work actually began, and the date when final approval was given of the completed work. No mention was made of his own apartment, which suggested to Brunetti that this information must be contained in the papers Rossi still held.

From what he could make out, Brunetti realized that the apartment directly below them had last been restored in 1977, when the current owners moved in. Last restored officially, that is. They'd had dinner with the Calistas more than a few times and had been pleased with the almost unimpeded view that spread out from the windows of their living room, yet the windows indicated on the plans looked quite small, and there seemed to be only four, not six. He saw that the small guest bathroom to the left of the Calistas' entrance hall was nowhere indicated. He wondered how that could be, but Rossi was certainly not the man to ask. The less the Ufficio Catasto knew about what got added to or shifted around inside the building, the better it would be for everyone living there.

Glancing across at Rossi, he asked, 'These records go back a long time. Have you any idea how old the building is?'

Rossi shook his head. 'Not precisely. But from the location and the windows on the ground floor, I'd say the original structure dates from the late fifteenth century, not earlier.' He paused and considered this for a moment, then added, 'And I'd say the top floor was added in the early nineteenth century.'

Brunetti looked up from the plans, surprised. 'No, it's much later than that. From after the war.' When Rossi didn't respond, he added,

'The Second World War.'

When Rossi still didn't comment, Brunetti asked, 'Wouldn't you say that's true?'

After a moment's hesitation, Rossi said, 'I was talking about the top floor.'

'So am I,' Brunetti said sharply, annoyed that this functionary of an office that dealt with building permits didn't understand something as simple as that. He softened his voice and continued, 'When I bought it, it was my understanding that it was added after the last war, not in the nineteenth century.'

Instead of answering him, Rossi nodded toward the papers that were still in Brunetti's hand. 'Perhaps you could take a closer look at the last page, Signor Brunetti.'

Puzzled, Brunetti read again through the last paragraphs, but as far as he could make out, they still concerned only the two apartments below him. 'I'm not sure what you want me to see, Signor Rossi,' he said, looking up and removing his glasses. 'This concerns the apartments below us, not this apartment. No mention is made of this floor.' He turned the paper over to see if something was written on the other side, but it was blank.

'That's why I've come,' Rossi said, sitting up straighter in his chair as he spoke. He bent down and set his briefcase on the floor to the left of his feet, keeping the folder on his lap.

'Yes?' Brunetti said, leaning forward to hand the other one back to him.

Rossi took it from him and opened the larger

9

folder. He carefully slipped the smaller one back in place and closed the file. 'I'm afraid there is some doubt as to the official status of your apartment.'

' "Official status"?' Brunetti repeated, looking off to the left of Rossi, to the solid wall and then up to the equally solid ceiling. 'I'm not sure I understand what you mean.'

'There's some doubt about the apartment,' Rossi said with a smile that Brunetti thought looked a bit nervous. Before Brunetti could again ask for clarification, Rossi went on, 'That is, there are no papers in the Ufficio Catasto to show that building permits were ever granted for this entire floor, or that they were approved when it was built or,' and here he smiled again, 'that, in fact, it was ever built.' He cleared his throat and added, 'Our records show the floor below this one as the top floor.'

At first Brunetti thought he was joking, but then he saw the smile disappear and realized that Rossi was serious. 'But all of the plans are in the papers we got when we bought it,' Brunetti said.

'Could you show them to me?'

'Of course,' Brunetti answered and got to his feet. Without excusing himself, he went down to Paola's office and stood for a moment, studying the spines of the books that lined three walls of the room. Finally he reached to the top shelf and pulled down a large manila envelope filled with papers and took it back to the other room. Pausing inside the door to open the envelope, he pulled out the grey folder they'd received, almost twenty years ago, from the notary who had handled the purchase of the apartment for them. He came back to Rossi and handed this folder to him.

Rossi opened it and began to read, his finger tracing slowly down each line. He turned the page, read the next and thus until the end. A muffled 'Hmm' escaped his lips, but he said nothing. He finished the file, closed it, and left it lying on his knees.

'Are these the only papers?' Rossi asked.

'Yes, only what's in there.'

'No plans? No building permissions?'

Brunetti shook his head. 'No, I don't remember anything like that. Those are the only papers we were given at the time of the purchase. I don't think I've looked at them since then.'

'You said you studied law, Signor Brunetti?' Rossi finally asked.

'Yes, I did.'

'Are you practising as a lawyer?'

'No, I'm not,' Brunetti answered and left it at that.

'If you were or if you had been at the time you signed these papers, I'd be surprised you didn't notice, on page three of the deed, the paragraph which states that you are buying the apartment in the state, both legal and physical, in which you found it on the day on which ownership passed to you.'

'I believe that's pretty standard language in

any deed of transfer,' Brunetti said, summoning up a vague memory from one of his classes in civil law and hoping it was.

'The part about physical state is, certainly, though that about legal is not. Nor is this following sentence,' Rossi said, opening the folder again and searching until he found the passage. ' "In the absence of the *condono edilizio*, the buyer accepts full responsibility to obtain the same in a timely manner and hereby absolves the sellers of any responsibilities or conse-quences which might occur in regard to the legal state of the apartment and/or from the failure to obtain this *condono*." ' Rossi looked up, and Brunetti thought he saw a deep sadness in his eyes at the thought that someone might have signed such a thing.

Brunetti had no memory of that particular sentence. Indeed, at the time, they had both been so intent on buying the apartment that he had done what the notary told him to do, signed what he told him to sign.

Rossi turned back to the cover, where the name of the notary was listed. 'Did you select this notary?' he asked.

Brunetti didn't even remember the name and had to look at the cover. 'No, the seller suggested we use him, and so we did. Why?'

'No reason,' Rossi said, too quickly.

'Why? Do you know something about him?'

'I believe he's no longer practising as a notary,' Rossi said in a soft voice.

Finally out of patience at Rossi's questions,

Brunetti demanded, 'I'd like to know what all this means, Signor Rossi. Is there some dispute about our ownership of this apartment?'

Rossi gave his nervous smile again. 'I'm afraid it's a bit more complicated than that, Signor Brunetti.'

Brunetti had no idea what could be more serious than that. 'What is it, then?'

'I'm afraid this apartment doesn't exist.'

2

'What?' Brunetti cried before he could stop himself. He could hear the outrage in his voice but made no attempt to modify it. 'What do you mean, it doesn't exist?'

Rossi leaned back in his chair as if to remove himself from the immediate orbit of Brunetti's anger. He looked as if he found it puzzling to have someone react strongly to his having called into question the very existence of a perceived reality. When he saw that Brunetti had no violent intention, he relaxed minimally, adjusted the papers on his lap, and said, 'I mean that it doesn't exist for us, Signor Brunetti.'

'And what does that mean, not for you?' Brunetti asked.

'It means there are no records of it in our

office. No requests for building permits, no plans, no final approval of the work that was done. In short, there exists no documentary evidence that this apartment was ever built.' Before Brunetti could speak, Rossi added, placing his hand upon the file Brunetti had given him, 'And, unfortunately, you can't provide us with any.'

Brunetti recalled a story Paola had once told about an English writer who, confronted with a philosopher who maintained that reality did not exist, had kicked a rock and told the philosopher to take *that*. He turned his mind to more immediate matters. His knowledge of the workings of other city offices was vague, but it was not his understanding that this sort of information would be kept at the Ufficio Catasto, where, as far as he knew, only documents regarding ownership were kept. 'Is it normal for your office to interest itself in this?'

'No, not in the past,' Rossi answered with a timid smile, as if he approved of Brunetti's being well informed enough to ask. 'But as the result of a new directive, our office has been commissioned to assemble a comprehensive, computerized file of all of the apartments in the city that have been declared historical monuments by the Fine Arts Commission. This building is one of them. We're in the process of assembling the papers and files from the various offices in the city. This way, one central office, ours, will have copies of the complete documentation regarding every apartment on the list. In the end, this centralized system will save enormous amounts of time.'

Two weeks ago, Brunetti reflected, observing the smile of satisfaction Rossi gave as he said this, *Il Gazzettino* had carried an article announcing that, because of lack of funds, the dredging of the canals in the city had stopped. 'How many apartments are there?' he asked.

'Oh, we have no idea. That's one of the reasons this survey is being done.'

'How long ago was the survey begun?' Brunetti asked.

'Eleven months,' Rossi answered at once, leaving Brunetti little doubt that, if asked, he could supply the exact date, as well.

'And how many of these composite files have you compiled so far?'

'Well, because some of us have volunteered to work on Saturdays, we've done more than a hundred,' Rossi said, making no attempt to disguise his pride.

'And how many of you are working on this project?'

Rossi looked down at his right hand and, beginning with his thumb, began to count out his fellow workers. 'Eight, I think.'

'Eight,' Brunetti repeated. He turned his mind away from the calculations he had been making and asked, 'What does all of this mean? For me, specifically?'

Rossi's answer was immediate. 'When we don't have the papers for an apartment, the first thing we do is ask the owner to supply them, but there's nothing suitable in this file.' He indicated the slim folder. 'All you have is the deed of transfer, so we have to assume you weren't given any records the previous owners may have had concerning the original construction.' Before Brunetti could interrupt, he continued, 'And that means they are either lost, which is to suggest that they once existed, or else they never did. Exist, that is.' He looked across at Brunetti, who said nothing. Rossi continued: 'If they are lost, and if you say you never had them, then they must be lost in one of the city offices.'

'In that case,' Brunetti asked, 'what will you do to find them?'

'Ah,' Rossi began, 'it's not as simple as that. We have no obligation to keep copies of those documents. The Civil Code makes it clear that this is the responsibility of the person who owns the property under consideration. Without your copies, you can't argue that we've lost ours, if you see what I mean,' he said with another small smile. 'And it's impossible for us to initiate a search for the papers because we can't afford to use manpower in a search that might prove futile.' Seeing Brunetti's look, he explained, 'Because they might not exist, you see.'

Brunetti bit his lower lip and then asked, 'And if they haven't been lost and, instead, they never existed?'

Rossi looked down and prodded at the face of his wristwatch, centring it on his wrist. 'In that case, Signore,' he finally explained, glancing up at Brunetti, 'it means that permits were never granted and the final work was never approved.'

'That's possible, isn't it?' Brunetti asked. 'There was a tremendous amount of building just after the war.'

'Yes, there was,' Rossi said with the feigned modesty of one who spent his working life dealing with just these things. 'But most of those projects, whether they were minor restorations or extensive renovations, most of them have received the *condono edilizio* and so have gained legal status, at least with our office. The problem here is that no *condono* exists,' he said and waved a hand to encompass the offending walls, floor, ceiling.

'If I might repeat my question, Signor Rossi,' Brunetti said, forcing sweet calm and Olympian reasonableness into his voice, 'what does this mean for me and for my apartment, specifically?'

'I'm afraid I haven't the authority to answer that, Signore,' Rossi said, handing the file back to Brunetti. He leaned down and picked up his briefcase. Holding it, he got to his feet. 'My responsibility is only to visit home-owners and see if the missing papers are in their possession.' His face sobered, and Brunetti thought he saw real disappointment there. 'I'm sorry to learn that you don't have them.'

Brunetti stood. 'What happens now?'

'That depends upon the Commission of the Ufficio Catasto,' Rossi said and took a step toward the door.

Brunetti moved to the left, not quite blocking Rossi's exit, but certainly creating an obstacle between Rossi and the door. 'You said you think the floor below was added in the nineteenth century. But if it was added later, at the same time as this one was, would that change things?' Try as he might, Brunetti could not disguise the raw hope in his voice.

Rossi considered this for a long time and eventually said, his voice a study in caution and reserve, 'Perhaps. I know that floor has all the permits and approvals, so if this floor could be shown to have been added at the same time, that could be used to argue that permits must once have been granted.' He thought about this, a bureaucrat presented with a novel problem. 'Yes, that might change things, though I'm certainly not in a position to judge.'

Momentarily buoyed by the possibility of a reprieve, Brunetti stepped over to the door to the terrace and opened it. 'Let me show you something,' he said, turning to Rossi and waving his hand through the open door. 'I've always thought the windows on the floor below were the same as ours.' Without looking back toward Rossi, he went on, 'If you just have a look, down here on the left, you can see what I mean.' With the ease of long familiarity, Brunetti leaned out over the waist-high wall, bracing himself on broad-spread palms, to look at the windows of the apartment below. Now that he studied them, however, he could see that they were not at all the same: those below had carved lintels of white Istrian marble; his own windows were nothing more than rectangles cut in the brick of the wall.

He pulled himself back upright and turned toward Rossi. The young man stood like one transfixed, his left arm raised in Brunetti's direction, his palm exposed, as if trying to ward off evil spirits. He stared at Brunetti, his mouth agape.

Brunetti took a step toward him, but Rossi stepped quickly back, his hand still raised.

'Are you all right?' Brunetti asked, stopping at the door.

The younger man tried to speak, but no sound came. He lowered his arm and said something, but his voice was so soft Brunetti couldn't hear what it was.

In an attempt to cover the awkwardness of the moment, Brunetti said, 'Well, I'm afraid I might not have been right about the windows. There's nothing to see at all.'

Rossi's face relaxed and he tried to smile, but his nervousness remained and was contagious.

Trying to move away from all thoughts of the terrace, Brunetti asked, 'Can you give me some idea of what the consequences of all of this will be?'

'Excuse me?' Rossi said.

'What's likely to happen?'

Rossi moved back a step and began to answer, his voice taking on the curiously incantatory rhythms of someone who has heard himself say the same thing countless times, 'In the case that permits were applied for at the time of construction but final approval was never granted, a fine is imposed, depending on the seriousness of the violation of the building codes in force at the time.' Brunetti remained immobile and the young man continued. 'In the event that neither application was made nor approval granted, the case is passed to the Sovraintendenza dei Beni Culturali and they make judgement in accordance with how much damage the illegal structure does to the fabric of the city.'

'And?' Brunetti prompted.

'And sometimes a fine is imposed.'

'And?'

'And sometimes the offending structure has to be demolished.'

'What?' Brunetti exploded, all pretence of calm abandoned.

'Sometimes the offending structure has to be demolished.' Rossi gave a weak smile, suggesting that he was in no way responsible for this possibility.

'But this is my home,' Brunetti said. 'This is my house you're talking about demolishing.'

'It seldom comes to that, believe me,' Rossi said, trying to sound reassuring.

Brunetti found himself incapable of speech. Seeing this, Rossi turned away and made toward the door of the apartment. Just as he reached it, a key turned in the lock, and the door was pushed open. Paola came into the apartment, her attention divided among two large plastic bags, her key, and the three newspapers just slipping out from under her left arm. She noticed Rossi only when he lunged forward instinctively to grab the papers before they fell. She gasped in surprise and dropped the bags, stepped violently back from him and hit the open door with her elbow. Her mouth fell open, either in alarm or pain, as she began to rub at her elbow.

Brunetti stepped quickly toward her, calling her name as he came, 'Paola, it's all right. He's here with me.' He walked around Rossi and placed a hand on Paola's arm. 'You surprised us,' he said, hoping to calm her.

'You surprised me, too,' she said and managed to smile.

Behind them, Brunetti heard a sound and turned to see Rossi, his briefcase set against the wall, kneeling on one knee and stuffing oranges back into a plastic bag.

'Signor Rossi,' Brunetti said. The younger man looked up, finished with the oranges, got to his feet, and set the bag on the table beside the door.

'This is my wife,' Brunetti said unnecessarily. Paola released her elbow and offered her hand to Rossi. They shook hands and said the appropriate things, Rossi apologizing for having startled her, and Paola dismissing it.

'Signor Rossi is from the Ufficio Catasto,' Brunetti said at last.

'The Ufficio Catasto?' she asked.

'Yes, Signora,' Rossi said. 'I came to speak to

your husband about your apartment.'

Paola glanced at Brunetti, and what she saw on his face led her to turn to Rossi with her most winning smile. 'It looks like you were just leaving, Signor Rossi. Please don't let me keep you. I'm sure my husband will explain everything to me. There's no reason you should waste your time, especially on a Saturday.'

'That's very kind of you, Signora,' Rossi said warmly. He turned to Brunetti and thanked him for his time, then apologized to Paola again, though he did not offer to shake hands with either of them. When Paola closed the door after him, she asked, 'The Ufficio Catasto?'

'I think they want to tear the apartment down,' Brunetti said by way of explanation.

3

'Tear it down?' Paola repeated, not at all certain whether to respond with astonishment or laughter. 'What are you talking about, Guido?'

'He's just told me some story about there being no papers on file at the Ufficio Catasto for this apartment. They've started a new sort of system to computerize all of their records, but they can't find any proof that the permits were ever granted – or requested, for that matter – for this apartment when it was built.'

'That's absurd,' Paola said, bending down. She handed him the newspapers, picked up the remaining plastic bag, and headed down the corridor toward the kitchen. She set the bags on the table and started to take the packages out of them. As Brunetti explained, she continued to take out tomatoes, onions, and some zucchini flowers no longer than her finger.

When Brunetti saw the flowers, he stopped talking about Rossi and asked, 'What are you going to do with those?'

'Risotto, I think,' she answered and bent to put a white-paper-covered package into the refrigerator. 'Remember how good that one was that Roberta made us last week, with the ginger?'

'Hmm,' Brunetti answered, glad to be diverted to the far more congenial topic of lunch.

'Many people at Rialto?'

'Not when I got there,' she answered, 'but by the time I was leaving, it was packed. Most of them were tourists, come, as far as I could see, to take pictures of other tourists. In a few years, we'll have to get there at dawn or we won't be able to move.'

'Why do they go to Rialto?' he asked.

'To see the market, I suppose. Why?'

'Don't they have markets in their countries? Don't they sell food?'

'God knows what they have in their countries,' Paola answered with the slightest suggestion of exasperation. 'What else did he say, this Signor Rossi?'

Brunetti leaned back against the kitchen counter. 'He said that, in some cases, all they do is impose a fine.'

'That's pretty standard,' she said, facing him now that all of the food was put away. 'That's what happened to Gigi Guerriero, when he put in that extra bathroom. His neighbour saw the plumber carrying a toilet into the house and called the police and reported it, and he had to pay a fine.'

'That was ten years ago.'

'Twelve,' Paola corrected, out of habit. She saw the tightening of Brunetti's lips and added, 'Never mind. Doesn't matter. What else can happen?'

'He said that in some cases, when the permits were never requested but the work was done anyway, they were forced to demolish whatever it was that had been built.'

'Surely he was joking,' she said.

'You had a look at Signor Rossi, Paola. Do you think he was the kind of man to joke about something like this?'

'I suspect Signor Rossi is not the kind of man to joke about anything at all,' she said. Idly, she went into the living room, where she straightened some magazines lying abandoned on the arm of a chair, then went out on to the terrace. Brunetti followed her. When they were standing side by side, the city lying stretched out before them, she waved at rooftops, terraces, gardens, skylights. 'I'd like to know how much of that is legal,' she said. 'And I'd like to know how much of it has the right permits and has received the *condono*.' Both of them had lived in Venice for most of their lives, so they had an endless repertoire of stories about bribes paid to building inspectors or walls made of plasterboard that were pulled down the day after the inspectors left.

'Half the city's like that, Paola,' he said. 'But we've been caught.'

'We haven't been caught at anything,' she said, turning toward him. 'We haven't done anything wrong. We bought this place in good faith. Battistini – wasn't that the man we bought it from – he should have got the permits and the *condono edilizio.*'

'We should have made sure he had them before we bought it,' Brunetti attempted to reason. 'But we didn't. All we had to do was see that' – he said, sweeping his hand in an arc that encompassed all that lay before them – 'and we were lost.'

'That's not the way I remember it,' Paola said, walking back into the living room and sitting down.

'That's the way I remember it,' Brunetti said.

Before Paola could object, he went on, 'It doesn't matter how we remember it. Or how rash we were at the time we bought it. What does matter is that we're stuck with this problem now.'

'Battistini?' she asked.

'He died about ten years ago,' Brunetti answered, thus putting an end to any plans she might have had to contact him.

'I didn't know,' she said.

'His nephew, the one who works on Murano, told me about it. A tumour.'

'I'm sorry to hear that,' she said. 'He was a nice man.'

'Yes, he was. And he certainly gave us a good price.'

'I think he fell in love with the newlyweds,' she said, a smile of recollection crossing her face. 'Especially newlyweds with a baby on the way.'

'You think that affected the price?' Brunetti asked.

'I always thought it did,' Paola said. 'Very un-Venetian of him, but still a decent thing to do.' She added quickly, 'But not if we've got to tear it down.'

'That's more than a bit ridiculous, don't you think?' Brunetti asked.

'You've been working for the city for twenty years, haven't you? You ought to have learned that the fact that something is ridiculous makes no difference at all.'

Wryly, Brunetti was forced to agree. He remembered a fruit seller telling him that, if a customer touched the fruit or vegetables on display, the dealer was subject to a fine of half a million lire. Absurdity seemed no impediment to any ordinance the city thought fit to impose.

Paola slumped down in the chair and stretched her feet out on to the low table between them. 'So what should I do, call my father?'

Brunetti had known the question would be asked, and he was glad it had come sooner, rather than later. Count Orazio Falier, one of the richest men in the city, could easily work this miracle with no more than a phone call or a remark made over dinner. 'No. I think I'd like to take care of this myself,' he said, emphasizing the last word.

At no time did it occur to him, as it did not occur to Paola, to approach the matter legally, to find out the names of the proper offices and officials and the proper steps to follow. Nor did it occur to either of them that there might be a clearly defined bureaucratic procedure by which they could resolve this problem. If such things did exist or could be discovered, Venetians ignored them, knowing that the only way to deal with problems like this was by means of *conoscienze*: acquaintances, friendships, contacts and debts built up over a lifetime of dealing with a system generally agreed, even by those in its employ, perhaps especially by those in its employ, to be inefficient to the point of uselessness, prone to the abuses resultant from centuries of bribery, and encumbered by a Byzantine instinct for secrecy and lethargy.

Ignoring his tone, she said, 'I'm sure he could take care of it.'

Before giving himself time to consider, Brunetti asked, 'Ah, where are the snows of yesteryear? Where the ideals of '68?'

Instantly alert, Paola snapped out, 'What's that supposed to mean?'

He considered her, head flung back, ready for anything, and he realized how intimidating she could be in the classroom. 'It means that we both used to believe in the politics of the left and in social justice and things like equality under the law.'

'And?'

'And now our first impulse is to jump the queue.'

'Say what you mean, Guido,' she began. 'Don't talk about "our", please, when I'm the one who made the suggestion.' She paused for a moment, then added, 'Your principles are safely intact.'

'And that means?' he asked, voice somewhere beyond sarcasm but still short of anger.

'That mine aren't. We've been fools and fooled for decades, all of us with our hopes for a better society and our idiotic faith that this disgusting political system and these disgusting politicians would somehow transform this country into a golden paradise, run by an endless succession of philosopher kings.' Her eyes sought his and rested on them. 'Well, I don't believe it any more, none of it: I have no faith and I have no hope.'

Though he saw the real tiredness in her eyes when she said this, the resentment he could never suppress crept into his voice, and he asked, 'And does that mean that any time there's trouble, you turn to your father, with his money and his connections and the power he carries around in his pockets like the rest of us carry loose change, and ask him to take care of it for you?'

'All I'm trying to do,' she began with a sudden change in tone, as if she wanted to defuse things while there was still time, 'is save us time and energy. If we try to do this the right way, we'll set foot in the world of Kafka, and we'll ruin our peace and our lives trying to find the correct papers, only to stumble up against another little bureaucrat like Signor Rossi who will tell us they aren't the right papers and we have to find others, and others, until we both run screaming mad.'

Sensing that Brunetti had warmed to the change in her tone, she continued, 'And so, yes, if I can spare us that by asking my father to help, then that's what I would prefer to do, because I don't have the patience or the energy to do it any other way.'

'And if I tell you I would prefer to do this myself, without his help?' Before she could answer, he added, 'It's our apartment, Paola, not his.'

'Do you mean do this by yourself in a legal way or' – and here even greater warmth came into her voice – 'do it by using your own friends and connections?'

Brunetti smiled, a sure sign that peace had been restored, 'Of course I'll use them.'

'Ah,' she said, smiling too, 'that's entirely different.' Her smile broadened and she turned her mind to tactics. 'Who?' she asked, all thought of her father swept from the room.

'There's Rallo, on the Fine Arts Commission.'

'The one whose son sells drugs?'

'Sold,' Brunetti corrected.

'What did you do?'

'A favour,' was Brunetti's only explanation.

Paola accepted this and asked only, 'But

what's the Fine Arts Commission got to do with it? Wasn't this floor built after the war?'

'That's what Battistini told us. But the lower part of the building is listed as a monument, so it might be affected by whatever happens to this floor.'

'Uh huh,' Paola agreed. 'Anyone else?'

'There's that cousin of Vianello's, the architect, who works in the Comune, I think in the office where they issue building permits. I'll get Vianello to ask him to see what he can find out.'

Both sat for a while, drawing up lists of favours they'd done in the past and that could be called in now. It was almost noon before they had compiled a list of possible allies and agreed on their probable usefulness. It was only then that Brunetti asked, 'Did you get the *moeche*?'

Turning, as was her decades-long habit, to the invisible person who she pretended listened to her husband's worst excesses, she asked, 'Did you hear that? We are about to lose our home, and all he thinks about is soft-shelled crabs.'

Offended, Brunetti objected: 'That's not all I think about.'

'What else, then?'

'Risotto.'

The children, who came home for lunch, were told about the situation only after the last of the crabs had been sent to their reward. At first, they refused to treat it seriously. When their parents managed to persuade them that the apartment really was in jeopardy, they immediately began to plan the move to a new home.

'Can we get a house with a garden so I can have a dog?' Chiara asked. When she saw her parents' faces, she amended this to, 'Or a cat?' Raffi displayed no interest in animals and opted, instead, for a second bathroom.

'If we got one, you'd probably move into it and never come out again, trying to grow that silly moustache of yours,' Chiara said – the family's first public recognition of a light shadow that had been gradually making itself visible under her older brother's nose for the last few weeks.

Feeling not unlike a blue-helmeted UN peacekeeper, Paola intervened. 'I think that's enough from the two of you. This isn't a joke, and I don't want to listen to you talk about it as though it were.'

The children looked at her, and then, like a pair of baby owls perched on a limb, watching to see which of two nearby predators would strike first, swivelled their heads to look at their father. 'You heard what your mother said,' Brunetti told them, a sure sign that things were serious.

'We'll do the dishes,' offered Chiara in a conciliatory way, knowing full well that it was her turn, anyway.

Raffi pushed his chair back and got to his feet. He picked up his mother's plate, then his father's, then Chiara's, stacked them on his own plate, and took them to the sink. More remarkably, he turned on the water and pushed up the sleeves of his sweater.

Like superstitious peasants in the presence of the numinous, Paola and Brunetti fled into the living room, but not before he had grabbed a bottle of grappa and two small glasses.

He poured the clear liquid out and handed a glass to Paola. 'What are you going to do this afternoon?' she asked after the first calming sip.

'I'm going back to Persia,' Brunetti answered. Kicking off his shoes, he lay back on the sofa.

'Rather an excessive response to Signor Rossi's news, I'd say.' She took another sip. 'This is that bottle we brought back from Belluno, isn't it?' They had a friend up there, who had worked with Brunetti for more than a decade but who had abandoned the police force after being wounded in a shootout and had gone back to take over his father's farm. Every fall, he set up a still and made about fifty bottles of grappa, an entirely illegal operation. He gave the bottles to family and friends.

Brunetti took another sip and sighed.

'Persia?' she finally asked.

He set his glass on the low table and picked up the book he had abandoned on Signor Rossi's arrival. 'Xenophon,' he explained, opening it to the marked page, back in that other part of his life.

'They managed to save themselves, didn't they, the Greeks? And get back home?' she asked.

'I haven't got that far yet,' Brunetti answered.

Paola's voice took on a faint edge. 'Guido, you've read Xenophon at least twice since we've been married. If you don't know whether or not they got back, then you weren't paying attention, or you've got the first symptoms of Alzheimer's.'

'I'm pretending I don't know what happens so I'll enjoy it more,' he explained and put on his glasses. He opened the book, found his place, and began reading.

Paola stared across at him for quite a long time, poured herself another glass of grappa, and took it back with her to her study, abandoning her husband to the Persians.

4

As happens with these things, nothing happened. That is, no further communication arrived from the Ufficio Catasto, and nothing further was heard from Signor Rossi. In the face of this silence, and perhaps moved by superstition, Brunetti made no attempt to speak to the friends who might have helped him clarify the legal status of his home. Early spring passed into mid-spring and that in its turn passed. The weather became warm, and the Brunettis began to spend more and more time on their terrace. On the fifteenth of April, they ate lunch there for the first time, though by dinnertime it was again too cold to think about eating outside. The days lengthened, but still nothing further was heard about the dubious legality of the Brunettis' home. Like farmers living beneath a volcano, the instant the earth ceased to rumble, they went back to tilling their fields, hoping that the gods who governed these things had forgotten about them.

With the change in season, more and more tourists began to flood into the city. A large number of gypsies followed in their wake. The gypsies had been suspected of countless burglaries in the cities, but now they started to be accused of pickpocketing and minor street crimes, as well. Because these crimes were a bother to tourists, the principal source of the city's revenue, and not merely to residents, Brunetti was assigned to see if something could be done about them. The pickpockets were too young to be prosecuted; they were repeatedly apprehended and taken to the Questura, where they were asked to identify themselves. When the few who carried papers turned out to be under age, they were cautioned and released. Many were back the next day; most were back within a week. Since the only viable options Brunetti could see were to change the law regarding juvenile offenders or expel them from the country, he found it difficult to write his report.

He was at his desk, devoting a great deal of thought to how best to avoid stating self-evident truths, when his phone rang. 'Brunetti,' he said and flipped over to the third page of the names of those arrested for petty theft in the last two months.

'Commissario?' a man's voice asked.

'Yes.'

'This is Franco Rossi.'

The name was the most common one a Venetian could have, equivalent to 'John Smith', so it took Brunetti a moment to sort through the various places he could expect to find a Franco Rossi, and it was only then that he found himself in the Ufficio Catasto.

'Ah, I've been hoping to hear from you, Signor Rossi,' he lied easily. His real hope was that Signor Rossi had somehow disappeared, taking the Ufficio Catasto and its records along with him. 'Is there some sort of news?'

'About what?'

'The apartment,' Brunetti asked, wondering what other sort of news he might be expecting to hear from Signor Rossi.

'No, nothing,' Rossi answered. 'The office has been given the report and will consider it.'

'Have you any idea when that might be?' Brunetti asked diffidently.

'No. I'm sorry. There's no way of telling when they'll get around to it.' Rossi's voice was brisk, dismissive.

Brunetti was momentarily struck by how apt a slogan these words would be for most of the city offices he had dealt with, both as a civilian and as a policeman. 'Did you want more information?' he asked, remaining polite, conscious that he might, some time in the future, have need of Signor Rossi's good will, even perhaps his material aid.

'It's about something else,' Rossi said. 'I mentioned your name to someone, and they told me where you worked.'

'Yes, how can I help you?'

'It's about something here at the office,' he said, then stopped and corrected himself, 'well, not here because I'm not at the office. If you understand.'

'Where are you, Signor Rossi?'

'On the street. I'm using my *telefonino*. I didn't want to call you from the office.' The reception faded out and when Rossi's voice came back, he was saying, '. . . because of what I wanted to tell you.'

If that was the case, Signor Rossi would have been well advised not to use his *telefonino*, a means of communication as open to the public as the newspaper.

'Is what you have to tell me important, Signor Rossi?'

'Yes, I think it is,' Rossi said, his voice lower.

'Then I think you'd better find a public phone and call me on that,' Brunetti suggested.

'What?' Rossi asked uneasily.

'Call me from a public phone, Signore. I'll be right here and I'll wait for your call.'

'You mean this call isn't safe?' Rossi asked, and Brunetti heard the same tightness that had choked him off when he refused to move out on to the terrace of Brunetti's apartment.

'That's an exaggeration,' Brunetti said, trying to sound calm and reassuring. 'But there will be no trouble if you make the call from a public phone, especially if you use my direct number.' He gave the number to Rossi and then repeated it as, he thought, the young man wrote it down.

'I've got to find some change or buy a phone card,' Rossi said and then, after a brief pause, Brunetti thought he heard him hang up, but the voice drifted back, and Rossi seemed to say, 'I'll call you back.'

'Good. I'll be here,' Brunetti started to say, but he heard the phone click before he could finish.

What had Signor Rossi discovered at the Ufficio Catasto? Payments made so that some incriminatingly accurate blueprint could be made to disappear from a file and another one, more inventive, could be put in its place? Bribes paid to a building inspector? The idea that a civil servant would be shocked by any of this, even more, that he would call the police, made Brunetti want to laugh out loud. What was wrong with them over at the Ufficio Catasto, that they would hire a man as innocent as this?

For the next few minutes, while Brunetti waited for Rossi to call him back, he attempted to work out what good might come to him were he to help Signor Rossi with whatever he had discovered. With a pang of conscience – though a very small one – Brunetti realized he had every intention of making use of Signor Rossi, knew that he would go out of his way to help the young man and give special attention to whatever problem he had, knowing that, in return, a debt would be chalked up to his own account. This way, if nothing else, any favour he asked in return would be charged against his account, not against Paola's father's.

He waited ten minutes, but the phone did not ring. When it did, half an hour later, it was Signorina Elettra, his superior's secretary, asking if he wanted her to bring up the photos and list of articles of jewellery that had been found out on the mainland, in the caravan of one of the gypsy children who had been arrested two weeks ago. The mother insisted that the pieces were all hers, that they had been in the family for generations. Given the value of the jewellery, that seemed a most unlikely claim. One piece, Brunetti knew, had already been identified by a German journalist as stolen from her apartment more than a month ago.

He glanced at his watch and saw that it was after five. 'No, Signorina, don't bother. It can wait until tomorrow.'

'All right, Commissario,' she said. 'You can pick them up when you come in.' She paused and he heard the rustle of papers at the other end of the line. 'If there's nothing else, I'll go home, then.'

'The Vice-Questore?' Brunetti asked, wondering how she dared leave more than an hour early.

'He left before lunch,' she answered, her voice neutral. 'He said he was going to lunch with the Questore, and I think they were going back to the Questore's office afterwards.'

Brunetti wondered what his superior would be getting up to when speaking to his own superior. Patta's excursions into the fields of power never resulted in anything good for the people who worked in the Questura: usually his attempt to flaunt his single-minded energy resulted in new plans and directives that were imposed, vigorously enforced, and then ultimately abandoned when they proved to be futile or redundant.

He wished Signorina Elettra a pleasant evening and hung up. For the next two hours, he waited for the phone to ring. Finally, a bit after seven, he left his office and went downstairs into the officers' squad room.

Pucetti was at the duty desk, a book open in front of him, chin propped on two fists as he looked down at the pages.

'Pucetti?' Brunetti said as he came in.

The young officer looked up and, seeing Brunetti, was instantly on his feet. Brunetti was glad to see that, for the first time since he'd come to work at the Questura, the young officer managed to resist the impulse to salute.

'I'm going home now, Pucetti. If anyone calls for me, a man, please give him my home phone number and ask him to call me there, would you?'

'Of course, sir,' the young officer answered, and this time he saluted.

'What are you reading?' Brunetti asked.

'I'm not reading, sir, not really. I'm studying. It's a grammar book.'

'Grammar?'

'Yes, sir. Russian.'

Brunetti looked down at the page. Sure enough, Cyrillic letters ran across the page. 'Why are you studying Russian grammar?' Brunetti asked, and then added, 'If I might ask, that is.'

'Of course, sir,' Pucetti said with a small smile. 'My girlfriend's Russian, and I'd like to be able to talk to her in her own language.'

'I didn't know you had a girlfriend, Pucetti,' Brunetti said, thinking of the thousands of Russian prostitutes flooding into Western Europe and striving to keep his voice neutral.

'Yes, sir,' he said, his smile broader.

Brunetti risked it. 'What is she doing here in Italy? Working?'

'She's teaching Russian and mathematics at my kid brother's high school. That's how I met her, sir.'

'How long have you known her?'

'Six months.'

'That sounds serious.'

Again, the young man smiled, and Brunetti was struck by the sweetness of his face. 'I think it is, sir. Her family's coming here this summer, and she wants them to meet me.'

'So you're studying?' he asked, nodding down at the book.

Pucetti ran a hand through his hair. 'She told me they don't like the idea of her marrying a policeman: both of her parents are surgeons, you see. So I thought it might help if I could speak to them, even a little bit. And since I don't speak German or English, I thought maybe it would show them I'm not just a dumb cop if I could speak to them in Russian.'

'That sounds very wise. Well, I'll leave you to your grammar,' Brunetti said.

He turned to leave, and from behind him, Pucetti said, '*Das vedanya.*'

Knowing no Russian, Brunetti could not respond in kind, but he said goodnight and left the building. The woman's teaching mathematics, and Pucetti's studying Russian to be good enough to please her parents. On his way home, Brunetti considered this, wondering if, in the end, he himself was nothing but a dumb cop.

On Fridays Paola did not have to go to the university, and so she usually spent the afternoon preparing a special meal. All of the family had come to expect it, and that night they were not disappointed. She had found a leg of lamb at the butcher's behind the vegetable market and served it with tiny potatoes sprinkled with rosemary, zucchini *trifolati*, and baby carrots cooked in a sauce so sweet that Brunetti could have continued to eat them for dessert, had that not been pears baked in white wine.

After dinner he lay, not unlike a beached whale, in his usual place on the sofa, permitting himself just the smallest glass of Armagnac, merely a whisper of liquid in a glass so small as barely to exist.

When Paola joined him after dismissing the children to their homework with the life-endangering threats they had come to anticipate, she sat down and, far more honest in these things than he, poured herself a healthy swig of Armagnac. 'Lord, this is good,' she said after the first sip.

As if in a dream, Brunetti said, 'You know who called me today?'

'No, who?'

'Franco Rossi. The one from the Ufficio Catasto.'

She closed her eyes and leaned back in her chair. 'Oh, God, and I thought it was all over or had gone away.' After a while she asked, 'What did he say?'

'He wasn't calling about the apartment.'

'Why else would he call you?' Before he could answer, she asked, 'He called you at work?'

'Yes. That's what's so strange about it. When he was here, he didn't know I worked for the police. He asked me, well, he sort of asked me what I did, and all I said was that I'd studied law.'

'Do you usually do that?'

'Yes.' He offered no other explanation, and she asked for none.

'But he found out?'

'That's what he said. Someone he knew told him.'

'What did he want?'

'I don't know. He was calling on his *telefonino*, and since it sounded like he was going to tell me something he didn't want made public, I suggested he call me back from a public phone.'

'And?'

'He didn't call.'

'Maybe he changed his mind.'

To the extent that a man can shrug when he is filled with lamb and lying on his back, Brunetti shrugged.

'If it's important, he'll call back,' she said.

'I suppose so,' Brunetti said. He considered having the slightest little sip more of Armagnac, but instead dropped off to sleep for half an hour. When he woke, all thought of Franco Rossi had fled, leaving him only with the desire for that sip of Armagnac before he went down the hall to bed.

5

As Brunetti had feared, Monday was to bring him the results of Vice-Questore Patta's lunch-time conversation with the Questore. The summons came at about eleven, soon after Patta's arrival at the Questura.

'Dottore?' Signorina Elletra called from the door of his office, and he glanced up to see her standing there, a blue folder in one hand. For a moment he wondered if she had chosen the folder to match the colour of her dress.

'Ah, good morning, Signorina,' he said, waving her toward his desk. 'Is that the list of the stolen jewellery?'

'Yes, and the photos,' she answered, handing him the file. 'The Vice-Questore asked me to tell you he'd like to speak to you this morning.' Her voice held no hint that peril lurked in the message, so Brunetti did no more than nod in acknowledgement. She remained where she was, and he opened the file. Four colour photos were stapled to the page, each of a single piece of jewellery, three rings and an elaborate gold bracelet containing what looked like a row of small emeralds.

'It looks like she was prepared for a robbery,' Brunetti said, surprised that anyone would go to the trouble of having what looked like studio photos taken of her jewellery and immediately suspicious of insurance fraud.

'Isn't everyone?' she asked.

Brunetti looked up, making no attempt to hide his surprise. 'You can't mean that, Signorina.'

'Perhaps I shouldn't mean it, especially as I work here, but I certainly *can* mean it.' Before he could question her, she added, 'It's all people talk about.'

'There's less crime here than in any other city in Italy. Just look at the statistics,' he said hotly.

She did not roll her eyes to the heavens but contented herself with saying, 'Surely you don't think they represent what really happens here, Dottore?'

'What do you mean?'

'How many break-ins or robberies do you think actually get reported?'

'I just told you. I've seen the crime statistics. We all have.'

'Those statistics aren't related to crime, sir.

Surely you should know that.' When Brunetti refused to rise to the bait, she asked, 'You don't really believe that people bother to report crimes here, do you?'

'Well, perhaps not all of them, but I'm sure most people do.'

'And I'm sure most people don't,' she said with a shrug that softened her posture but did nothing to soften her voice.

'Can you give me some reason why you believe this?' Brunetti asked, laying the folder down on his desk.

'I know three people whose apartments have been robbed in the last few months who haven't reported it.' She waited for Brunetti to speak, and when he didn't, she added, 'No, one of them did. He went down to the *Carabinieri* station next to San Zaccaria and told them his apartment had been robbed, and the sergeant in charge told him to come back the next day to report it because the lieutenant wasn't there that day, and he was the only one who could handle robbery reports.'

'And did he go?'

'Of course not. Why bother?'

'Isn't that a negative attitude to have, Signorina?'

'Of course it's negative,' she shot back with far more impudence than she usually directed at him. 'What sort of attitude do you expect me to have?' At the heat of her tone, the comfort usually provided by her presence fled the room, leaving Brunetti feeling the same tired sadness he felt whenever he and Paola had an argument. In an attempt to free himself of this sensation, he looked down at the photos and asked, 'Which piece did the gypsy woman have?'

Signorina Elettra, equally relieved by the change of atmosphere, leaned over the photos and pointed to the bracelet. 'The owner's identified it. And she's got the original receipt which describes it. I doubt that it will make any difference or be much use, but she said she saw three gypsies in Campo San Fantin the afternoon her place was robbed.'

'No,' Brunetti agreed. 'It won't be any use.'

'What is?' she asked rhetorically.

In ordinary circumstances, Brunetti would have made a light remark to suggest that the laws were no different for the gypsies than for anyone else, but he didn't want to endanger the easy mood that had been restored between them. Instead, he asked, 'How old is the boy?'

'His mother says he's fifteen, but of course there are no documents, no birth certificate and no school records, so he could be any age from fifteen to eighteen. So long as she maintains he's fifteen, he can't be prosecuted, and he's guaranteed a few more years of getting away with anything he wants to.' Brunetti once again noted the quick flame of her anger and did his best to turn away from it.

'Hmm,' he muttered, closing the file. 'What does the Vice-Questore want to talk to me about? Do you have any idea?'

'Probably something that came out of his

meeting with the Questore.' Her voice revealed nothing.

Brunetti sighed audibly and got to his feet; though the issue of the gypsies remained unresolved between them, his sigh was enough to bring a smile to her lips.

'Really, Dottore, I have no idea. All he did was ask me to tell you he'd like to see you.'

'Then I'll go and see what he wants.' He paused at the door to allow her to go through first, then side by side they went down the stairs and toward Patta's office and her own small alcove just outside of it.

Her phone was ringing as they entered, and she leaned across her desk to answer it. 'Vice-Questore Patta's office,' she said. 'Yes, Dottore, he is. I'll put you through.' She pressed one of the buttons at the side of the phone and replaced the receiver. Looking up at Brunetti, she pointed at Patta's door. 'The Mayor. You'll have to wait until . . .' The phone rang again, and she picked it up. From the quick look she gave him, Brunetti guessed that it was a personal call, so he picked up that morning's edition of *Il Gazzettino* that lay folded on her desk and went over to the window to have a look at it. He glanced back for an instant, and their eyes met. She smiled, wheeled her chair around, pulled the receiver closer to her mouth, and started to talk. Brunetti stepped out into the corridor.

He had picked up the second section of the paper, which he hadn't had time to read that morning. The top half of the first page was dedicated to the ongoing examination – it was so half-hearted that one could hardly call it an investigation – of the process by which the contract for the rebuilding of the La Fenice Theatre had been awarded. After years of discussion, accusation, and counter-accusation, even those few people who could still keep the chronology straight had lost all interest in the facts and all hope in the promised rebuilding. Brunetti unfolded the paper and glanced at the articles at the bottom of the page.

To the left was a photo; he recognized the face but couldn't place it until he read the name in the caption: 'Francesco Rossi, city surveyor, in a coma after falling from scaffolding.'

Brunetti's hands tightened on the pages of the newspaper. He glanced away and then back to the story below the photo.

Francesco Rossi, a surveyor in the employ of the Ufficio Catasto, fell on Saturday afternoon from the scaffolding in front of a building in Santa Croce, where he was conducting the inspection of a restoration project. Rossi was taken to the emergency room at the Ospedale Civile, where his condition is given as 'riservata'.

Long before he became a policeman, Brunetti had abandoned any belief he had ever had in coincidence. Things happened, he knew, because other things had happened. Since becoming a policeman, he had added to this a conviction that the connections between events, at least such events as it became his duty to consider, were seldom innocent. Franco Rossi had failed to make much of an impression on Brunetti, save for that one moment of near-panic when he had raised his hand defensively as if to press away Brunetti's invitation that he step out on to the terrace to have a look at the windows below. In that one instant, and for that one instant, he had ceased to be the dedicated, colourless bureaucrat able to do little more than recite the regulations of his department and had become, for Brunetti, a man like himself, filled with the weaknesses that make us human.

Not for a moment did it occur to Brunetti that Franco Rossi had *fallen* from that scaffolding. Nor did he waste his time considering the possibility that Rossi's attempted phone call concerned some minor problem at his office, someone detected trying to get a building permit approved illegally.

These certainties fixed in his mind, Brunetti stepped back into Signorina Elettra's office and placed the newspaper on her desk. Her back was still to him, and she laughed softly at something said to her. Without bothering to attract her attention and without giving a thought to Patta's summons, Brunetti left the Questura, heading for the Ospedale Civile.

6

As he approached the hospital, Brunetti found himself thinking of all the times his work had brought him here; not so much recalling the specific people he had been called to visit as the times when he'd passed, Dante-like, through the yawning portals beyond which lurked pain, suffering, and death. Over the course of the years, he'd come to suspect that, no matter how great the physical pain, the emotional suffering which surrounded that pain was often far worse. He shook his head to clear it of these thoughts, reluctant to enter with these miserable reflections already in his care.

At the porter's desk Brunetti asked where he'd find the man, Franco Rossi, who had been injured in a fall during the weekend. The porter, a dark-bearded man who looked faintly familiar to Brunetti, asked if he knew which ward Signor Rossi had been taken to: Brunetti had no idea but guessed he was probably in Intensive Care. The porter made a call, spoke for a moment, then made another call. After speaking briefly, he told Brunetti that Signor Rossi was neither in Intensive Care nor in Emergency.

'Neurology, then?' suggested Brunetti.

With the calm efficiency of long experience, the porter dialled another number from memory, but with the same result.

'Then where could he be?' Brunetti asked.

'Are you sure he was brought here?' the porter asked.

'That's what was in *Il Gazzettino*.'

If the porter's accent had not already told Brunetti he was Venetian, the look he gave in response to this would have. All he said, however, was, 'He hurt himself in a fall?' At Brunetti's nod, he suggested, 'Let me try Orthopaedics, then.' He made another call and gave Rossi's name. Whatever he heard made him glance quickly toward Brunetti. He listened for a moment, covered the phone with his hand, and asked Brunetti, 'Are you a relative?'

'No.'

'Then what? A friend?'

Without hesitation, Brunetti made the claim. 'Yes.'

The porter said a few more words into the phone, listened, then set it down. He kept his eyes on the phone for a moment, then looked up at Brunetti. 'I'm sorry to tell you this, but your friend died this morning.'

Brunetti felt the shock and then a hint of the sudden pain he would have felt had it been a real friend who had died. But all he could say was, 'Orthopaedics?'

The porter gave a small shrug to distance himself from any information he had been given or had passed on. 'They told me they took him there because both his arms were broken.'

'But what did he die of?'

The porter paused, giving death the silence it was due. 'The nurse didn't say. But maybe they'd give you more information if you went and talked to them. Do you know the way?'

He did. As he stepped back from the desk, the porter said, 'I'm sorry about your friend, Signore.'

Brunetti nodded his thanks and started through the high-arched entrance hall, blind to its beauty. By a conscious effort of will, he prevented himself from counting over, like the beads on the rosary of myth, the stories he'd heard of the legendary inefficiency of the hospital. Rossi had been taken to Orthopaedics, and there he had died. And that was all he needed to think about right now.

In London and New York, he knew, there were musical shows that had been running for years. The casts changed, new actors took over the roles from those who retired or went on to different shows, but the plots and the costumes remained the same, year after year. It seemed to

Brunetti that much the same happened here: the patients changed, but their costumes and the general air of misery that surrounded them did not. Men and women shuffled through the arcades and stood at the bar in their dressing gowns and pyjamas, supporting themselves on casts and crutches, while the same stories were played out endlessly: some of the players went on to other roles. Some, like Rossi, left the stage.

When he arrived at Orthopaedics, he found a nurse standing outside the door, lounging at the top of the stairs, smoking a cigarette. As he approached, she stabbed out the cigarette in a paper cup she held in her other hand and opened the door, heading back into the ward.

'Excuse me,' Brunetti said, walking quickly through the door close behind her.

She tossed the paper cup into a metal wastepaper basket and turned to look at him. 'Yes?' she asked, barely glancing at him.

'I've come for Franco Rossi,' he said. 'The porter told me he was here.'

She looked at him more closely, and her professional opacity softened, as if his proximity to death made him worthy of better treatment. 'Are you a relative?' she asked.

'No, a friend.'

'I'm sorry for your loss,' she said, and in her tone there was nothing of her profession, only the sincere acknowledgement of human grief.

Brunetti thanked her and then asked, 'What happened?'

She moved off slowly and Brunetti walked

along with her, assuming she was leading him toward Franco Rossi, his friend Franco Rossi. 'They brought him in here Saturday afternoon,' she explained. 'They could see downstairs when they examined him that both arms were broken, so they sent him up here.'

'But it said in the paper that he was in a coma.'

She hesitated, then suddenly began to walk faster, toward a pair of swinging doors at the end of the corridor. 'I can't say anything about that. But he was unconscious when they brought him up.'

'Unconscious from what?'

She paused again, as if considering how much she could tell him. 'He must have hit his head when he fell.'

'How far was it that he fell? Do you know?'

She shook her head and pushed a door open with her hand, holding it to allow him to pass through and into a large open area at one side of which there was a desk, empty now.

When he sensed that she was not going to answer his question, he asked, 'Was there much damage?'

She started to speak and then said, 'You'll have to ask one of the doctors.'

'Is that what caused his death, the wound to his head?'

He didn't know if he was imagining it, but it seemed that she drew herself up straighter with his every question, as her voice became more professional and less warm. 'That's something else you'll have to ask the doctors.'

'But I still don't understand why he was brought up here,' Brunetti said.

'Because of his arms,' she said.

'But if his head . . .' Brunetti started to say, but the nurse turned away from him and toward another swinging door to the left of the desk.

Just as she reached it, she turned and called back over her shoulder, 'Perhaps they could explain things to you downstairs. In Emergency. Ask for Dottor Carraro,' and she was gone.

He did as she suggested and went quickly downstairs. In the Emergency Room he explained to the nurse that he was a friend of Franco Rossi, a man who had died after being seen in the ward, and asked if he could speak to Dottor Carraro. She asked his name and told him to wait while she spoke to the doctor. He went over to one of the plastic chairs that lined one wall and sat, suddenly grown very tired.

After about ten minutes, a man in a white jacket pushed his way through the swinging doors that led to the treatment room and walked a few steps toward Brunetti before he stopped. Standing with his hands jammed into the pockets of his jacket, it was obvious that he expected Brunetti to come toward him. He was short, with the swinging, aggressive walk many men of his stature adopt. He had wiry white hair that he wore slicked to his head with oily pomade, and reddened cheeks that spoke of drink rather than good health. Brunetti rose politely to his feet and walked over toward the doctor. He stood at least a head taller than the other man.

'Who are you?' Carraro asked, looking up at the other man and showing a lifetime's resentment at having to do so.

'As the nurse may have told you, Dottore, I'm a friend of Signor Rossi,' Brunetti began by way of introduction.

'Where's his family?' the doctor asked.

'I don't know. Have they been called?'

The doctor's resentment turned to irritation, no doubt provoked by the thought that there existed a person so ignorant as to think he had nothing better to do than sit around making phone calls to the relatives of dead people. He didn't answer and, instead, asked, 'What do you want?'

'I'd like to know the cause of Signor Rossi's death,' Brunetti answered in an equable voice.

'What business is it of yours?' the doctor demanded.

They were understaffed at the hospital, *Il Gazzettino* often reminded its readers. The hospital was overcrowded, so many doctors ended up working long hours.

'Were you on duty when he was brought in, Dottore?' Brunetti asked by way of reply.

'I asked you who you were,' the doctor said in a louder voice.

'Guido Brunetti,' he answered calmly. 'I learned that Signor Rossi was in the hospital from the newspaper, and I came to see how he was. The porter told me he'd died, and so I came here.'

'What for?'

'To learn the cause of his death,' Brunetti said, and then added, 'among other things.'

'What other things?' the doctor demanded, his face suffusing with a colour it would not take a doctor to realize was dangerous.

'To repeat myself, Dottore,' Brunetti said with an unctuously polite smile, 'I'd like to know the cause of death.'

'You said you were a friend, right?'

Brunetti nodded.

'Then you have no right to know. No one but the immediate family can be told.'

As if the doctor hadn't spoken, Brunetti asked, 'When will the autopsy be performed, Dottore?'

'The *what*?' Carraro asked, emphasizing the patent absurdity of Brunetti's question. When Brunetti made no response, Carraro turned on his heel and started to walk away, his swagger bespeaking his professional contempt for the layman and his stupidity.

'When will the autopsy be held?' Brunetti repeated, this time omitting Carraro's title.

The doctor wheeled around, not without a hint of the melodramatic in his gesture, and walked quickly back towards Brunetti. 'There will be whatever the medical direction of this hospital decides, Signore. And I hardly think you'll be asked to take any part in that decision.' Brunetti was not interested in the heat of Carraro's anger, only in what could have caused it.

He pulled out his wallet and took his warrant

card from it. He held it by a corner and extended it toward Carraro, careful to hold it at such a height that the other man had to tilt his head far back to see it. The doctor grabbed the card, lowered it, and studied it with some attention.

'When will the autopsy be held, Dottore?'

Carraro kept his head lowered over Brunetti's warrant card, as if reading the words there could make them change or take on some new significance. He turned it over and looked at the back, found it as empty of useful information as his mind of the proper response. At last, he looked up at Brunetti and asked, the arrogance in his voice replaced by suspicion, 'Who called you?'

'I don't think it's important why we're here,' Brunetti began, deliberately using the plural and hoping to suggest a hospital filled with policemen requisitioning records, X-rays, and patient charts, questioning nurses and other patients, all bent on discovering the cause of Franco Rossi's death. 'Isn't it enough to know that we are?'

Carraro handed the card back to Brunetti and said, 'We don't have an X-ray machine down here, so when we saw his arms, we sent him to Radiology and then Orthopaedics. It was the obvious thing to do. Any doctor would have done the same thing.' Any doctor in the Ospedale Civile, Brunetti reflected, but said nothing.

'Were they broken?' Brunetti asked.

'Of course they were, both of them, the right

in two places. We sent him up there to have them set and cast. There was nothing else we could do. It was standard procedure. As soon as that was taken care of, they could have sent him somewhere else.'

'Neurology, for example?' Brunetti asked.

By way of answer, Carraro did no more than shrug his shoulders.

'I'm sorry, Dottore,' Brunetti said with oily sarcasm, 'I'm afraid I didn't hear your answer.'

'Yes, they could have.'

'Did you observe any damage that would suggest he should be sent to Neurology? Did you make mention of it on your records?'

'I think so,' Carraro said evasively.

'You think so or you know so?' Brunetti demanded.

'I know so,' Carraro finally admitted.

'Did you make note of damage to the head? As if from a fall?' Brunetti asked.

Carraro nodded. 'It's on the chart.'

'But you sent him to Orthopaedics?'

Carraro's face coloured again with sudden anger. What would it be, Brunetti wondered, to have your health in the hands of this man? 'The arms were broken. I wanted to get them attended to before he went into shock, so I sent him to Orthopaedics. It was their responsibility to send him to Neurology.'

'And?'

Under Brunetti's eyes, the doctor was replaced by the bureaucrat, retreating at the thought that any suspicion of negligence was more likely to fall on his shoulders than on those who had actually treated Rossi. 'If Orthopaedics failed to send him on for further treatment, that's not my responsibility. You should be talking to them.'

'How serious was the injury to his head?' Brunetti asked.

'I'm not a neurologist,' Carraro answered instantly, just as Brunetti had thought he would.

'A moment ago, you said you noted the injury on his chart.'

'Yes, it's there,' Carraro said.

Brunetti was tempted to tell him that his own presence there had nothing to do with a possible charge of malpractice, but he doubted that Carraro would believe him or, even if he did, that it would make a difference. He'd dealt with many bureaucracies in his career, and bitter and repeated experience had taught him that only the military and the Mafia, and perhaps the Church, were as likely as the medical profession to fall into the instant goosestep of mutual protection and denial, regardless of the cost to justice, truth, or life.

'Thank you, Dottore,' Brunetti said with a finality the other man clearly found surprising. 'I'd like to see him.'

'Rossi?'

'Yes.'

'He's in the morgue,' Carraro explained, his voice as cool as the place itself. 'Do you know the way?'

'Yes.'

7

Mercifully, Brunetti's path took him outside and along the main courtyard of the hospital, and so he had a brief glimpse of sky and blossoming trees; he wished he could somehow store up the beauty of the plump clouds glimpsed through the pink blossoms and take it with him. He turned into the narrow passageway that led to the *obitorio*, vaguely troubled to realize how familiar he was with the way to death.

At the door, the attendant recognized him and greeted him with a nod. He was a man who, through decades of dealing with the dead, had taken on their silence.

'Franco Rossi,' Brunetti said by way of explanation.

Another nod and the man turned away from

the door, leading Brunetti into the room where a number of white-sheeted forms lay on hip-high tables. The attendant led Brunetti to the far side of the room and stopped by one of the tables, but he made no effort to remove the cloth. Brunetti looked down: the raised pyramid of the nose, a dropping off at the chin, and then an uneven surface broken by two horizontal lumps that must be the plaster-cast arms, and then two horizontal tubes that ended where the feet jutted off to the sides.

'He was my friend,' Brunetti said, perhaps to himself, and pulled the cloth back from the face.

The indentation above the left eye was blue and destroyed the symmetry of the forehead, which was strangely flattened, as if it had been pushed in by an enormous palm. For the rest, it was the same face, plain and unremarkable. Paola had once told him that her hero, Henry James, had referred to death as 'the distinguished thing', but there was nothing distinguished about what lay under Brunetti's gaze: it was flat, anonymous, cold.

He pulled the cloth back over Rossi's face, distracted by the desire to know how much of what lay there was Rossi; and if Rossi was no longer there, why what was left deserved so much respect. 'Thank you,' he said to the attendant and left the room. His response to the greater warmth of the courtyard was completely animal: he could almost feel the hair on the back of his neck smooth itself down. He thought about going to Orthopaedia to see what sort of justification they might engage in, but the sight of Rossi's battered face lingered, and he wanted nothing so much as to get out of the confines of the hospital. He gave in to this desire and left. He paused again at the desk, this time showing his warrant card, and asked for Rossi's address.

The porter found it quickly and added the phone number. It was a low number in Castello, and when Brunetti asked the porter if he knew where it was, he said he thought it must be down by Santa Giustina, near the shop that used to be the Doll Hospital.

'Has anyone been here to ask for him?' Brunetti asked.

'No one while I've been here, Commissario. But his family will have been called by the hospital, so they'll know where to go.'

Brunetti looked at his watch. It was almost one, but he doubted that the usual summons to lunch would be heeded by Franco Rossi's family, if he had one, that day. He knew that the dead man worked in the Ufficio Catasto and had died after a fall. Beyond that, he knew only what little he had inferred from their one brief meeting and even briefer phone conversation. Rossi was dutiful, timid, almost a cliché of the punctilious bureaucrat. And, like Lot's wife, he had turned solid when Brunetti suggested he step out on to the terrace.

He started down Barbaria delle Tolle, heading in the direction of San Francesco della Vigna. On his right, the fruit vendor, the one with the wig, was just closing, draping a green cloth over the open boxes of fruit and vegetables in a gesture Brunetti found disturbingly reminiscent of the way he had pulled the cloth over Rossi's face. Around him, things went on as normal: people hurried home to lunch and life went on.

The address was easy to find, on the right side of the *campo*, two doors beyond what had now become yet another real estate agency. ROSSI, FRANCO, was engraved on a narrow brass plaque next to the doorbell for the second floor. He pressed the bell, waited, then pressed it again, but there was no answer. He pressed the one above but got the same result, and so he tried the one below it.

After a moment, a man's voice answered through the speakerphone, 'Yes, who is it?'

'Police.'

There was the usual pause, then the voice said, 'All right.'

Brunetti waited for the click that would open the large outer door to the building, but instead he heard the sound of footsteps, and then the door was pulled open from within. A short man stood in front of him, his size not immediately apparent because he stood at the top of the high step the residents no doubt hoped would raise their front hall above the level of *acqua alta*. The man still held his napkin in his right hand and looked down at Brunetti with the initial suspicion he was long accustomed to encountering. The man wore thick glasses, and Brunetti noticed a red stain, probably tomato sauce, to the left of his tie.

'Yes?' he asked without smiling.

'I've come about Signor Rossi,' Brunetti said.

At Rossi's name, the man's expression softened and he leaned down to open the door more fully. 'Excuse me. I should have asked you to come in. Please, please.' He moved aside and made room for Brunetti on the small landing then extended his hand as if to take Brunetti's. When he noticed that he still held his napkin, he quickly hid it behind his back. He leaned down and pushed the door closed with his other hand then turned back to Brunetti.

'Please, come with me,' he said, turning back toward a door that stood open halfway down the corridor, just opposite the stairs that led to the upper floors of the building.

Brunetti paused at the door to allow the man to enter before him, then followed him in. There was a small entrance, little more than a metre wide, up from which rose two steps, further evidence of the Venetians' eternal confidence that they could outwit the tides that gnawed away perpetually at the foundations of the city. The room to which the steps led was clean and neat and surprisingly well lit for an apartment located on a *piano rialzato*. Brunetti noticed that at the back of the apartment a row of four tall windows looked across to a large garden on the other side of a wide canal.

'I'm sorry. I was eating,' the man said, tossing his napkin on to the table.

'Don't let me stop you,' Brunetti insisted.

'No, I was just finishing,' the man said. A

large helping of pasta still lay on his plate, an open newspaper spread out to its left. 'It doesn't matter,' he insisted and gestured Brunetti into the centre of the room, to a sofa that stood facing the windows. He asked, 'May I offer you something? *Un' ombra*?'

There was nothing Brunetti would have liked better than a small glass of wine, but he refused. Instead, he put out his hand and introduced himself.

'Marco Caberlotto,' the man answered, taking his hand.

Brunetti sat on the sofa, and Caberlotto sat opposite him. 'What about Franco?' he asked.

'You know he was in the hospital?' Brunetti asked by way of answer.

'Yes. I read the article in the *Gazzettino* this morning. I'm going to see him as soon as I finish,' he said, waving toward the table, where his lunch sat, slowly growing cold. 'How is he?'

'I'm afraid I have bad news for you,' Brunetti began, using the formulaic introduction he'd become so familiar with in the last decades. When he saw that Caberlotto understood, he continued, 'He never came out of the coma and died this morning.'

Caberlotto murmured something and put one hand to his mouth, pressing his fingers against his lips. 'I didn't know. The poor boy.'

Brunetti paused for a moment, then asked softly, 'Did you know him well?'

Ignoring the question, Caberlotto asked, 'Is it true that he fell? That he fell and hit his head?'

Brunetti nodded.

'He fell?' Caberlotto insisted.

'Yes. Why do you ask?'

Again, Caberlotto did not respond directly. 'Ah, the poor boy,' he repeated, shaking his head. 'I never would have believed something like this could have happened. He was always so cautious.'

'On the job, do you mean?'

Caberlotto looked across at Brunetti and said, 'No, about everything. He was just . . . well, he was just like that: cautious. He worked in that office, and part of their job means they have to go out and keep an eye on what's being done, but he preferred to stay in the office and work with the plans and projects, seeing how buildings were put together, or how they would be when they were put back together after a restoration. It's what he loved, that part of the job. He said that.'

Remembering the visit Rossi had made to his own home, Brunetti said, 'But I thought part of his job was to visit sites, to inspect houses that had building violations.'

Caberlotto shrugged. 'I know he had to go to houses sometimes, but the impression I got was that he did that only to be able to explain things to the owners so that they'd understand what was happening.' Caberlotto paused, perhaps trying to recall conversations with Rossi, but then went on. 'I didn't know him all that well. We were neighbours, so we'd talk on the street sometimes or have a drink together. That was when he told me about liking to study the plans.'

'You said he was always so cautious,' Brunetti prompted.

'About everything,' Caberlotto said and seemed almost to smile at the memory. 'I used to joke with him about it. He'd never carry a box downstairs. He said he needed to see both feet when he walked.' He paused, as though considering whether to continue, and then did. 'One time he had a light bulb blow up on him, and he called me to get the name of an electrician. I asked him what it was, and when he told me, I told him to change the bulb himself. All you've got to do is wrap some tape backwards around a piece of cardboard and stick it in the base of the bulb and unscrew it. But he said he was afraid to touch it.' Caberlotto stopped.

'What happened?' Brunetti prodded.

'It was a Sunday, so it would have been impossible to get someone, anyway. So I went up and did it for him. I just turned off the current and took the broken bulb out.' He looked across at Brunetti and made a turning gesture with his right hand. 'I did it just like I'd told him, with the tape, and it came right out. It took about five seconds, but there was no way he could have done it himself. He wouldn't have used that room until he could find an electrician, just would have let it stay dark.' He smiled and glanced across at Brunetti. 'It's not really that he was afraid, you see. It's just the way he was.'

'Was he married?' Brunetti asked.

Caberlotto shook his head.

'A girlfriend?'

'No, not that either.'

Had he known Caberlotto better, Brunetti would have asked about a boyfriend. 'Parents?'

'I don't know. If he still has them, I don't think they're in Venice. He never spoke of them, and he was always here on holidays.'

'Friends?'

Caberlotto gave this some thought and then said, 'I'd see him on the street with people occasionally. Or having a drink. You know the way it is. But I don't remember anyone in particular or seeing him with the same person.' Brunetti made no answer to this, so Caberlotto tried to explain. 'We weren't really friends, you know, so I guess I would see him and not really pay much attention, just recognize him.'

Brunetti asked, 'Did people come here?'

'I suppose so. I don't have much of an idea of who comes in and out. I hear people going up and down, but I never know who they are.' Suddenly he asked, 'But why are you here?'

'I knew him, too,' Brunetti answered. 'So when I found out he was dead, I came to talk to his family, but I came as a friend, nothing more than that.' Caberlotto didn't think to question why Brunetti, if he was a friend of Rossi's, should know so little about him.

Brunetti got to his feet. 'I'll leave you to finish your lunch, Signor Caberlotto,' he said, extending his hand.

Caberlotto took it and returned the pressure.

He went with Brunetti down the hall to the outer door and pulled it open. There, standing on the higher step and looking down at Brunetti, he said, 'He was a good man. I didn't know him well, but I liked him. He always said kind things about people.' He leaned forward and placed his hand on Brunetti's sleeve, as if to impress him with the importance of what he had just said, and then he closed the door.

8

On the way back to the Questura, Brunetti stopped to call Paola and tell her he wouldn't be home for lunch, then went into a small trattoria and ate a plate of pasta he didn't taste and a few pieces of chicken that served only as fuel to propel him into the afternoon. When he returned to work, he found a note on his desk, saying that Vice-Questore Patta wanted to see him in his office at four.

He called the hospital and left a message with Dottor Rizzardi's secretary, asking the pathologist if he'd perform the autopsy on Francesco Rossi himself, then made another call that set in motion the bureaucratic process that would order that autopsy to be performed. He went down to the officers' room to see if his assistant, Sergeant Vianello, was there. He was, at his desk, a thick file open before him. Though he wasn't much taller than his superior, Vianello seemed somehow to take up much more space.

He looked up when Brunetti came in and started to get to his feet, but Brunetti waved him back to his seat. Then, noticing the three other officers who were there, he changed his mind and gave a quick lift of his chin to Vianello, then nodded in the direction of the door. The sergeant closed the file and followed Brunetti up to his office.

When they were seated facing one another, Brunetti asked, 'Did you see the story about the man who fell from the scaffolding over in Santa Croce?'

'The one from the Ufficio Catasto?' Vianello asked, but it really wasn't a question. When Brunetti confirmed that it was, Vianello asked, 'What about it?'

'He called me on Friday,' Brunetti said and paused to allow Vianello to question him. When he did not, Brunetti went on, 'He said he wanted to talk to me about something that was going on at his office, but he was calling me on his *telefonino*, and when I told him it wasn't secure, he said he'd call me back.'

'And didn't?' Vianello interrupted.

'No,' said Brunetti with a shake of his head. 'I waited here until after seven. I even left my home number, in case he called, but he didn't. And then, this morning, I saw his picture in the paper. I went over to the hospital as soon as I saw it, but it was too late.' He stopped and again waited for Vianello to comment.

'Why did you go to the hospital, sir?'

'He was afraid of heights.'

'I beg your pardon?'

'When he came to my apartment, he . . .' Brunetti began, but Vianello cut him off.

'He came to your apartment? When?'

'Months ago. It was about the plans or the records they have for my apartment. Or that they don't have. It doesn't really matter; anyway, he came and asked to see some papers. They'd sent me a letter. But it's not important why he came; what's important is what happened when he was there.'

Vianello said nothing, but his curiosity was written large on his broad face.

'I asked him, when we were talking about the building, to come out on the terrace and have a look at the windows in the apartment below ours. I thought they'd show that both floors had been added at the same time, and that, if they had, it might affect their decision about the apartment.' As he spoke, Brunetti realized he had no idea at all what decision, if any, the Ufficio Catasto had come to.

'I was out there, leaning over and looking down at the windows on the floor below us, and when I turned back to him, it was as if I'd shown him a viper. He was paralysed.' When he saw the scepticism with which Vianello greeted this, he temporized, 'Well, that's what it looked like to me. Frightened, at any rate.' He stopped talking and glanced at Vianello.

Vianello said nothing.

'If you had seen him, you'd understand what I mean,' Brunetti said. 'The idea of leaning over the terrace terrified him.'

'And so?' Vianello asked.

'And so there was no way he would dare to go out on scaffolding, and even less that he would do it alone.'

'Did he say anything?'

'About what?'

'Being afraid of heights?'

'Vianello, I just told you. He didn't have to say anything; it was written all over his face. He was terrified. If a person is that frightened of something, he can't do it. It's impossible.'

Vianello tried a different tack. 'But he didn't say anything to you, sir. That's what I'm trying to make you see. Well, make you consider. You don't know it was the idea of looking over the side of the terrace that frightened him. It could have been something else.'

'Of course it could have been something else,' Brunetti admitted with exasperation and disbelief. 'But it wasn't. I saw him. I talked to him.'

Gracious, Vianello asked, 'And so?'

'And so if he didn't go up that scaffolding willingly, he didn't fall off it accidentally.'

'You think he was killed?'

'I don't know that that's true,' Brunetti admitted. 'But I don't think he went there willingly, or if he went to the place willingly, he didn't go out on the scaffolding because he wanted to.'

'Have you seen it?'

'The scaffolding?'

Vianello nodded.

'There's been no time.'

Vianello pushed back the sleeve of his jacket and looked at his watch. 'There's time now, sir.'

'The Vice-Questore wants me in his office at four,' Brunetti answered, glancing down at his own watch. He had twenty minutes to wait before his meeting. He caught Vianello's look. 'Yes,' Brunetti said, 'let's go.'

They stopped in the officers' room and picked up Vianello's copy of that day's *Gazzettino*, which gave the address of the building in Santa Croce. They also picked up Montisi, the chief pilot, and told him they wanted to go over to Santa Croce. On the way, the two men standing on the deck of the police boat studied a street directory and found the number, on a *calle* that led off of Campo Angelo Raffaele. The boat took them toward the end of the Zattere, in the waters beyond which loomed an enormous ship, moored to the embankment and dwarfing the area beside it.

'My God, what's that?' Vianello asked as their boat approached.

'It's that cruise ship that was built here. It's said to be the biggest in the world.'

'It's horrible,' Vianello said, head back and staring at its upper decks, which loomed almost twenty metres above them. 'What's it doing here?'

'Bringing money to the city, Sergeant,' Brunetti observed drily.

Vianello looked down at the water and then up to the rooftops of the city. 'What whores we are,' he said. Brunetti did not see fit to demur.

Montisi pulled to a stop not far from the enormous ship, stepped off the boat, and began tying it to the mushroom-shaped metal stanchion on the embankment, so thick it must have been intended for larger boats. As he got off, Brunetti said to the pilot, 'Montisi, there's no need for you to wait for us. I don't know how long we'll be.'

'I'll wait if you don't mind, sir,' the older man answered, then added, 'I'd rather be here than back there.' Montisi was only a few years short of retirement and had begun to speak his mind as the date began to loom, however distantly, on the horizon.

The agreement of the others with Montisi's sentiments was no less strong for remaining unspoken. Together, they turned from the boat and walked back toward the *campo*, a part of the city Brunetti seldom visited. He and Paola used to eat in a small fish restaurant over here, but it had changed hands a few years ago, and the quality of the food had rapidly deteriorated, so they'd stopped coming. Brunetti had had a girlfriend who lived over here, but that had been when he was still a student, and she had died some years ago.

They crossed the bridge and walked through Campo San Sebastiano, toward the large area of Campo Angelo Raffaele. Vianello, leading the way, turned immediately into a *calle* on the left, and up ahead they saw the scaffolding attached to the façade of the last building in the row, a four-storey house that looked as if it had been abandoned for years. They studied the signs of its emptiness: the leprous paint peeling away from the dark green shutters; the gaps in the marble gutters that would allow water to pound down on to the street and probably into the house itself; the broken piece of rusted antenna hanging out a metre from the edge of the roof. There was, at least for people born in Venice – which means born with an interest in the buying and selling of houses – an emptiness about the house which would have registered on them even if they had not been paying particular attention.

As far as they could tell, the scaffolding was abandoned: all the shutters were tightly closed. There was no evidence that work was being conducted here, nor was there any sign that a man had injured himself fatally, though Brunetti was not at all sure how he thought that fact would be indicated.

Brunetti stepped back from the building until he was leaning against the wall of the one opposite. He studied the entire façade, but there was no sign of life. He crossed the *calle*, turned, and this time studied the building that faced the scaffolding. It too showed the same signs of abandonment. He looked to his left: the *calle* ended in a canal, and beyond it was a large garden.

Vianello had, at his own pace, duplicated Brunetti's actions and had given the same attention to both buildings and to the garden. He came and stood next to Brunetti. 'It's possible, isn't it, sir?'

Brunetti nodded in acknowledgement, and thanks. 'No one would notice a thing. There's no one in the building that looks across at the scaffolding, and there's no sign that anyone is taking care of the garden. So there was no one to see him fall,' he said.

'If he fell,' Vianello added.

There was a long pause, and then Brunetti asked, 'Do we have anything on it?'

'Not that I know of. It was reported as an accident, I think, so the Vigili Urbani from San Polo would have come over to have a look. And if they decided that it was, an accident, I mean, that would have been the end of it.'

'I think we'd better go and talk to them,' Brunetti pushed himself away from the wall and turned to the door of the house. A padlock and chain were attached to a circle of iron set into the lintel to hold the door to the marble frame.

'How did he get inside to get up on the scaffolding?' Brunetti asked.

'Maybe the Vigili can tell us that,' Vianello said.

*

They couldn't. Montisi took them over in the boat, up the Rio di San Agostino to the police station near Campo San Stin. The policeman at the door recognized them both and took them at once to Lieutenant Turcati, the officer in charge. He was a dark-haired man whose uniform seemed to have been made for him by a tailor. This was enough for Brunetti to treat him with formality and address him by rank.

When they were seated and after listening to what Brunetti had to say, Turcati had the file on Rossi brought up. The man who called about Rossi had also called for an ambulance after phoning the police. Because the much-nearer Giustiniani had no ambulances available, Rossi had been taken to the Ospedale Civile.

'Is he here? Officer Franchi?' Brunetti asked, reading the name at the bottom of the report.

'Why?' the lieutenant asked.

'I'd like him to describe a few things to me,' Brunetti answered.

'Like what?'

'Why he thought it was an accident. Whether Rossi had keys to the building in his pocket. Whether there was blood on the scaffolding.'

'I see,' the lieutenant said, and reached for his phone.

While they waited for Franchi, Turcati asked if they would like coffee, but both men refused.

After a few minutes of idle talk, a young policeman came in. He had blond hair cut so short as almost not to be there and looked barely old enough to need to shave. He saluted the lieutenant and stood to attention, not looking at either Brunetti or Vianello. Ah, that's the way Lieutenant Turcati runs his shop, Brunetti thought.

'These men have some questions for you, Franchi,' Turcati said.

The policeman stood a bit more easily, but Brunetti saw little evidence that he had relaxed.

'Yes, sir,' he said but still did not look towards them.

'Officer Franchi,' Brunetti began, 'your report on the finding of the man over near Angelo Raffaele is very clear, but I have a few questions I'd like to ask you about it.'

Still facing the lieutenant, Franchi said, 'Yes, sir?'

'Did you search the man's pockets?'

'No, sir. I got there just as the men from the ambulance did. They picked him up and put him on a stretcher and were taking him toward the boat.' Brunetti did not ask the policeman why it had taken him the same time to travel the short distance from the police station as for the ambulance to cross the entire city.

'You wrote in your report that he had fallen from the scaffolding. I wondered if you examined the scaffolding to see if there were signs of that. Perhaps a broken board or a piece of fabric from his clothing. Or perhaps a bloodstain.'

'No, sir.'

Brunetti waited for an explanation, and when it didn't come, he asked, 'Why didn't you do that, officer?'

'I saw him there on the ground, next to the scaffolding. The door to the house was open, and when I opened his wallet, I saw that he worked in the Ufficio Catasto, so I just figured he was there on a job.' He paused and, into Brunetti's silence, added, 'If you see what I mean, sir.'

'You said he was being carried to the ambulance by the time you got there?'

'Yes, sir.'

'Then how was it you had his wallet?'

'It was on the ground, sort of hidden by an empty cement bag.'

'And where was his body?'

'On the ground, sir.'

Keeping his voice level, Brunetti asked patiently, 'Where was his body in relation to the scaffolding?'

Franchi considered the question and then answered, 'To the left of the front door, sir, about a metre from the wall.'

'And the wallet?'

'Under the cement bag, sir, as I told you.'

'And when did you find it?'

'After they took him to the hospital. I thought I should have a look around, so I went inside the house. The door was open when I got there, as I wrote in the report. And I'd already seen that the shutters just above where he was lying were open, so I didn't bother to go upstairs. It was when I came out that I saw the wallet lying there, and when I picked it up, there was an identification card from the Ufficio Catasto, so I assumed he was there to check on the building or something like that.'

'Was there anything else in the wallet?'

'There was some money, sir, and some cards. I brought it all back here and put it in an evidence bag. I think that's listed in the report.'

Brunetti turned to the second page of the report and saw that mention of the wallet was made.

Looking up, he asked Franchi, 'Did you notice anything else while you were there?'

'What sort of thing, sir?'

'Anything at all that seemed unusual or out of place in any way?'

'No, sir. Nothing at all.'

'I see,' Brunetti said. 'Thank you, Officer Franchi.' Before anyone else could speak, Brunetti asked him, 'Could you go and get that wallet for me?'

Franchi looked toward the lieutenant, who nodded.

'Yes, sir,' Franchi said and turned sharply on his heel and left the office.

'He seems an eager young man,' Brunetti said.

'Yes,' the lieutenant said, 'he's one of my best men.' He gave a brief account of how well Franchi had done in his training classes, but before he could finish, the young officer was back with the plastic evidence bag. Inside was a brown leather wallet.

Franchi stood at the door, uncertain to whom to give the bag.

'Give it to the Commissario,' Lieutenant Turcati said, and Franchi couldn't disguise his start of astonishment at learning the rank of the man who had questioned him. He walked over to Brunetti, handed him the bag, and saluted.

'Thank you, officer,' Brunetti said, taking the bag by one corner. He took out his handkerchief and carefully wrapped the bag in it. Then, turning to the lieutenant, he said, 'I'll sign a receipt for this if you like.'

The lieutenant passed a sheet of paper across his desk, and Brunetti wrote the date, his name, and a description of the wallet. He signed it at the bottom and passed it back toward Turcati, before leaving the office with Vianello.

When they emerged into the broad *calle*, it had started to rain.

9

They made their way through the increasing
rain back toward the boat, glad that Montisi
had insisted on waiting for them. When they
climbed on board, Brunetti looked at his watch
and saw that it was well after five, which meant
it was high time to go back to the Questura. They
emerged into the Grand Canal; Montisi turned
right and into the long S that would take them
up past the Basilica and Bell Tower, down
toward the Ponte della Pietà and the Questura.

Down in the cabin, Brunetti pulled his
handkerchief and the wallet it contained from
his pocket and handed them to Vianello. 'When
we get back, could you take this to the lab and
have it dusted for prints?' As Vianello took
them, Brunetti added, 'Any prints on the plastic

bag will be Franchi's, I'd guess, so they can exclude those. And you better send someone over to the hospital to get a set of Rossi's.'

'Anything else, sir?'

'When they've finished, send the wallet up to me. I'd like to have a look at what's in it. And could you tell them it's urgent,' he said.

Vianello looked across at him and asked, 'And when isn't it, sir?'

'Well, tell Bocchese that there's a dead person involved. That might make him work a little faster.'

'Bocchese would be the first person to say that's proof there's no need for hurry,' remarked Vianello.

Brunetti chose to ignore this.

Vianello slipped the handkerchief into the inside pocket of his uniform jacket and asked, 'What else, sir?'

'I want Signorina Elettra to check the records to see if there's anything about Rossi.' He doubted that there would be, couldn't conceive of Rossi as ever having been involved in anything criminal, but life had given him larger surprises than that, so it would be best to check.

Vianello raised the fingers of one hand. 'I'm sorry, sir. I don't mean to interrupt you, but does this mean we're going to treat it as a murder investigation?'

Both of them knew the difficulty of this. Until a magistrate had been assigned, neither of them could begin an official investigation, but before a magistrate would take it on and begin to treat it as a case of murder, there had to be persuasive evidence of a crime. Brunetti doubted that his impression of Rossi as a man terrified of heights would count as persuasive evidence of anything: not crime and certainly not murder.

'I'll have to try to persuade the Vice-Questore,' Brunetti said.

'Yes,' Vianello answered.

'You sound sceptical.'

Vianello raised an eyebrow. It sufficed.

'He won't like this, will he?' Brunetti volunteered. Again, Vianello didn't respond. Patta allowed the police to accept crime when it was, in a sense, thrust upon them and could not be ignored. There was little chance that he would permit an investigation of something that so clearly appeared to be an accident. Until such time as it could not be ignored, until such time as evidence could be presented that would convince even the most sceptical that Rossi had not fallen to his death, it was destined to remain an accident in the eyes of the authorities.

Brunetti was blessed, or cursed, with a psychological double vision that forced him to see at least two points of view in any situation, and so he knew how absurd his suspicions must seem and could be made to seem by someone who did not share them. Good sense declared that he abandon all of this and accept the obvious: Franco Rossi had died after an accidental fall from scaffolding. 'Tomorrow morning, get his keys from the hospital and have a look at his apartment.'

'What am I looking for?'

'I have no idea,' Brunetti answered. 'See if you can find an address book, letters, names of friends or relatives.'

Brunetti had been so immersed in his speculations that he had not noticed them turning into the canal, and it was only the gentle thump of the boat against the Questura landing that told him they had arrived.

Together, they climbed up to the deck. Brunetti waved his thanks to Montisi, who was busy mooring the ropes that held the boat to the quay. He and Vianello walked through the rain to the front door of the Questura, which was pulled open before them by a uniformed officer. Before Brunetti could thank him, the young man said, 'The Vice-Questore wants to see you, Commissario.'

'He's still here?' He sounded surprised.

'Yes, sir. He said I was to tell you as soon as you got here.'

'Yes, thank you,' he said, and to Vianello, 'I better go up, then.'

They went up the first flight of stairs together, neither willing to speculate on what Patta might want. At the first floor, Vianello headed down the corridor that led to the back stairs to the laboratory where Bocchese, the technician, reigned, unquestioned, unhurried, and unwilling to defer to rank.

Brunetti made his silent way toward Patta's office. Signorina Elettra sat at her desk and looked up when he came in. She waved him toward her at the same time as she picked up her phone and pressed a button. After a moment she said, 'Commissario Brunetti's here, Dottore.' She listened to Patta, replied, 'Of course, Dottore,' and replaced the receiver.

'He must want to ask you a favour. It's the only reason he hasn't been screaming for your blood all afternoon,' she had time to say before the door opened and Patta appeared.

His grey suit, Brunetti observed, had to be cashmere, and the tie was what passed in Italy for an English club tie. Though it had been a rainy, cool spring, Patta's handsome face was taut and tanned. He wore a pair of thin-rimmed oval glasses. This was the fifth pair of glasses Brunetti had seen Patta wear in the years he'd been at the Questura, the style always a few months ahead of what everyone else would soon be wearing. Brunetti had once, caught without his own reading glasses, picked up Patta's from his desk and held them up to take a closer look at a photograph, only to discover that the lenses were clear glass.

'I was just telling the Commissario to go in, Vice-Questore,' Signorina Elettra said. Brunetti noticed that there were two files and three pieces of paper on her desk that he was sure had not been there a moment ago.

'Yes, do come in, Dottor Brunetti,' Patta said, extending a hand in a gesture that Brunetti found unsettlingly similar to that with which he imagined Clytemnestra had lured Agamemnon down from his chariot. He had time only to cast one last glance at Signorina Elettra before his arm was taken by Patta and he was pulled gently into the office.

Patta closed the door and walked across the room toward the two armchairs he'd had placed in front of the windows. He waited for Brunetti to join him. When he did, Patta gestured him to sit, then himself sat down; an interior decorator would have called the placement of the chairs a 'conversation angle'.

'I'm glad you could spare me the time, Commissario,' Patta said. Hearing the tinge of angry sarcasm in the words, Brunetti felt himself on easier ground.

'I had to go out,' he explained.

'I thought that was this morning,' Patta said but then remembered to smile.

'Yes, but then I had to go out this afternoon, too. It was so sudden I didn't have time to get word to you.'

'Don't you have a *telefonino*, Dottore?'

Brunetti, who loathed them and refused to carry one out of what he realized was stupid, Luddite prejudice, said only, 'I didn't have it with me, sir.'

He wanted to ask Patta why he was there, but Signorina Elettra's warning was enough to keep him silent, a neutral expression on his face, as though they were two strangers waiting for the same train.

'I wanted to talk to you, Commissario,' Patta began. He cleared his throat and continued, 'It's

93

about something . . . well, it's about something personal.'

Brunetti worked hard to keep his face motionless, with an expression of passive interest in what he was hearing.

Patta sat back in his chair, stretched his feet out in front of him, and crossed his ankles. For a moment, he contemplated the gleaming shine on his wingtips; then he uncrossed his feet, pulled them back, and leaned forward. In the few seconds it took him to do this, Brunetti was astonished to realize, Patta seemed to have aged years.

'It's my son,' he said.

Brunetti knew that he had two, Roberto and Salvatore. 'Which one, sir?'

'Roberto, the baby.'

Roberto, Brunetti quickly calculated, must be at least twenty-three. Well, his own daughter Chiara, though she was fifteen, was still his baby and would surely always be. 'Isn't he studying at the university, sir?'

'Yes, Economia Commerciale,' Patta answered but then stopped and looked down at his feet. 'He's been there a few years,' he explained as he lifted his gaze towards Brunetti.

Brunetti again worked hard at keeping his face absolutely immobile. He did not want to appear overly curious about what might be a family problem, nor did he want to seem uninterested in whatever Patta chose to tell him. He nodded in what he thought was an encouraging way, the same gesture he used with nervous witnesses.

'Do you know anyone in Jesolo?' Patta asked, confusing Brunetti.

'I beg your pardon, sir?'

'In Jesolo, on the police there. Do you know anyone?'

Brunetti thought about it for a moment. He had contacts with some police on the mainland, but none out there on the Adriatic coast among the nightclubs, hotels, discos, and the scores of daytripping tourists who stayed in Jesolo and came across the Laguna by boat every morning. A woman he'd studied with at university was on the police in Grado, but he knew no one in the nearer city. 'No, sir, I don't.'

Patta failed to disguise his disappointment. 'I had hoped you would,' he said.

'Sorry, sir.' Brunetti considered his options, studying the motionless Patta, who had gone back to looking at his feet, and decided to risk it. 'Why do you ask, sir?'

Patta looked up at him, away, and then back. Finally he said, 'The police there called me last night. They have someone working for them, you know how it is.' This must mean an informer of some sort. 'This person told them a few weeks ago that Roberto was selling drugs.' Patta stopped.

When it was obvious that the Vice-Questore was not going to say anything more, Brunetti asked, 'Why did they call you, sir?'

Patta went on as though Brunetti had not asked the question. 'I thought perhaps you might know someone there who could give us a clearer idea of what was happening, who this person is, how far along their investigation is.' Again, the word 'informer' sprang to Brunetti's mind, but he kept his own counsel. Responding to his silence, Patta added, 'That sort of thing.'

'No, sir, I'm sorry to tell you, but I really don't know anyone there.' After a pause, he volunteered, 'I could ask Vianello, sir.' Before Patta could respond, Brunetti added, 'He's discreet, sir. There's nothing to worry about there.'

Still Patta just sat and looked away from Brunetti. Then he shook his head in a firm negative, dismissing the possibility of accepting help from a uniformed man.

'Will that be all, sir?' Brunetti said and put his hands on the arms of his chair to show his readiness to leave.

Seeing Brunetti's gesture, Patta said, his voice now lower, 'They arrested him.' He glanced at Brunetti, but seeing that he had no questions, Patta continued: 'Last night. They called me at about one. There was a fight at one of the discos, and when they got there to break it up, they stopped a couple of people and searched them. It must have been because of what this person had told them that they searched Roberto.'

Brunetti remained silent. Once witnesses had gone this far, he knew from long experience, there was no stopping them: it would all come out.

'In the pocket of his jacket, they found a

plastic envelope with Ecstasy in it.' He bent towards Brunetti and asked, 'You know what that is, don't you, Commissario?'

Brunetti nodded, amazed that Patta could believe it possible for a policeman not to know. He knew that any word from him could break the momentum. He relaxed his posture as best he could, took one hand from the arm of the chair, and settled into what he hoped would appear to be a more comfortable position.

'Roberto told them that someone must have put it into the pocket of his jacket when they saw the police arrive. That sort of thing often happens.' Brunetti knew that. He also knew that, just as often, it didn't happen.

'They called me, and I went out there. They knew who Roberto was, so they suggested I go. When I got there, they gave him into my custody. On the way back, he told me about the envelope.' Patta stopped, and it seemed a final stop.

'Did they keep it as evidence?'

'Yes, and they took his fingerprints to match against any they found on the envelope.'

'If he took it out and gave it to them, then his fingerprints were bound to be on it,' Brunetti said.

'Yes, I know,' Patta said. 'So I wasn't worried about that. I didn't even bother to call my lawyer. There was no proof, even if the prints were there. What Roberto said could have been true.'

Brunetti nodded in silent agreement, waiting

to learn why Patta spoke of it as no more than a possibility.

Patta leaned back in the chair and gazed out the window. 'They called me this morning, after you'd gone out.'

'Is that why you wanted to see me, sir?'

'No, this morning I wanted to ask you about something else. It isn't important now.'

'What did they tell you, sir?' Brunetti finally asked.

Patta returned his gaze from whatever he could see beyond the window. 'That inside the large envelope, they found forty-seven smaller ones, each of them with an Ecstasy tablet inside.'

Brunetti tried to calculate the weight and value of the drugs in order to work out the seriousness with which a judge was likely to view their possession. Well, it didn't sound as if he had an enormous amount of the stuff, and if Roberto stuck to his story that someone else had put them into his jacket, he could see no serious legal danger for the boy.

'His fingerprints were on the small envelopes, too,' Patta dropped into the silence. 'On all of them.'

Brunetti resisted the impulse to reach across and place his hand on Patta's arm. Instead, he waited a few moments and then said, 'I'm sorry, sir.'

Still not looking at him, Patta nodded, either in acknowledgement or thanks.

After a full minute had passed, Brunetti asked, 'Was it in Jesolo itself or out on the Lido?'

Patta looked at Brunetti and shook his head, a fighter shaking off a soft blow. 'What?'

'Where it happened, sir. Was it Jesolo or Jesolo Lido?'

'On the Lido.'

'And where was he when he was . . .' Brunetti began, intending to use the word 'arrested'. Instead he said, '. . . detained?'

'I just told you,' Patta snapped in a voice that showed how close he was to anger. 'Lido di Jesolo.'

'But in what place, sir? A bar? A disco?'

Patta closed his eyes, and Brunetti wondered how much time he must have spent thinking about all of this, recalling events in his son's life.

'At a place called Luxor, a disco,' he finally said.

A small 'Ah' escaped Brunetti's lips, but that was enough to force Patta to open his eyes. 'What?'

Brunetti dismissed the question. 'I knew someone once who used to go there,' he said.

As his formless hope died, Patta turned his attention away.

'Have you called a lawyer, sir?' Brunetti asked.

'Yes. Donatini.' Brunetti hid his surprise in a curt nod, as if the lawyer most often called upon to defend those accused of Mafia association was an obvious choice for Patta.

'I'd be glad, Commissario. . .' Patta began and stopped as he considered how best to put it.

'I'll give it some more thought, sir,' Brunetti

interrupted. 'And I'll say nothing about this to anyone, of course.' Much as he despised many of the things Patta did, there was no way he could allow the man the embarrassment of having to ask him to keep silent about this.

Patta responded to the finality in Brunetti's voice and pushed himself to his feet. He went with Brunetti to the door and opened it for him. He did not offer to shake hands, but he did utter a curt 'Thank you' before going back into his office and closing the door.

Brunetti saw that Signorina Elettra was at her desk, though the files and papers had been replaced by what looked suspiciously thick and glossy enough to be the spring fashion issue of *Vogue*.

'His son?' she asked, looking up from the magazine.

It escaped before he could stop himself. 'Do you have his office wired?' He had meant it as a joke, but when he heard himself asking the question, he wasn't all that sure that he did.

'No. He had a call from the boy this morning, sounding very nervous, then one from the Jesolo police. And as soon as he'd spoken to them, he asked me to get him Donatini's number.' Brunetti wondered if he could ask her to give up secretarial work and join the force. But he knew she'd die before she'd wear the uniform.

'Do you know him?' Brunetti asked.

'Who, Donatini or the boy?'

'Either. Both.'

'I know them both,' she said, then added

casually, 'they're both shits, but Donatini dresses better.'

'Did he tell you what it's about?' he asked with a backward nod of his head towards Patta's office.

'No,' she said with no trace of disappointment. 'If it was rape, it would have been in the papers. So I guess it's drugs. Donatini ought to be good enough to get him off.'

'Do you think he's capable of rape?'

'Who, Roberto?'

'Yes.'

She considered this for a second and then said, 'No, I suppose not. He's arrogant and self-important, but I don't think he's completely bad.'

Something led Brunetti to ask, 'And Donatini?'

Without hesitation, she answered, 'He'd do anything.'

'I didn't know you knew him.'

She glanced down at the magazine and turned a page, making it look like an idle gesture. 'Yes.' She turned another page.

'He asked me to help him.'

'The Vice-Questore?' she asked, looking up in surprise.

'Yes.'

'And are you going to?'

'If I can,' Brunetti answered.

She looked at him for a long time, then turned her attention back to the page below her. 'I don't think grey is much longer for this world,' she said. 'We're all tired of wearing it.'

She was wearing a peach-coloured silk blouse with a high-collared black jacket in what he thought he recognized as raw silk.

'You're probably right,' he said, wished her a good evening, and went back up to his office.

10

He had to call Information to get the number of Luxor, but when he dialled it, whoever answered the phone at the disco told him that Signor Bertocco was not there and refused to give his home number. Brunetti did not say it was the police calling. Instead, he called Information again and was given Luca's home number without any difficulty at all.

'Self-important fool,' Brunetti muttered as he dialled the number.

It was picked up on the third ring and a deep voice with a rough edge said, 'Bertocco.'

'*Ciao*, Luca, it's Guido Brunetti. How are you?'

The formality of the answering voice disappeared, replaced with real warmth. 'Fine,

Guido. I haven't heard from you in ages. How are you, and Paola, and the kids?'

'Everyone's fine.'

'You've finally decided to accept my offer and come out and dance till you drop?'

Brunetti laughed at this, a joke that had run for more than a decade. 'No, I'm afraid I have to disappoint you again, Luca. Much as you know how I long to come and dance till dawn among people as young as my own children, Paola refuses to allow it.'

'The smoke?' Luca asked. 'Thinks it's bad for your health?'

'No, the music, I think, but for the same reason.'

There was a brief pause, after which Luca said, 'She's probably right.' When Brunetti said nothing more he asked, 'Then why are you calling? About the boy who was arrested?'

'Yes,' Brunetti said, not even pretending to be surprised that Luca knew about it already.

'He's your boss's son, isn't he?'

'You seem to know everything.'

'A man who runs five discos, three hotels, and six bars has to know everything, especially about the people who get themselves arrested in any of those places.'

'What do you know about the boy?'

'Only what the police tell me.'

'Which police? The ones who arrested him or the ones who work for you?'

The silence that followed his question reminded Brunetti, not only that he had gone too far, but also that, however much Luca was a friend, he would always view Brunetti as a policeman.

'I'm not sure how to answer that, Guido,' Luca finally said. His voice was interrupted by the explosive bark of a heavy smoker.

The coughing went on for a long time. Brunetti waited for it to stop, and when it did, he said, 'I'm sorry, Luca. It was a bad joke.'

'It's nothing, Guido. Believe me, anyone who's involved with the public as much as I am needs all the help they can get from the police. And they're glad to get all the help they can from me.'

Brunetti, thinking of small envelopes changing hands discreetly in city offices, asked, 'What sort of help?'

'I've got private guards who work the parking lots of the discos.'

'What for?' he asked, thinking of muggers and the vulnerability of the kids who staggered out at three in the morning.

'To take their car keys away from them.'

'And no one complains?'

'Who's to complain? Their parents, that I stop them from driving off dead drunk or out of their minds on drugs? Or the police, because I stop them from slamming into the trees at the side of the highways?'

'No, I suppose not. I didn't think.'

'It means they don't get woken up at three to go out to watch bodies being cut out of cars. Believe me, the police are very happy to give me any help they can.' He paused and Brunetti listened to the sharp snap of a match as Luca lit a cigarette and took the first deep breath. 'What is it you'd like me to do – get this hushed up?'

'Could you?'

If shrugs made sounds, Brunetti heard one on the phone. Finally Luca said, 'I won't answer that until I know whether you want me to or not.'

'No, not hushed up in the sense that it disappears. But I would like you to keep it out of the papers if it's possible.'

Luca paused before he answered this. 'I spend a lot of money on advertising,' he said at last.

'Does that translate as yes?'

Luca laughed outright until the laugh turned into a deep, penetrating cough. When he could speak again, he said, 'You always want things to be so clear, Guido. I don't know how Paola stands it.'

'It makes things easier for me when they are.'

'As a policeman?'

'As everything.'

'All right, then. You can consider it as meaning yes. I can keep it out of the local papers, and I doubt that the big ones would be interested.'

'He's the Vice-Questore of Venice,' Brunetti said in a perverse burst of local pride.

'I'm afraid that doesn't mean much to the guys in Rome,' Luca answered.

Brunetti considered this. 'I suppose you're right.' Before Luca could agree, Brunetti asked,

'What do they say about the boy?'

'They've got him cold. His fingerprints were all over the small envelopes.'

'Has he been charged yet?'

'No. At least I don't think so.'

'What are they waiting for?'

'They want him to tell them who he got the stuff from.'

'Don't they know?'

'Of course they know. But knowing isn't proving, as I'm sure you're in a position to understand.' This last was said not without irony. At times Brunetti thought Italy was a country where everyone knew everything while no one was willing to say anything. In private, everyone was eager to comment with absolute certainty on the secret doings of politicians, Mafia leaders, movie stars; put them into a situation where their remarks might have legal consequences, and Italy turned into the largest clam bed in the world.

'Do you know who it is?' Brunetti asked. 'Would you give me his name?'

'I'd rather not. It wouldn't serve any purpose. There's someone above him, and then someone else above him.' Brunetti could hear him lighting another cigarette.

'Will he tell them? The boy?'

'Not if he values his life, he won't,' Luca said but immediately added, 'No, that's an exaggeration. Not if he wants to avoid being beat up pretty badly.'

'Even in Jesolo?' Brunetti asked. So big city

crime had come to this sleepy Adriatic town.

'Especially in Jesolo, Guido,' Luca said but offered no explanation.

'So what will happen to him?' Brunetti asked.

'You should be able to answer that better than I can,' Luca said. 'If it's a first offence, they'll slap his wrist and send him home.'

'He's already home.'

'I know that. I was speaking figuratively. And the fact that his father is a policeman won't hurt.'

'Not unless the papers get it.'

'I told you. You can be sure about that.'

'I hope so,' Brunetti said.

Luca failed to rise to this. Into the long, growing silence, Brunetti said, 'And what about you? How are you, Luca?'

Luca cleared his throat, a wet sound that made Brunetti uncomfortable. 'The same,' he finally said and coughed again.

'Maria?'

'That cow,' Luca said with real anger. 'All she wants is my money. She's lucky I let her stay in the house.'

'Luca, she's the mother of your children.'

Brunetti could hear Luca fighting the impulse to rage at Brunetti for daring to comment on his life. 'I don't want to talk about this with you, Guido.'

'All right, Luca. You know I say it only because I've known you a long time.' He stopped and then added, 'Known you both.'

'I know that, but things change.' There was

another silence, and then Luca said again, his voice sounding distant, 'I don't want to talk about this, Guido.'

'All right,' Brunetti agreed. 'I'm sorry I haven't called for so long.'

In the easy concession of long friendship, Luca said, 'I haven't called, either, have I?'

'Doesn't matter.'

'No, it doesn't, does it?' Luca agreed with a laugh that brought back both his old voice and his old cough.

Encouraged, Brunetti asked, 'If you hear anything else, will you let me know?'

'Of course,' Luca agreed.

Before the other man could hang up, Brunetti asked, 'Do you know anything else about the men he got it from, and the ones they got it from?'

Caution returned to Luca's voice as he asked, 'What sort of things are you talking about?'

'Whether they . . .' he was not quite certain how to define what it was they did. 'Whether they do business in Venice.'

'Ah,' Luca sighed. 'From what I understand, there's not a lot of business for them there. The population's too old, and it's too easy for the kids to come out to the mainland to find what they want.'

Brunetti realized it was nothing more than selfishness that made him so glad to hear this: any man with two teenaged children, no matter how certain he was of their characters and dispositions, would be glad to learn that there

109

was little drug traffic in the city in which they lived.

Instinct told Brunetti that he had got as much as he was going to get from Luca. Knowing the names of the men who sold the drugs wouldn't make any difference, anyway.

'Thanks, Luca. Take care of yourself.'

'You, too, Guido.'

That night, talking to Paola after the kids had gone to bed, he told her about the conversation and about Luca's outburst of rage at the mention of his wife's name. 'You've never liked him as much as I do,' Brunetti said, as if that would somehow explain or excuse Luca's behaviour.

'What's that supposed to mean?' Paola asked, but without rancour.

They were sitting at opposite ends of the sofa and had put down their books when they began to talk. Brunetti thought about her question for a long time before he answered, 'I guess it's supposed to mean that you'd have to be more sympathetic to Maria than to him.'

'But Luca's right,' Paola said, turning her head and then her entire body to face him. 'She is a cow.'

'But I thought you liked her.'

'I do like her,' Paola insisted. 'Still, that doesn't stop Luca from being right in saying she's a cow. But it was he who turned her into one. When they got married, she was a dentist, but he asked her to stop working. And then after Paolo was born, he told her she didn't have to go back to work, that he was making enough money with the clubs to support them all well. So she stopped working.'

'So?' Brunetti interrupted. 'How does that make him responsible if she's become a cow?' Even as he asked the question, he was conscious of both how insulting and how absurd the very word was.

'Because he moved them all out to Jesolo where it would be more convenient for him to oversee the clubs. And she went.' Her voice grew truculent, reciting the beads of a very old rosary.

'No one held a gun to her head, Paola.'

'Of course no one held a gun to her head: no one had to,' she fired back. 'She was in love.' Seeing his look, she amended this. 'All right, *they* were in love.' She stopped briefly, then continued, 'So she leaves Venice to go out to live in Jesolo, a summer beach town, for God's sake, and becomes a housewife and mother.'

'They're not dirty words, Paola.'

However fiery the glance this earned, she remained cool. 'I know they're not dirty words. I don't mean to suggest that they are. But she gave up a profession she enjoyed and that she was very good at, and she went out to the middle of nowhere to raise two children and take care of a husband who drank too much and smoked too much and fooled around with too many women.' Brunetti knew better than to pour oil on these particular flames. He waited for her to continue, and she did.

'So now, after more than twenty years out there, she's turned into a cow. She's fat and she's boring and all she seems able to talk about is her children or her cooking.' She glanced in Brunetti's direction, but he still didn't say anything. 'How long has it been since we saw them together? Two years? Remember how painful it was the last time, with her hovering around, asking us if we'd like more food or showing us more pictures of their two very unexceptional children?'

It had been a painful evening for everyone except, strangely enough, Maria, who had seemed unaware of how tedious the others found her behaviour.

With childlike candour, Brunetti asked, 'This isn't turning into an argument, is it?'

Paola put her head back against the sofa and laughed outright. 'No, it isn't.' She added, 'I suppose my tone shows how little real sympathy I have for her. And the guilt I feel about that.' She waited to see how Brunetti reacted to her confession, and then continued, 'There were a lot of things she could have done, but she chose not to. She refused to have anyone help her with the kids so that she could work even part-time in someone else's office; then she let her membership in the dental association lapse; then she gradually lost interest in anything that didn't have to do with the two boys; and then she got fat.'

When he was sure she was finished, Brunetti observed, 'I'm not sure how you're going to take this, but those sound suspiciously like the arguments I've heard lots of faithless husbands give.'

'For being faithless?'

'Yes.'

'I'm sure they are.' Her tone was determined but not in any way angry.

Clearly she was not going to add to that, so he asked, 'And?'

'And nothing. Life offered her a series of choices that might have made things different, and she made the choices she did. My guess is that each of those choices made the next one inevitable, once she agreed to stop working and to move out of Venice, but she still made them when no one, as you said, was pointing a gun at her head.'

'I feel sorry for her,' Brunetti said. 'For them both.'

Paola, head resting against the back of the sofa, closed her eyes and said, 'So do I.' After a long time, she asked, 'Are you glad I kept my job?'

He gave this the consideration it deserved and answered, 'Not particularly; I'm just happy you didn't get fat.'

11

The next day, Patta did not appear at the Questura, and the only explanation he gave was to call Signorina Elettra and tell her what had, by then, become self-evident: he would not be there. Signorina Elettra asked no questions, but she did call Brunetti to tell him that the Vice-Questore's absence left him in charge, the Questore being on vacation in Ireland.

At nine, Vianello called to say that he had already got Rossi's keys from the hospital and been to see his apartment. Nothing seemed out of place, and the only papers were bills and receipts. He'd found an address book by the phone, and Pucetti was in the process of calling everyone listed in it. So far, the only relative was an uncle in Vicenza, who had already been called by the hospital and was taking care of the funeral. Bocchese, the lab technician, called soon after this to say he was sending one of the officers up to Brunetti's office with Rossi's wallet.

'Anything on it?'

'No, only his own prints and some that came off that kid who found him.'

Immediately curious about the possibility that there might be another witness, Brunetti asked, 'Kid?'

'The officer, the young one. I don't know his name. They're all kids to me.'

'Franchi.'

'If you say so,' Bocchese said with little interest. 'I've got his prints on file here, and they match the others on the wallet.'

'Anything else?'

'No. I didn't look at the stuff inside, just lifted the prints.'

A young officer, one of the new ones Brunetti found it so difficult to call by name, appeared at his door. At Brunetti's wave, he came in and placed the wallet, still wrapped in a plastic bag, on the desk.

Brunetti shifted the phone, clamping it under his chin, and picked up the envelope. Opening it, he asked Bocchese, 'Any prints inside?'

'I said those were the only prints,' the technician said and hung up.

Brunetti put the phone down. A *Carabiniere* colonel had once remarked that Bocchese was so good that he could find fingerprints even on a substance as oily as a politician's soul, and so he was given more latitude than most of the other people working in the Questura. Brunetti had long since become accustomed to the man's constant irascibility; indeed, years of exposure had dulled him to it. His surliness was compensated for by the flawless efficiency of his work, which had more than once held up to the fierce scepticism of defence attorneys.

Brunetti zipped open the envelope and tilted the wallet on to the desk. It was curved, having taken on the shape of Rossi's hip, against which it must have been kept for years. The brown leather was creased down the middle and a small strip of the binding had been rubbed away, exposing a thin grey cord. He opened the wallet and pressed it flat on his desk. A series of slots on the left side held four plastic cards: Visa, Standa, his identification card from the Ufficio Catasto, and his Carta Venezia that would qualify Rossi to pay the lower fare imposed on residents by the transport system. He pulled them out and studied the photo that appeared on the last two. It had been impressed into the cards by some sort of holographic process and so lapsed into invisibility when the light struck it from certain angles, but it was definitely Rossi.

On the right side of the wallet was a small change purse, its flap held closed by a brass snap. Brunetti opened it and poured the change out on to his desk. There were some of the new thousand-lire pieces, a few five-hundred-lire coins, and one of each of the three different sized one-hundred-lire coins currently in circulation. Did other people find it as strange as he did that there should be three different sizes? What could explain such madness?

Brunetti pulled apart the back section of the wallet and lifted out the banknotes. They were arranged in strict order, with the largest bills toward the back of the wallet, descending to the thousand-lire bills at the front. He counted the notes: one hundred and eighty-seven thousand lire.

He pulled the back section apart to see if he had overlooked anything, but there was nothing else. He slipped his fingers into the slot on the left side and pulled out some unused vaporetto tickets, a receipt from a bar for three thousand, three hundred lire, and some eight-hundred-lire stamps. On the other side he found another receipt from a bar, on the back of which was written a phone number. As it did not begin with 52, 27, or 72, he assumed it was not a Venice number, though no city code was given. And that was all. No names, no note from the deceased man, leaving a message to be read in the event that something happened to him, none of those things that never really are found in the wallets of people who may have died by wilful violence.

Brunetti put the money back into the wallet, the wallet back into the plastic bag. He pulled the telephone across the desk and dialled Rizzardi's number. The autopsy should have been done by now, and he was curious to know more about that strange indentation on Rossi's forehead.

The doctor answered the phone on the second ring, and they exchanged polite greetings. Rizzardi then said, 'You calling about Rossi?' When Brunetti said he was, Rizzardi said, 'Good. If you hadn't called me, I would have called you.'

'Why?'

'The wound. Well, the two wounds. On his head.'

'What about them?'

'One's flat, and cement's ground into it. That happened when he hit the pavement. But to the left of it there's another one, tubular. That is, it was made by something cylindrical, like the pipes used to build the *impalcatura* they put up around the building, though the circumference seems smaller than the pipes I remember seeing on those things.'

'And?'

'And there's no rust at all in the wound. Those pipes are usually filthy with all sorts of dirt and rust and paint, but the wound had no sign of any of those things.'

'They could have washed it at the hospital.'

'They did, but traces of metal in the smaller wound were ground into the bones of his skull. Only metal. No dirt, no rust, and no paint.'

'What kind of metal?' Brunetti asked, suspecting that there would have to be more than

118

the absence of something to have inspired Rizzardi's call.

'Copper.' When Brunetti made no comment, Rizzardi ventured, 'It's not my business to tell you how to run yours, but it might be a good idea to get a crime scene team over there today or as soon as you can.'

'Yes, I will,' Brunetti said, glad that he was in charge of the Questura that day. 'What else did you find?'

'Both arms were broken, but I suspect you know that. There were bruises on his hands, but that could have resulted from the fall.'

'Do you have any idea how far he fell?'

'I'm not really an expert on that sort of thing: it happens so infrequently. But I had a look at a couple of books, and I'd guess it was about ten metres.'

'Third floor?'

'Possibly. At least the second.'

'Can you tell anything from the way he landed?'

'No. But it looks like he tried to push himself forward for a while after he did. The knees of his pants are scraped raw, his knees too; there's also some scraping on the inside of one ankle that I'd say came from dragging it on the pavement.'

Brunetti interrupted the doctor here. 'Is there any way to tell which wound killed him?'

'No.' Rizzardi's answer was so immediate that Brunetti realized he must have been waiting for the question. He waited for Brunetti to go on. But Brunetti could think of nothing better to ask than a vague, 'Anything else?'

'No. He was healthy and would have lived a long time.'

'Poor devil.'

'The man in the morgue said you knew him. Was he a friend?'

Brunetti didn't hesitate. 'Yes, he was.'

12

Brunetti called the office of Telecom and identified himself as a police officer. He explained that he was trying to trace a phone number but lacked the city code, as he had only the last seven digits, and asked if Telecom could give him the names of the cities where this number existed. Without thinking of verifying the authenticity of his call, without so much as the suggestion that she call him back at the Questura, the woman asked him to hang on a moment while she consulted her computer, and put him on hold. At least there was no music. She was quickly back and told him that the possibilities were Piacenza, Ferrara, Aquilea, and Messina.

Brunetti then asked to be given the names of

the people for whom those four numbers were listed, at which point the woman retreated behind Telecom rules, the law of privacy, and 'approved policy'. She explained that she needed a phone call from the police or from some other organ of the state. Patiently, keeping his voice calm, Brunetti explained again that he was a commissario of police: she could call him at the Questura of Venice. When she asked for the number, Brunetti resisted the temptation to ask if she might not be better advised to check the number in the phone book to be sure she was in fact calling the Questura. Instead, he gave her the number, repeated his name, and hung up. The phone rang almost immediately, and the woman read out four names and addresses.

The names told him nothing. The Piacenza number was a car rental agency, that of Ferrara was for joint names that could be a business office or even a shop. The other two were, presumably, private residences. He dialled the Piacenza number, waited, and when the phone was answered by a man, said he was calling from the Venice police and would like them to check their records and see if they had rented a car to or were familiar with a man called Franco Rossi from Venice. The man asked Brunetti to hold on, covered the phone, and spoke to someone else. A woman then asked him to repeat his request. After he had, he was again told to wait a moment. The moment stretched into a few minutes, but eventually the woman came back and said she was sorry to report they had no record of a client by that name.

On the Ferrara number there was only a message announcing that he had reached the office of Gavini and Cappelli and asking him to leave his name, number, and the reason for his call. He hung up.

In Aquilea he reached what sounded like an old woman who said she had never heard of Franco Rossi. The Messina number was no longer in service.

He had found no driver's licence in Rossi's wallet. Even though many Venetians didn't drive, he might still have had one: the absence of roads was hardly enough to prevent an Italian from exercising his lust for speed. He called down to the drivers' licence office and was told that licences had been given to nine Franco Rossis. Brunetti checked Rossi's identification card from the Ufficio Catasto and gave Rossi's date of birth: no licence had been issued to him.

He tried the number in Ferrara again, but there was still no answer. His phone rang.

'Commissario?' It was Vianello.

'Yes.'

'We've just had a call from the station over in Cannaregio.'

'The one by Tre Archi?'

'Yes, sir.'

'What is it?'

'They responded to a call from a man who said there was a smell coming from the apartment above his, a bad smell.'

Brunetti waited; it took very little imagination

to know what was coming: police commissari were not called about bad plumbing or abandoned garbage.

'He was a student,' Vianello said, cutting off further speculation.

'What was it?'

'It looks like an overdose. At least that's what they said.'

'How long ago did the call come in?'

'About ten minutes.'

'I'll come along.'

When they left the Questura, Brunetti was surprised by the heat. Strangely enough, although he always knew the day and usually the date, he very often had to pause to recall whether it was spring or autumn. So when he felt the heat of the day, he had to shake himself free of this strange disorientation before he recalled that it was spring and that the growing heat was to be expected.

There was a different pilot that day, Pertile, a man Brunetti found *antipatico*. They climbed aboard, Brunetti and Vianello and the two men from the technical squad. One of them cast off and they headed out into the *bacino* and then quickly turned back into the Arsenale Canal. Pertile turned on the siren and sped through the dead calm waters of the Arsenale, cutting in front of a 52 vaporetto that was just pulling away from the Tana boat stop. 'This isn't a nuclear evacuation, Pertile,' Brunetti said.

The pilot looked back at the men on deck, lowered one hand from the wheel, and the noise of the siren was cut off. It seemed to Brunetti that the pilot urged the boat to greater speed, but he stopped himself from saying anything. At the back of the Arsenale, Pertile swung sharply to the left and past the usual stops: the hospital, Fondamenta Nuove, La Madonna dell'Orto, San Alvise, and then turned into the beginning of the Cannaregio Canal. Just after the first boat stop, they saw a police officer standing on the *riva* and waving to them as they approached.

Vianello tossed him the rope, and he bent to fix it to an iron ring. When he saw Brunetti, the officer on the *riva* saluted, then extended a hand to help him from the boat.

'Where is he?' Brunetti asked as soon as his feet were again on firm ground.

'Down this *calle*, sir,' he said, turning away from Brunetti and into a narrow street that ran back from the water toward the interior of Cannaregio.

The others filed off the boat, and Vianello turned to tell Pertile to wait for them. Brunetti walking next to the officer, the others in single file behind them, they started down the narrow *calle*.

They didn't have far to go, and they didn't have any trouble in finding the right house: about twenty metres along, a small crowd of people stood clustered in front of a doorway, in which a uniformed officer stood, arms folded.

As Brunetti approached, a man broke away from the crowd but made no attempt to walk toward the policemen. He simply moved away from the others and stood still, hands on his hips, watching the police draw near. He was tall, almost cadaverous, and had the worst drinker's nose Brunetti had ever seen: inflamed, enlarged, pitted, and virtually blue at the end. It made Brunetti think of faces he'd once seen in a painting by some Dutch Master – was it of Christ carrying His cross? – horrible, distorted faces boding nothing but pain and evil for all who came within their malignant compass.

In a low voice, Brunetti asked, 'That the man who found him?'

'Yes, sir,' answered the policeman who had met the boat. 'He lives on the first floor.'

They approached the man, who stuffed his hands into his pockets and started to rock back and forth on his heels, as if he had important work to get on with and resented the police for keeping him from it.

Brunetti stopped in front of him. 'Good morning, sir. Is it you who called us?' he asked.

'Yes, I did. I'm surprised you took the trouble to get here so fast,' he said, his voice as filled with rancour and hostility as his breath was with alcohol and coffee.

'You live below him?' Brunetti asked neutrally.

'Yeah, I've been there for seven years, and if that shit, my landlord, thinks he can get me out by giving me an eviction notice, I'll tell him where he can shove it.' He spoke with the accent of Giudecca and, like many of the natives of that island, seemed to think that scurrility was as essential to speech as air to breathing.

'How long has he lived here?'

'Doesn't live here any more, does he?' the man asked and bent over to engage in a prolonged laugh that ended in a bout of coughing.

'How long *had* he lived here?' Brunetti asked when the man stopped coughing.

The man stood upright and took a closer look at Brunetti. In his turn, Brunetti observed the white patches that peeled away from the reddened skin of the man's face and the yellowed eyes that told of jaundice.

'A couple of months. You'll have to ask the landlord. I just saw him on the stairs.'

'Did anyone come to visit him?'

'I don't know,' the man said with sudden truculence. 'I keep my business to myself. Besides, he was a student. I don't have anything to say to people like that. Little shits, think they know everything.'

'Did he behave like that?' Brunetti asked.

The man considered this for a moment, surprised at having to examine a specific case to see if it conformed to his general prejudice. After a long time, he said, 'No, but like I told you, I just saw him a few times.'

'Give your name to the sergeant, please,' Brunetti said and turned away, indicating the young man who had greeted the boat. He walked up the two steps that led to the front door, where he was saluted by the officer standing there. From behind him he heard the man he'd questioned call out, 'His name was Marco.'

When Vianello approached, Brunetti asked him to see what he could learn from the people in the neighbourhood. The sergeant turned away and the officer stepped forward. 'Second floor, sir,' he said.

Brunetti looked up the narrow staircase. Behind him, the policeman snapped on the light, but the low-wattage bulb made little difference, as if reluctant to illuminate the general squalor. Paint and cement had flaked off the walls and been kicked into small dunes on either side by the people who used the stairs. Here and there, cigarette butts and bits of paper lay on top of or stuck out from the dunes.

Brunetti climbed the steps. The smell met him on the first landing. Close, dense, penetrating, it spoke of rot and vileness and something inhumanly unclean. As he drew closer to the second floor, the smell grew stronger, and Brunetti had a terrible moment in which he visualized the avalanche of molecules, falling over him, clinging to his clothing, cascading into his nose and throat, always carrying with it the horrible reminder of mortality.

A third policeman, looking very pale in the dim light, stood at the door to the apartment. Brunetti was sorry to see that it was closed because it meant the smell would be much worse when they opened it again. The officer saluted and stepped away very quickly, and didn't stop until he was four steps from the door.

'You can go downstairs,' Brunetti said, aware that the boy must have been there for almost an hour. 'Go outside.'

'Thank you, sir,' he said and saluted again before walking very quickly around Brunetti and launching himself down the stairs.

Behind him, Brunetti heard the various clumps and clatters of the technical team as they carried up their bags of tools.

He resisted the impulse to draw a deep breath; instead he drew up his courage and reached for the door. Before he could open it, however, one of the technical men called out, 'Commissario, take this first.' When Brunetti turned, the man was ripping open the plastic covering around a surgical mask. He handed one to Brunetti, then one to his colleague. They all slipped the elastic strings around their ears and pulled the masks up over their mouths and noses, all of them glad to breathe in the sharp odour of the chemicals with which the masks had been treated.

Brunetti opened the door, and the smell assaulted them, slicing through the chemicals. He glanced up and saw that all of the windows had been opened, probably by the police, and that the crime scene was, in a sense, contaminated. There was, however, little need to protect this scene; Cerberus himself would have fled, howling, from the smell.

His body stiff with the desire not to move, Brunetti stepped through the door, and the others crowded in after him. The living room was what he would have expected to find in the apartment of a student: indeed, it reminded him of the way his friends had lived when they were at university. A battered sofa was covered with a length of colourful Indian cloth, tossed over the back and tucked in tight under the seats and beside the arms to make it look like upholstery. A long table stood against the wall, its surface covered with papers, books, and an orange on which green mould had begun to grow. Books and an assortment of clothing covered two other chairs.

The boy was on the floor of the kitchen, sprawled on his back. His left arm was flung out behind his head, the needle that had killed him still stuck into the vein of his arm, just below the turn of the elbow. His right hand was curved around the top of his head, and Brunetti recognized the gesture his son made whenever he realized he had made a mistake or done something stupid. On the table lay what was to be expected: a spoon, a candle, and the tiny plastic envelope that had held whatever killed him. Brunetti turned his eyes away. The open window of the kitchen looked across at another window, shuttered and blind.

One of the lab men came in behind him and looked down at the boy. 'Should I cover him, sir?'

'No. Better leave him until the doctor's seen him. Who's coming?'

'Guerriero, sir,'

'Not Rizzardi?'

'No, sir. Guerriero's on duty today.'

Brunetti nodded and went back into the living room. The elastic had begun to rub against his cheek, so he removed the surgical mask and stuffed it into his pocket. The smell was worse for a while, but then it wasn't. The second lab man went into the kitchen, carrying camera and tripod, and he heard the muted sound of their voices as they discussed how best to record this scene for the little part of history that Marco, a student at the university and dead with a needle stuck in his arm, would fill in the police archives of Venice, pearl of the Adriatic. Brunetti went over to the boy's desk and stood looking down at a jumble of papers and books, so like the one he had created on his own desk when he was a student, so like the mess his own son left in his wake each morning when he went off to school.

On the inside cover of a history of architecture, Brunetti found his name: Marco Landi. Slowly he went through the papers on the desk, occasionally stopping to read a paragraph or a sentence. Marco, he discovered, had been working on a paper that dealt with the gardens of four of the eighteenth-century villas between Venice and Padova. Brunetti found books and photocopies of articles on landscape architecture, even some sketches of gardens that seemed to have been made by the dead boy. For a long time, Brunetti studied a large drawing of an elaborate formal garden, each plant and tree drawn in exact detail. He could even read the time on the enormous sundial that stood to the left of a fountain: four fifteen. At the bottom of the right side of the drawing, he noticed a pair of rabbits behind a fat oleander, peering curiously at the viewer, both of them seeming content and well fed. He replaced the drawing and picked up another, this one apparently for some other project because it showed a severely modern house, cantilevered out over an open space that could have been a canyon or a cliff. Brunetti studied the drawing, noticing the rabbits again, this time quizzically looking out from behind what appeared to be a piece of modern sculpture on the lawn in front of the house. He set it down and leafed through more of Marco's drawings. In each of them, the rabbits appeared, sometimes almost impossible to find, so cleverly had they been hidden: once in the window of an apartment building, once peering through the windshield of a car parked in front of a house. Brunetti wondered how Marco's professors would have greeted the appearance of the rabbits in each new assignment, whether it would have amused or annoyed them. And then he allowed himself to wonder about the boy who put them there, in every drawing. Why rabbits? And why two of them?

He turned his attention from the drawings to a handwritten letter to the left of them. It bore no return address and was postmarked from somewhere in the province of Trento. The postmark was smudged, making the name of the town illegible. He glanced quickly down the page and saw that it was signed '*Mamma*'.

Brunetti looked away a moment before he began to read. It contained the usual family news: *Papà* busy with the spring planting; Maria, whom Brunetti inferred must be Marco's younger sister, doing well in school. Briciola had run after the postman again; she herself was well and hoped that Marco was studying and doing well at school and not having any more trouble. No, Signora, your Marco will never have any trouble again, but all that you will have now, and for the rest of your lives, is loss and pain and the terrible sense that you somehow failed this boy. And no matter how deep your knowledge that you were not responsible for it, your certainty that you were will always be deeper and more absolute.

He set the letter down and quickly went through the rest of the papers on the desk. There were more letters from the boy's mother, but Brunetti did not read them. Finally, in the top drawer of the pine dresser to the left of the table, he found an address book, and in it he found Marco's parents' address and phone number. He slipped the small book into the side pocket of his jacket.

A sound at the door made him turn around to see Gianpaolo Guerriero, Rizzardi's assistant. To Brunetti, Guerriero's ambition was easily read on his lean young face and in the quickness of his every gesture, or perhaps it was nothing more than that Brunetti knew him to be ambitious and so saw that quality – Brunetti could never bring himself to call it a virtue – in everything the man did. Brunetti wanted to like him because he had seen that he was respectful of the dead with whom he worked, but there was a humourless sincerity in the man that made it difficult for Brunetti to feel toward him anything stronger than respect. Like his superior, he was a careful dresser and today wore a grey woollen suit which complemented his elegant good looks. Behind him came two white-clad attendants from the morgue. Brunetti nodded towards the kitchen, and the men went inside, taking their rolled-up stretcher with them.

'Don't touch anything,' Guerriero called unnecessarily after them. He gave Brunetti his hand.

'They told me it was an overdose,' Guerriero said.

'It looks like it.' No sounds came from the other room.

Guerriero went into the kitchen, carrying a bag Brunetti couldn't help noticing bore the Prada logo.

Brunetti remained in the living room and, while he waited for Guerriero to finish, propped himself on the table on his outstretched palms and looked down again at Marco's drawings. He wanted to smile at the rabbits, but he could not.

Guerriero was inside the room no more than a few minutes. He paused at the door to remove the surgical mask he had put on. 'If it was heroin,' the doctor said, 'and I think it was, it would have been instant. You saw him: he didn't even have time to get the needle out of his arm.'

Brunetti asked, 'What would do that to him? Or why would it, if he was an addict?'

Guerriero considered this then answered, 'If it was heroin, it could have had just about any sort of crap mixed up in it. That could have done it. Or, if he hadn't been using it for a while, then it could have been no more than an over-reaction to a dosage that wouldn't have harmed him while he was using it regularly. That is, if he got some stuff that was particularly pure.'

'What do you think?' Brunetti asked, and when he saw Guerriero begin to give an automatic, no doubt cautious, reply, he raised his hand and added, 'entirely unofficially'.

Guerriero thought about this for a long time before he answered, and Brunetti couldn't escape the idea that the young doctor was weighing up the professional consequences of being discovered to have made an entirely unofficial judgement. Finally, he said, 'I think it might be the second.'

Brunetti didn't prod, simply stood there and waited for him to continue.

'I didn't check the entire body,' Guerriero said. 'Just the arms, but there are no fresh marks, though there are a lot of old ones. If he's been using heroin recently, he would have been using his arms. Addicts tend to use the same place. I'd say he's been off the stuff for a couple of months.'

'But then he went back to it?'

'Yes, it would seem so. I'll be able to tell you more after I have a better look at him.'

'Thank you, Dottore,' Brunetti said. 'Will they take him out now?'

'Yes. I've told them to put him in a bag. With the windows open, it should be better in here soon.'

'Good. Thank you.'

Guerriero raised a hand in acknowledgement.

'When can you do the autopsy?' Brunetti asked.

'Tomorrow morning, most likely. Things are slow at the hospital at the moment. It's strange, the way so few people die in the spring.

'I left his wallet and the things from his pockets on the kitchen table,' Guerriero went on, opening his bag and stuffing the surgical mask inside.

'Thank you. Call me when you have anything, will you?'

'Of course,' Guerriero said and, after shaking hands in farewell, left the apartment.

During their brief conversation, Brunetti had been aware of sounds coming from the kitchen. As soon as Guerriero was gone, the two attendants emerged, stretcher now unrolled and filled with its bagged burden suspended between them. With an effort of will, Brunetti kept himself from thinking about how they would manipulate their burden down the narrow, twisting steps of the building. The men nodded in his direction but did not stop.

The sound of their departure growing fainter as they descended the stairs, Brunetti went back into the kitchen.

The taller of the two technicians – Brunetti thought his name was Santini but wasn't sure – looked up and said, 'Nothing here, sir.'

'You check his papers?' Brunetti asked, indicating the wallet and small pile of crumpled papers and coins that lay on the table.

Santini's partner answered for him. 'No, sir. We thought you'd want to do that.'

'How many more rooms are there?' Brunetti asked.

Santini pointed toward the back of the apartment. 'Just the bathroom. He must have slept on that sofa in the other room.'

'Anything in the bathroom?'

Santini left it to the other to answer. 'No needles in there, sir, no sign of them. Just the regular stuff you'd expect to find in a bathroom: aspirin, shaving cream, a package of plastic razors; no drug paraphernalia at all.'

Brunetti found it interesting that the technician should comment on this and so asked, 'What do you make of it?'

'I'd say the kid was clean,' he answered without hesitation. Brunetti glanced at Santini, who nodded in agreement with his partner. The other continued, 'We've seen a lot of these kids, and most of them are a mess. Sores all over their bodies, not just their arms.' He raised a hand and waved it back and forth a few times, as if brushing away the memory of the young bodies he'd seen, lying in their drug-bought deaths. 'But this kid didn't have any other fresh marks.' No one spoke for a time.

Santini finally asked, 'Is there anything else you'd like us to do, sir?'

'No, I don't think so.' He noticed that both of them were no longer wearing their masks and that the smell was fainter now, even here, where the boy had been lying for no one knew how long. 'You two go and have a coffee. I'll have a look at that,' he said, waving towards the wallet and papers. 'Then I'll lock up and come down.'

Neither objected. When they were gone, Brunetti picked up the wallet and blew on it to remove some of the fine grey powder. It contained fifty-seven thousand lire. There was another two thousand, seven hundred in coins on the table, where someone had put it after taking it from Marco's pockets. Inside he found Marco's *Carta d'identità*, which gave his birthdate. With a sudden motion, he swept all of the money and paper on the desk into his hand and stuffed it into the pocket of his jacket. He had seen a set of keys on the table just inside the door. Carefully checking that all of the shutters held fast, he closed them and then the windows of the apartment. He locked the door and went downstairs.

Outside, Vianello was standing by an old man, leaning forward to listen to whatever he had to say. When he saw Brunetti emerge, he patted the old man on the arm and turned away. As Brunetti approached, Vianello shook his head. 'No one saw anything. No one knows anything.'

13

With Vianello and the men from the technical squad, Brunetti rode back to the Questura on the police boat, glad of the air and the wind that, he hoped, would blow them free of the smell they had taken with them from the apartment. None of them mentioned it, but Brunetti knew he would not feel entirely clean until he had stripped himself of every piece of clothing he had worn that day and stood for a long time under the cleansing water of a shower. Even in the burgeoning heat of this late spring day, he longed equally for hot, steaming water and the hard feel of a rough cloth against every centimetre of his body.

The technicians carried the means of Marco's death back to the Questura with them and, even though there was little chance of getting a second set of prints from the syringe that had killed him, there was some hope that the plastic bag he'd left lying on the kitchen table would provide them with something, even a fragment that might be matched with prints already on file.

When they arrived at the Questura, the pilot brought the boat in too quickly, slamming it up against the landing so hard that they were jostled about on the deck. One of the technicians grabbed Brunetti's shoulder to prevent himself from falling down the steps and into the cabin. The pilot cut the motor and jumped ashore, grabbing the end of the rope that would anchor the boat to the landing deck and keeping himself busy with the knots. A silent Brunetti led the others off the boat and into the Questura.

Brunetti went directly to Signorina Elettra's small office. She was talking on the phone when he came in, and when she saw him, she held up a hand, signalling him to wait. He came in slowly, concerned that he would carry in with him the terrible smell that still filled his imagination, if not his clothing. He noticed that the window was open, so he went and stood by it, beside a large vase of lilies whose oily sweetness filled the air around them with a sickly odour he had always loathed.

Sensing his restlessness, Signorina Elettra glanced across at him, held the receiver away from her ear and waved her other hand in the air, as if to suggest her lack of patience with the caller. She pulled the receiver back to her ear and muttered, '*Sì*' a few times without letting her impatience show in her voice. A minute passed, she held the phone away again, and then pulled it suddenly toward her, said thank you and goodbye, and hung up.

'All that to tell me why he can't come tonight,' was all she offered by way of explanation. It wasn't much, but it was enough to cause Brunetti to wonder what and where. And who. He said nothing.

'How was it?' she asked.

'Bad,' Brunetti answered. 'He was twenty. And no one knows how long he'd been there.'

'In this heat,' she said, not as a question but as an expression of general sympathy.

Brunetti nodded. 'It was drugs, an overdose.'

She said nothing to this but closed her eyes and then said, 'I've been asking some people I know about drugs, but they all say the same thing, that Venice is a very small market.' She paused, then added, 'But it must be big enough for someone to have sold this boy whatever killed him.' How strange, it seemed to Brunetti, to hear her refer to Marco as a 'boy': she couldn't be much more than a decade older herself.

'I have to call his parents,' Brunetti said.

She looked at her watch, and Brunetti looked at his, amazed to discover that it was only ten past one. Death made real time meaningless, and it seemed to him that he had spent days in the apartment.

'Why don't you wait a little while, sir?' Before

he could ask, she explained. 'That way, the father might be there and they'll have finished lunch. It would be better for them if they were together when you tell them.'

'Yes,' he said. 'I hadn't thought of that. I'll wait.' He had no idea of what he would do to fill the time between now and then.

Signorina Elettra reached forward and touched something on her computer. It made a sudden droning noise, and then the screen went blank. 'I thought I'd stop now and go and have *un' ombra* before lunch. Would you like to join me, sir?' She smiled at her own flagrant boldness: a married man, her boss, and she was inviting him for a drink.

Brunetti, moved by the charity of it, said, 'Yes, I'd like that, Signorina.'

He made the call a little after two. A woman answered the phone, and Brunetti asked to speak to Signor Landi. He breathed silent, directionless thanks when she displayed no curiosity and said she'd get her husband.

'Landi,' a deep voice answered.

'Signor Landi,' Brunetti said, 'this is Commissario Guido Brunetti. I'm calling from the Questura of Venice.'

Before he could go on, Landi cut him off, his own voice suddenly tight and loud. 'Is it Marco?'

'Yes, Signor Landi, it is.'

'How bad is it?' Landi asked in a softer voice.

'I'm afraid it couldn't be worse, Signor Landi.'

Silence drifted across the line. Brunetti imagined the man, the newspaper in his hand, standing at the phone and looking back toward the kitchen, where his wife was clearing up after the last peaceful meal she would ever have.

Landi's voice grew almost inaudible, but there was only one thing he could have asked, so Brunetti filled in the missing sounds. 'Is he dead?'

'Yes, I'm sorry to tell you, he is.'

There was another pause, this one even longer, and then Landi asked, 'When?'

'We found him today.'

'Who did?'

'The police. A neighbour called.' Brunetti could not bring himself to give the details or to talk about the time that had passed since Marco died. 'He said he hadn't seen Marco recently and called us to check on the apartment. When we did, we found him.'

'Was it drugs?'

No autopsy had been performed. The mechanism of the state had not yet considered the evidence surrounding the boy's death, had not weighed and considered it and brought judgement as to the cause of his death; thus it would be rash and so irresponsible as to merit official reprimand for an officer of the law to venture his own opinion in this matter. 'Yes,' Brunetti said.

The man on the other end of the line was crying. Brunetti heard the long, deep gasps as he choked on his grief and fought for air. A minute passed. Brunetti held the phone away from him and looked off to the left, where a plaque on the wall gave the names of police officers who had died in the First World War. He started to read their names, the dates of their birth and the dates of their death. One had been only twenty, the same age as Marco.

From the receiver, he heard the dim sound of a higher voice, raised in curiosity or fear, but then the sound was cut off as Landi covered the phone with his hand. Another minute passed. Then he could hear Landi's voice. Brunetti pulled the phone to his ear, but all he heard was Landi saying, 'I'll call you back,' and the connection was broken.

While he sat and waited, Brunetti considered the nature of this crime. If Guerriero was right and Marco had died because his body had grown unaccustomed to the terrible shock of heroin during the time he hadn't been using it, then what crime had been committed other than the sale of a prohibited substance? And what sort of crime was that, to sell heroin to an addict, and where existed the judge to treat it as more than a misdemeanour? If, instead, the heroin that killed him had been laced with something dangerous or lethal, how to determine at what point along the trail that stretched from the poppy fields of the East to the veins of the West that that substance had been added, and by whom?

No matter how he considered it, there was no way Brunetti could see that this crime would have serious legal consequences. Nor could he see much likelihood that the identity of the person responsible would ever be discovered. And yet the young student who drew the whimsical rabbits and had the wit to hide them in different places in each of his drawings was no less dead for that.

He got up from his desk and stood at the window. The sun beat down on Campo San Lorenzo. All of the men who lived in the old-age home had answered the summons to sleep, leaving the *campo* to the cats and the people who crossed it at this hour. Brunetti leaned forward, resting his hands on the sill, and watched the *campo* as if in search of an omen. After half an hour, Landi called to say that he and his wife would arrive in Venice at seven that evening and asked how they could get to the Questura.

When Landi answered that, yes, they would be coming by train, Brunetti said he would meet them and take them to the hospital by boat.

'The hospital?' Landi asked, hopeless hope springing into his voice.

'I'm sorry, Signor Landi. It's where they're taken.'

'Ah,' was Landi's only answer, and again he broke the connection.

Later that afternoon, Brunetti called a friend who ran a hotel in Campo Santa Marina and asked if he had a double room available that he would hold for some people who might stay the night. People called somewhere by disaster forgot about things like eating and sleeping and all those intrusive details showing that life continued.

He asked Vianello to come with him, telling himself it would be easier for the Landis to recognize the police if someone in uniform met their train, though part of him knew that Vianello was the best person to take along, for himself as much as for the Landis.

The train was on time, and Marco's parents were easy to spot as they came down the platform. She was a tall, spare woman in a grey dress that had been badly wrinkled by the trip: she wore her hair in a small bun at the back of her head, a fashion that was decades out of date. Her husband held her arm, and anyone who saw them could see that it was not a gesture of courtesy or habit: she walked unsteadily, as if in the grip of drink or illness. Landi was short and muscular, with an iron-hard body that spoke of a lifetime spent at work, hard work. In other circumstances, Brunetti might have seen the contrast between them as comic, but not now. Landi's face was to the darkness of leather; his pale hair provided thin protection to his scalp, which was tanned the same colour as his face. He had the look of a man who spent all of his days outside, and Brunetti remembered the mother's letter about spring planting.

They saw Vianello's uniform, and Landi led his wife toward it. Brunetti introduced himself and his sergeant and explained that they had a boat waiting. Only Landi shook hands; only he was capable of speech. His wife could do no more than nod toward them and wipe at her eyes with her left hand.

It was quickly done. At the hospital, Brunetti suggested that Signor Landi alone identify Marco, but they both insisted on going into the room to see their son. Brunetti and Vianello waited outside, neither speaking. When the Landis emerged, some minutes later, both were sobbing openly. Procedure demanded that some formal identification be made, that the person who identified the body do so in speech or writing to the accompanying official.

When they had calmed down, the only thing Brunetti said was, 'I've taken the liberty of reserving you a room for the night, if you'd prefer to stay.'

Landi turned to his wife, but she shook her head.

'No. We'll go back, sir. I think it's better. There's a train at eight thirty. We checked before we came.'

He was right: it was better this way, Brunetti knew. Tomorrow would be the autopsy, and any parent should be spared that or the knowledge of that. He led them out the emergency entrance of the hospital and back to the police boat at the dock. Montisi saw them coming and had the boat unmoored even before they reached it. Vianello took Signora Landi's arm and helped her on board and then down into the cabin. Brunetti took Landi's arm as they stepped aboard but with gentle pressure stopped him from following his wife down the steps into the cabin.

As accustomed to boats as to breathing, Montisi moved them smoothly away from the dock, running the motor at a low speed so that their passage was virtually silent. Landi kept his eyes lowered toward the water, unwilling to look at this city that had taken his son's life.

'Can you tell me something about Marco?' Brunetti asked.

'What do you want to know?' Landi asked, his eyes still lowered.

'You knew about the drugs?'

'Yes.'

'Had he stopped?'

'I thought so. He came home to us late last year. He said he had stopped and wanted to spend time at home before coming back here. He was healthy, and he did a man's work this winter. Together we put a new roof on the barn. You can't do that kind of work if you're taking those things or your body is sick with them.' Landi kept his eyes on the water as the boat glided across it.

'Did he ever talk about it?'

'The drugs?'

'Yes.'

'Only once. He knew I couldn't stand hearing about it.'

'Did he tell you why he did it or where he got them?'

Landi looked up at Brunetti. His eyes were the blue of glaciers, his face curiously unlined, though roughened by sun and wind. 'Who can understand why they do that to their bodies?'

He shook his head and returned his gaze to the water.

Brunetti quelled the impulse to apologize for his questions and asked, 'Did you know about his life here? His friends? What he did?'

Landi answered a different question. 'He always wanted to be an architect. Ever since he was a little boy, all he was ever interested in was buildings and how to make them. I don't understand that. I'm just a farmer. That's all I know about, farming.' As the boat moved out into the waters of the *laguna*, a wave lurched against them, but Landi kept his balance as though he'd felt nothing. 'There's no future in the land, not any more, and there's no living to be made from it. We all know that, but we don't know what else to do.' He sighed.

Still not looking up, he went on. 'Marco came here to study. Two years ago. And when he came home at the end of the first year, we knew something was wrong, but we didn't know what.' He looked up at Brunetti. 'We're simple people: we don't know about things like that, about drugs.' He looked away, saw the buildings that faced the *laguna*, and looked down at the water again.

The wind freshened, and Brunetti had to lean down to hear what he said. 'He came back at Christmas last year, and he was very troubled. So I talked to him, and he told me. He said he had stopped and didn't want to do it any more, that he knew it would kill him.' Brunetti shifted his weight and he saw Landi's work-hardened hands clenched to the railing of the boat.

'He couldn't explain why he did it or what it was like, but I know he meant it when he said he didn't want to do it any more. We didn't tell his mother.' Landi stopped.

Brunetti finally asked, 'What happened?'

'He stayed with us for the rest of the winter, and we worked together on the barn. That's why I know he was all right. Then, two months ago, he said he wanted to come back to school and start to study again, that there wasn't any danger any more. I believed him. So he came back here to Venice, and it seemed that he was all right. And then you called.'

The boat swung out of the Canale di Cannaregio and into the Grand Canal. Brunetti asked, 'Did he ever mention friends? A girlfriend?'

The question seemed to trouble Landi. 'He has a girlfriend at home.' He paused, his answer obviously unfinished. 'But there was someone here, I think. Marco called here in the winter, three or four times, and a girl called a few times and asked to talk to him. But he never told us anything.'

The motor slipped into reverse for a second, and the boat glided to a stop in front of the station. Montisi stopped the motor and came out of the cabin. Silently, he tossed the rope around a stanchion and stepped ashore, then pulled the boat up parallel with the landing. Landi and Brunetti turned, and the farmer helped his wife up the last step from the cabin.

Holding her arm, he helped her from the boat.

Brunetti asked Landi for his tickets and, when he handed them to him, gave them to Vianello, who walked quickly ahead to stamp them and find the correct platform. By the time the three of them reached the top of the stairs, Vianello was back. He led them to platform five, where the train for Verona was waiting. In silence, they walked along until Vianello, glancing up through the windows of the waiting train, saw an empty compartment. He walked to the door at the head of the carriage, stood to one side, and offered his arm to Signora Landi. She took it and pulled herself wearily up into the train. Landi followed her, then turned and reached down and extended his hand, first to Vianello, then to Brunetti. He nodded once but had no more words to give them. He turned and followed his wife down the corridor toward the empty compartment.

Brunetti and Vianello waited by the door until the conductor blew his whistle and waved a green cloth in the air before stepping up into the now-moving train; the door slammed shut automatically and the train started on its way toward the bridge and the world that lay beyond Venice. As the compartment moved slowly past them, Brunetti saw that the Landis sat together, his arm around her shoulder. Both stared at the seat opposite them and did not turn to look out the window as the train pulled past the two policemen.

14

From a phone in front of the station, surprised at himself for remembering to do it, Brunetti called and cancelled the hotel reservation. After that, the only thing he had the energy to do was to go home. He and Vianello boarded the number 82 but found little to say to one another as the boat took them to Rialto. Their farewell was sub-dued, and Brunetti took his misery with him across the bridge, down through the now-closed market, and toward home. Even the explosion of orchids in Biancat's window did nothing to lift his spirits, nor did the smell of rich cooking on the second-floor landing of his building.

The smells were richer still inside his own home: someone had taken a shower or bath and had used the rosemary-scented shampoo Paola had brought home last week; and she had prepared sausages and peppers. He hoped that she had gone to the trouble of making fresh pasta to put under them.

He hung his jacket in the closet. As soon as he walked into the kitchen, Chiara, who was sitting at the table doing what looked like some sort of geography project – the surface of the table was covered with maps, a ruler, and a protractor – launched herself at him and wrapped herself around him. He thought of the smell from Marco's apartment and by a conscious act of will did not move away from her.

'*Papà*,' she said, even before he had time to kiss her or say hello, 'could I take sailing lessons this summer?'

Brunetti looked, but looked in vain, for Paola, who might have been able to give him some explanation.

'Sailing lessons?' he repeated.

'Yes, *Papà*,' she said, looking up and smiling. 'I've got a book and I'm trying to teach myself navigation, but I think someone else will have to teach me how to sail a boat.' She took his hand and pulled him toward the kitchen table, which, he saw, was indeed covered with maps of all sorts, but maps of shoals and coastlines, only the edges where countries and continents kissed the water.

She moved away from him and stood over the table, looking down at the book that lay open below her, another book propping it open. 'Look, *Papà*,' she said, jabbing a finger down at a list of numbers, 'if they don't have any clouds, and they have an accurate set of charts and a chronometer, they can tell just about where they are, anywhere in the world.'

'Who can, angel?' he asked, opening the refrigerator and pulling out a bottle of Tokai.

'Captain Aubrey and his crew,' she said, in a voice that suggested the answer should have been obvious.

'And who is Captain Aubrey?' he asked.

'He's the captain of the *Surprise*,' she said, looking at him as if he'd just admitted not knowing his own address.

'The *Surprise*?' he asked, no closer to illumination.

'In the books, *Papà*, the ones about the war with the French.' Before he could admit his ignorance, she added, 'They're wicked, aren't they, the French?'

Brunetti, who thought they were, said nothing, still having no idea of what they were talking about. He poured himself a small glass of wine and took a large sip, then another. Again, he glanced down at the maps and noticed that the blue parts contained many ships, but old-fashioned ones, surmounted by billowing clouds of white sails, and what he took to be tritons in the maps' corners, rising up from the waters with conch shells raised to their lips.

He gave in. 'What books, Chiara?'

'The ones *Mamma* gave me, in English, about the English sea captain and his friend and the war against Napoleon.'

Ah, those books. He took another sip of his wine. 'And do you like them as much as *Mamma* does?'

'Oh,' Chiara said, looking up at him with a serious expression, 'I don't think anyone could like them as much as she does.'

Four years ago, Brunetti had been abandoned by his wife of almost twenty years for a period of more than a month while she systematically read her way through, at his count, eighteen sea novels dealing with the unending years of war between the British and the French. The time had seemed no less long to him, for it was a time when he, too, ate hasty meals, half-cooked meat, dry bread, and was often driven to seek relief in excessive quantities of grog. Because she seemed to have no other interest, he had taken a look at one of the books, if only to have something to talk about at their thrown-together meals. But he had found it discursive, filled with strange facts and stranger animals, and had abandoned the attempt after only a few pages and before making the acquaintance of Captain Aubrey. Fortunately, Paola was a fast reader, and she had returned to the twentieth century after finishing the last one, apparently none the worse for the shipwreck, battle, and scurvy that had menaced her during those weeks.

Thus the maps. 'I'll have to talk to your mother about it,' he said.

'About what?' Chiara asked, head again bent over the maps, her left hand busy with her calculator, a device Brunetti thought Captain Aubrey might have envied her.

'The sailing lessons.'

'Ah yes,' Chiara said, slipping into English with eel-like ease, 'I long to sail a ship.'

Brunetti left her to it, refilled his glass and poured out another, then went towards Paola's study. The door was open, and she lay on the sofa, only her forehead visible over the top of her book.

'Captain Aubrey, I presume,' he said in English.

She put the book down on her stomach and smiled at him. Without a word, she reached up and took the glass he offered. She took a sip, pulled her legs up toward her to give him room to sit and, when he did, asked, 'Bad day?'

He sighed, leaning back in the sofa and placing his right hand on her ankles. 'Overdose. He was only twenty, an architectural student at the university.'

Neither spoke for a long time, and then Paola said, 'How lucky we were to be born when we were.'

He glanced at her and she went on. 'Before drugs. Well, before everyone used drugs.' She sipped at her wine, then added, 'I think I might have smoked marijuana twice in my whole life. And thank God it never did anything to me.'

'Why, "Thank God"?'

'Because if I had liked it or if it had done for me what it's supposed to do for people, I might have liked it enough to use it again. Or to move on to something stronger.'

He thought of his similar good fortune.

'What killed him?' she asked.

'Heroin.'

She shook her head.

'I was with his parents until just now.' Brunetti sipped again at his wine. 'His father's a farmer. They came down from the Trentino to identify him and then went back.'

'Do they have other children?'

'There's one younger sister; I don't know if there are others.'

'I hope so,' Paola said. She stretched out her legs and stuck her feet under his thigh. 'Do you want to eat?'

'Yes, but I want to take a shower first.'

'All right,' she said, pulling her feet out and setting them on the floor. 'I've made the sauce with peppers and sausage.'

'I know.'

'I'll send Chiara to get you when it's ready.' She got to her feet and set her own glass, still more than half full, on the table in front of the sofa. Leaving him there in her study, she went back to the kitchen to finish preparing dinner.

By the time they all sat down, Raffi having returned home just as Paola was serving the pasta, Brunetti's spirits had lifted a bit. The sight of his two children swirling the freshly made pappardelle around their forks filled him with an animal sense of security and well-being, and he began to eat his own with gusto. Paola had gone to the trouble of scorching and removing the skins of the red peppers, so they were soft and sweet, just as he liked them. The sausages contained large flecks of red and white peppercorns which lay inside the tender filling like depth charges of taste, ready to burst open at the first bite, and Gianni the butcher had used a lot of garlic when making them.

Everyone had second helpings, embarrassingly similar in size to the first. Afterwards, no one had room for anything except green salad, but when that was gone, each of them discovered a tiny space capable of holding just the smallest serving of fresh strawberries flavoured with a drop of balsamic vinegar.

During all of this, Chiara continued in her role as Ancient Mariner, endlessly cataloguing the flora and fauna of far-off lands, presenting them with the shocking information that most eighteenth-century sailors could not swim, and, until Paola reminded her they were eating, describing the symptoms of scurvy.

The children disappeared, Raffi to the Greek aorist and Chiara, if Brunetti understood her aright, to shipwreck in the South Atlantic.

'Is she going to read all of those books?' he asked, sipping at his grappa and keeping Paola company as she did the dishes.

'I certainly hope so,' Paola answered, attention on the serving platter.

'Is she reading them because you liked them so much or because she likes them herself?'

Her back to him as she scoured at the bottom

of a pot, Paola asked, 'How old is she?'

'Fifteen,' Brunetti answered.

'Can you name one living fifteen-year-old, indeed, one fifteen-year-old who has ever existed, who does what her mother wants her to do?'

'Does that mean adolescence has struck?' he asked. They'd gone through it with Raffi, about twenty years of it, if he remembered correctly, so he did not relish the idea of experiencing it again with Chiara.

'It's different with girls,' Paola said, turning around and wiping her hands on a towel. She poured herself a whisper of grappa and leaned back against the sink.

'Different how?'

'They just oppose their mothers, not their fathers, too.'

He considered this. 'Is that a good thing or a bad thing?'

She shrugged. 'It's in the genes or in the culture, so there's no way we can get around it, whether it's good or bad. We can just hope it doesn't last a long time.'

'How long would that be?'

'Until she's eighteen.' Paola took another sip, and together they considered the prospect.

'Would the Carmelites take her until then?'

'Probably not,' Paola said, voice rich with winsome regret.

'Do you think this is why the Arabs let their daughters marry so young, to avoid all of this?'

Paola remembered the heated defence Chiara

had made that morning of her need to have her own telephone. 'I'm certain of it.'

'No wonder people speak of the Wisdom of the East.'

She turned and set her glass in the bottom of the sink. 'I've still got some papers to grade. Want to come and sit with me and see how your Greeks are doing on their trip home while I do it?'

Gratefully Brunetti got to his feet and followed her down the hall to her study.

15

The next morning, and with considerable reluctance, Brunetti did something he seldom did: he involved one of his children in his work. Raffi didn't have to get to school until eleven and had a date to meet Sara Paganuzzi before then, so he appeared at breakfast looking bright and cheerful, qualities which seldom accompanied him at that hour. Paola was still asleep, and Chiara was in the bathroom, so they sat alone in the kitchen, eating the fresh brioche that Raffi had gone downstairs to get at the local pastry shop.

'Raffi,' Brunetti began, as they ate their first brioche, 'do you know anything about who sells drugs here?'

Raffi paused with the remaining piece of

brioche halfway to his mouth. 'Here?'

'In Venice.'

'Drugs like hard drugs or light stuff like marijuana?'

Though he was faintly troubled by the distinction Raffi made and would have liked to know more about the reason for Raffi's casual dismissal of 'light stuff like marijuana', he didn't ask. 'Hard drugs: heroin specifically.'

'Is this about that student who OD'd?' he asked, and when Brunetti looked surprised his son opened the *Gazzettino* and showed him the article. A postage-stamp-sized photo of a young man looked up at him: it could have been any young man with dark hair and two eyes. It could easily have been Raffi.

'Yes.'

Raffi broke the remainder of his brioche in two pieces and dipped one into his coffee. After some time he said, 'There's talk that there are people at the university who can get it for you.'

'People?'

'Students. At least I think so. Well,' he said after a moment's reflection, 'people who are enrolled for classes there.' He picked up his cup and sat with his elbows propped on the table, the cup encircled in both hands, a gesture he must surely have picked up from Paola. 'You want me to ask around?'

'No.' Brunetti's answer was immediate. Before his son could respond to the sharpness of his voice, Brunetti added, 'I'm just curious in general, wondered what people were saying.'

He finished his brioche and sipped at his coffee.

'Sara's brother's there, in the Department of Economics. I could ask him what he knows.'

The temptation was strong, but Brunetti dismissed it with a bored, 'No, don't bother. It was just an idea.'

Raffi lowered his cup to the table. 'I'm not interested in them, you know, *Papà*.'

Brunetti was struck by how deep his voice had become. Soon he'd be a man. Or maybe his need to comfort his father meant that he already was one.

'I'm glad to hear that,' Brunetti said. He reached across the table and patted his son's arm. Once, twice, and then he got up and went over to the stove. 'Shall I make some more?' he asked, carrying the coffee pot to the sink and opening it.

Raffi glanced down at his watch. 'No. Thanks, *Papà*, but I've got to go.' He pushed back his chair, got to his feet, and left the kitchen. A few minutes later, as Brunetti waited for the coffee, he heard the front door close. He listened to Raffi's footsteps thundering down the first flight, but the sudden eruption of coffee wiped them out.

Because it was still early enough for the boats not to be crowded, Brunetti took the 82 and got off at San Zaccaria. He bought two newspapers there and took them to his office. No further mention was made of Rossi's death, and the article about Marco Landi gave little more than his name and age. Above it there was the by now routine story about a car full of young people that had splattered itself, and their lives, against a plane tree at the side of one of the state highways leading to Treviso.

He'd read the same grim story so many times during the last few years that he hardly had to bother to look at this one to know what had happened. The youths – in this case, two boys and two girls – had left a disco after three in the morning and had driven off in a car belonging to the father of the driver. Some time later, the driver had been struck by what the newspapers ritually referred to as, *un colpo di sonno*, and the car had gone off the road and into a tree. It was still too early to know the cause of the attack of sleepiness, but it generally turned out to be alcohol or drugs. Usually, though, that wasn't determined until the autopsy was performed on the driver and on however many others he had killed along with himself. And by that time the story had dropped off the front pages and been forgotten, replaced by the photos of other young people, victims of their youth and its many desires.

He left the newspaper on the desk and went down to Patta's office. Signorina Elettra was nowhere in sight, so he knocked at the door and, when he heard Patta's shouted response, went in.

It was a different man who sat behind the desk, at least different from the one who had sat behind it the last time Brunetti was there. Patta was back: tall, handsome, dressed in a light-weight suit that caressed his broad shoulders with respectful, gossamer fingers. His skin glowed with health, his eyes with serenity.

'Yes, what is it, Commissario?' he asked, looking up from the single sheet of paper which lay on the desk in front of him.

'I'd like a word with you, Vice-Questore,' Brunetti said, coming to stand next to the chair in front of Patta's desk, waiting to be told to sit down.

Patta flicked back a starched cuff and glanced down at the golden wafer on his wrist. 'I have a few minutes. What is it?'

'It's about Jesolo, sir. And your son. I wondered if you'd come to any decision.'

Patta pushed himself back in his chair. Seeing that Brunetti could easily look down at the paper in front of him, he turned it over and folded his hands on its blank back. 'I'm not sure that there's any decision to be made, Com-missario,' he said, sounding puzzled that Brunetti should think of asking such a question.

'I wanted to know if your son was willing to talk about the people from whom he got the drugs.' With habitual caution, Brunetti restrained himself from saying, bought the drugs.

'If he knew who they were, I'm sure he would be more than willing to tell the police whatever he could.' In Patta's voice he heard the same injured confusion he'd heard in the voice of a generation of unwilling witnesses and suspects, and on his face he saw that same patently innocent, faintly bewildered, smile. His tone invited no contradiction.

'If he knew who they were?' Brunetti repeated, turning it into a question.

'Exactly. As you know, he has no idea of how these drugs came into his possession, nor of who might have planted them.' Patta's voice was as calm as his eyes were steady.

Ah, that's how it's going to be played, Brunetti thought. 'And his fingerprints, sir?'

Patta's smile was broad, and it appeared to be genuine. 'I know. I know how that must have appeared when he was first questioned. But he told me, and he's told the police, that he found the envelope in his pocket when he came back from dancing and reached into his pocket to get a cigarette. He had no idea of what it was, so, as anyone would do, he opened the envelope to see what was inside, and when he did that, he must have touched some of the packages.'

'Some?' Brunetti asked, his voice deliberately free of all scepticism.

'Some,' Patta repeated with a finality that put an end to discussion.

'Have you seen today's paper, sir?' Brunetti asked, surprising himself as much as his superior with the question.

'No,' Patta answered, then added, Brunetti thought gratuitously, 'I've been too busy since I got here to have time to read the paper.'

'Four teenagers were involved in an accident near Treviso last night. Coming back from a disco, their car went off the road and into a tree.

One boy's dead, a university student, and the others are badly injured.' Brunetti stopped, an entirely diplomatic pause.

'No, I haven't seen it.' Patta said. He too paused for a moment, but this was the pause of an artillery commander, deciding how heavy to make the next salvo. 'Why do you mention it?'

'He's dead, sir, one of the passengers. The paper said their car was going about a hundred and twenty kilometres an hour when they hit the tree.'

'That's certainly unfortunate, Commissario,' Patta observed with much the same involvement one might devote to a remark about the decline of the banded nuthatch. He returned his attention to his desk, turned the paper over and studied it, then glanced up at Brunetti. 'If it happened in Treviso, then I imagine the case belongs to them, not to us.' He looked studiedly down at the paper, read a few lines, then looked back up at Brunetti, as if surprised to see him still there. 'Was that all, Commissario?' he asked.

'Yes, sir. That's all.'

Outside the office, Brunetti found that his heart was pounding so hard he had to lean against the wall, glad that Signorina Elettra was not at her desk. He stood still until his breathing quieted, and when he was again in control of himself, he went back up to his office.

He did what he knew he had to do: routine would direct his mind away from the rage he felt toward Patta. He pushed papers around on his desk until he found the number that had been in Rossi's wallet. He dialled the Ferrara number. This time, the phone was picked up on the third ring. 'Gavini and Cappelli,' a woman's voice answered.

'Good morning, Signora. This is Commissario Guido Brunetti of the Venice police.'

'One moment, please,' she said, as though she'd been waiting for his call. 'I'll put you through.'

The line went dead as she transferred the call, then a man's voice said, 'Gavini. I'm glad someone finally answered our call. I hope you can tell us something.' The voice was deep and rich and gave every sign of eagerness to hear Brunetti's news, whatever it should be.

It took a moment for Brunetti to respond. 'I'm afraid you have the advantage of me, Signor Gavini. I haven't received any message from you.' When Gavini said nothing, he added, 'But I'd like to know what you're expecting the Venice police to call you about.'

'About Sandro,' Gavini said. 'I called there after his death. His wife told me he'd said he'd found someone in Venice who might be willing to talk.'

Brunetti was on the point of interrupting him when Gavini paused and asked, 'Are you sure no one there got my message?'

'I don't know, Signore. Whom did you speak to?'

'I spoke to one of the officers; I don't remember his name.'

'And could you repeat to me what you told him?' Brunetti asked, pulling a sheet of paper toward him.

'I told you: I called after Sandro's death,' Gavini said, and then asked, 'Do you know about that?'

'No.'

'Sandro Cappelli,' Gavini said, as if the name would explain everything. It did strike a faint chord in Brunetti's memory: he couldn't remember why he knew the name, but he was sure that whatever he knew of it was bad. 'He was my partner in the practice here,' Gavini added.

'What sort of practice, Signor Gavini?'

'Legal. We're lawyers. Don't you know anything about this?' For the first time, a note of exasperation slipped into his voice, the note that inevitably came into the voice of anyone who spent enough time dealing on the phone with an unresponsive bureaucracy.

Gavini's saying that they were lawyers jogged Brunetti's memory. He remembered Cappelli's murder, almost a month ago. 'Yes, I know the name. He was shot, wasn't he?'

'Standing at the window of his office, a client sitting behind him, at eleven in the morning. Someone shot him through the window with a hunting rifle.' As he rapped out the details of his partner's death, Gavini's voice took on the staccato rhythm of real anger.

Brunetti had read the newspaper accounts of the murder, but he knew no facts. 'Is there a suspect?' he asked.

'Of course not,' Gavini shot back, making no attempt to stop his anger from boiling over. 'But we all know who did it.'

Brunetti waited for Gavini to spell it out for him. 'The moneylenders. Sandro'd been after them for years. He had four cases running against them when he died.'

The policeman in Brunetti caused him to ask, 'Is there any evidence of this, Signor Gavini?'

'Of course not,' the lawyer all but spat down the line. 'They sent someone, paid someone and sent him to do it. It was a contract killing: the shot came from the roof of a building on the opposite side of the street. Even the police here said it had to be a contract killing; who else would want to murder him?'

Brunetti had too little information to be able to answer questions about Cappelli's death, even rhetorical ones, and so he said, 'I ask you to excuse my ignorance about your partner's death and the people responsible, Signor Gavini. I was calling you about something entirely different, but after what you've said, I wonder if it is so different.'

'What do you mean?' Gavini asked. Though the words were abrupt, his voice was curious, interested.

'I'm calling about a death we've had here in Venice, a death that looks accidental but might not be.' He waited for Gavini's questions, but none came, and so he continued. 'A man fell from scaffolding here, and died. He worked in the Ufficio Catasto and had a phone number in his wallet when he died, but without any city code. This is one of the numbers it might have been.'

'What was his name?' Gavini asked.

'Franco Rossi.' Brunetti allowed him a moment for reflection or memory, then asked, 'Does it mean anything to you?'

'No, it doesn't.'

'Is there any way you could find out if it meant something to your colleague?'

Gavini was a long time in answering. 'Do you have his number? I could check the phone logs,' he suggested.

'One moment,' Brunetti said and bent to pull open his bottom drawer. From it, he took the phone book and checked through the listings for Rossi: there were seven columns of them, and about a dozen of those were Francos. He found the address and read the phone number to Gavini, then asked him to wait while he flipped to the pages for the Comune of Venice and found the number for the Ufficio Catasto. If Rossi had been rash enough to call the police from his *telefonino*, he might easily have called the lawyer from his office or received calls there.

'It will take me a while to check the logs,' Gavini said. 'I've got someone waiting to see me. But as soon as he's gone, I'll call you back.'

'Perhaps you could ask your secretary to do it for you.'

Gavini's voice suddenly took on an odd note of excessive formality, almost of caution. 'No, I think I'd prefer to do this myself.'

Brunetti said that he'd wait for Gavini's call, gave his direct number, and the two men hung up.

A phone that had been disconnected months ago, an old woman who knew no one named Franco Rossi, a car rental agency with no such client, but now the partner of a lawyer whose death had been as violent as Rossi's: Brunetti well knew the time that could be wasted in following false scents and chasing down misleading trails, but this had the right feel to it, however uncertain he might be of what it was or where it might be leading.

Like the plagues inflicted upon the children of Egypt, moneylenders afflicted the children of Italy and caused them to suffer. Banks extended credit reluctantly and generally only with the guarantee of the sort of financial security that would obviate the need to borrow. Short-term credit for the businessman who had little cash at the end of the month or the salesman whose clients were slow in paying was virtually non-existent. And all of this was compounded by a habitual sloth in the paying of bills which could be said to characterize the entire nation.

Into this breach stepped, as everyone knew but few would say, the moneylenders, *gli strozzini*, those shadowy persons who were willing and able to lend at short notice and with little security from the borrowers. Their rates of interest more than compensated for any risk they might incur. And, in a sense, the idea of risk was academic at best, for the *strozzini* had methods which greatly reduced the possibility that their clients – if that is the right name for them – would fail to repay the money they had borrowed. Men had children, and children could disappear; men had daughters, and young girls might be raped; men had their lives, and these had been known to be lost. Occasionally the press carried stories which, without being entirely clear, managed nevertheless to suggest that certain actions, often unpleasant or violent, had resulted from the failure to repay borrowed money. But seldom did the people involved in these stories end up under prosecution or close police examination: a wall of silence hedged them safely round. Brunetti had to struggle to recall a case where enough evidence had been gathered to lead to a conviction for moneylending, a crime with a place in the statutes, however infrequently it appeared in the courtroom.

Brunetti sat at his desk and allowed his imagination and his memory to consider the many possibilities offered by the fact that Franco Rossi might have been carrying Sandro Cappelli's office phone number in his wallet when he died. He tried to recall Rossi's visit and to reconstruct his sense of the man. Rossi had been serious about his work: that was perhaps the most lasting impression he had left with Brunetti. A bit humourless, more earnest than seemed possible in a man so young, Rossi had still been likeable and eager to provide what help he could.

All of this thinking, in the absence of any clear idea of what was going on, got Brunetti nowhere, but it did manage to pass the time until Gavini called.

Brunetti answered on the first ring. 'Brunetti.'

'Commissario,' Gavini said and identified himself. 'I've been through both the client files and the phone logs.' Brunetti waited for more. 'No client named Franco Rossi is listed, but Sandro called Rossi's number three times during the month before he died.'

'Which one? At home or at work?' Brunetti asked.

'Does it make a difference?'

'Everything might make a difference.'

'At his office,' Gavini offered.

'How long did the calls last?'

The other man must have had the paper under his hand because he said, without hesitation, 'Twelve minutes, then six, then eight.' Gavini waited for Brunetti to respond, and when he didn't, asked, 'What about Rossi? Do you know if he called Sandro?'

'I haven't checked his phone records yet,' Brunetti admitted, feeling not a little embarrassed. Gavini said nothing, and Brunetti went on: 'I'll have them by tomorrow.' Suddenly he remembered that this man was a lawyer, not a fellow officer, which meant he had no responsibility to him and no need to share information with him.

'What's the name of the magistrate handling the case there?' he asked.

'Why do you want to know?'

'I'd like to talk to him,' Brunetti said.

A long silence greeted this.

'Do you have his name?' Brunetti prodded.

'Righetto, Angelo Righetto,' came the terse reply. Brunetti decided to ask nothing at this point. He thanked Gavini, made no promise to phone him about any numbers Rossi might have called, and hung up, wondering about the chill in Gavini's voice as he pronounced the name of the man in charge of the investigation of his partner's murder.

He immediately called down to Signorina Elettra and asked her to get copies of all of the calls made from Rossi's home number during the last three months. When he asked her if it would be possible to find out the number of Rossi's extension at the Ufficio Catasto and check that, she asked if he wanted the last three months of calls.

While he had her on the line, he asked her if she could call Magistrato Angelo Righetto in Ferrara and connect him as soon as she did.

Brunetti pulled a piece of paper toward him and started making a list of the names of people he thought might be able to give him information about moneylenders in the city. He knew nothing about the usurers, at least nothing more real than his vague certainty that they were there, burrowed into the social fabric as deeply as maggots into dead meat. Like certain forms of bacteria, they needed the security of an airless, dark place in which to thrive, and certainly the fearful state into which their debtors were intimidated provided neither light nor air. In secrecy, and with the unspoken threat of the consequences of late payment or default ever present in the minds of their debtors, they prospered and grew fat. The wonder of it, to Brunetti, was his ignorance of their names, faces, and histories as well as, he realized as he looked down at the still blank piece of paper, any idea of who to ask for help about how he might try to drive them out into the light.

A name came to him, and he pulled out the phone book to find the number of the bank where she worked. As he looked, his phone rang. He answered it with his name.

'Dottore,' Signorina Elettra said, 'I have Magistrato Righetto on the line, if you'd like to speak to him.'

'Yes, Signorina, I would. Please put him through.' Brunetti put down his pen and moved the paper to the side of his desk.

'Righetto,' a deep voice said.

'Magistrato, this is Commissario Guido Brunetti, from Venice. I'm calling to ask what you can tell me about the murder of Alessandro Cappelli.'

'Why are you interested in it?' Righetto asked, no sign of great curiosity audible in the question. He spoke with an accent Brunetti thought might be from the Sud Tirol; definitely a northerner, at any rate.

'I have a case here,' Brunetti explained, 'another death, that might be related to his, and

I wonder what you've managed to discover about Cappelli.'

There was a long pause, and then Righetto said, 'I'd be surprised if any other death was related to it.' He allowed a brief pause for Brunetti to question him, but as Brunetti said nothing he went on, 'It looks like we're dealing with a case of mistaken identity here, not murder.' Righetto halted for an instant and then corrected himself. 'Well, murder, of course it's that. But it wasn't Cappelli they were trying to kill, and we're not even sure they were trying to kill the other man so much as frighten him.'

Sensing that it was time he displayed an interest, Brunetti asked, 'What happened, then?'

'It was his partner, Gavini, they were after,' the magistrate explained. 'At least that's what our investigation suggests.'

'Why?' Brunetti asked, openly curious.

'It made no sense from the beginning that anyone would want to kill Cappelli,' Righetto began, making it sound as though no importance whatsoever was to be given to Cappelli's position as a declared enemy of usurers. We've looked into his past, even checked the current cases he was working on, but there's no indication at all of an involvement with anyone who would want to do something like this.'

Brunetti made a little noise, one that could be interpreted as a sigh of mingled understanding and agreement.

'On the other hand,' Righetto continued, 'there's his partner.'

'Gavini,' Brunetti supplied unnecessarily.

'Yes, Gavini,' Righetto said with a dismissive laugh. 'He's well known in the area, has the reputation as quite a ladies' man. Unfortunately, he has the habit of getting himself involved with married women.'

'Ah,' Brunetti said with a worldly sigh which he managed to infuse with the appropriate level of manly tolerance. 'So that was it?' he asked with bland acceptance.

'It would seem so. In the last few years, he's been involved with four different women, all of them married.'

Brunetti said, 'Poor devil.' He waited long enough to allow himself to consider the comic implications of what he'd just said and then added with a quick laugh, 'Maybe he should have limited himself to only one of them.'

'Yes, but how's a man to decide?' the magistrate shot back, and Brunetti rewarded his wit with another hearty laugh.

'Do you have any idea which one it was?' Brunetti asked, interested in how Righetto would handle the question, which in its turn would suggest how he was going to handle the investigation.

Righetto allowed himself a pause, no doubt he wanted it to seem like a thoughtful pause, and then said, 'No. We've questioned the women, and their husbands, but all of them can prove they were somewhere else when it happened.'

'I thought the papers said it was a professional hit,' Brunetti said, sounding confused.

The temperature of Righetto's voice dropped. 'If you're a policeman, you should know better than to believe what you read in the papers.'

'Of course,' Brunetti said, making himself laugh genially, as at a well-earned reproach from a colleague with greater experience and wisdom. 'You think maybe there was still another woman?'

'That's the trail we're following,' Righetto said.

'It happened at their offices, didn't it?' Brunetti asked.

'Yes,' Righetto answered, willing now, after Brunetti's hint at another woman, to give further information. 'The two men look alike: they're both short and have dark hair. It happened on a rainy day; the killer was on the roof of a building across the street. So there's little question he mistook Cappelli for Gavini.'

'But what about all this talk that Cappelli was killed because of his investigation of money-lenders?' Brunetti asked, putting enough scepticism into his voice to make it clear to Righetto that he wouldn't believe such nonsense for a minute but perhaps wanted to have the right answer in case someone else, more innocent than he and thus willing to believe everything he read in the papers, should ask him about it.

'We started by examining that possibility, but there's nothing there, just nothing. So we've excluded it from our investigation.'

'*Cherchez la femme*,' Brunetti said, intentionally mispronouncing the French and adding another laugh.

Righetto rewarded him with his own broad laugh and then asked, quite casually, 'You said you had another death there. A murder?'

'No, no, after what you've told me, Magistrato,' Brunetti said, attempting to sound as dull and ploddish as he could, 'I'm sure there's no connection. What we're dealing with here has got to be an accident.'

16

Like most Italians, Brunetti believed that records were kept of all phone calls made anywhere in the country and copies made of all faxes; like very few Italians, he had reason to know this was true. Belief or certainty, however, made little difference to behaviour: nothing of substance and nothing that could in any way be incriminating to either of the speakers or interesting to any of the agencies of government which chose to eavesdrop was ever discussed on the phone. People spoke in code where 'money' became 'vases' or 'flowers' and investments or bank accounts were referred to as 'friends' in foreign countries. Brunetti had no idea of how widespread the belief and the resultant caution were, but he knew enough when he called his friend at the Banca di Modena to suggest they meet for a coffee rather than attempt to make his request directly.

Because the bank was on the other side of Rialto, they agreed to have a drink before lunch in Campo San Luca and thus meet halfway. It was a long way for Brunetti to go just to ask a few questions, but a meeting was the only way he could get Franca to talk openly. Explaining nothing, telling no one, he left his office and walked out to the *bacino* and up towards San Marco.

As he walked along the Riva degli Schiavoni, he looked off to his left, expecting to see the tugboats, only to be caught up short by their absence and then by the immediate realization that they'd been gone for years but that he'd forgotten about it. How could he have forgotten something he knew so well? It was rather like not remembering his own phone number or the face of the baker. He didn't know where the tugs had been sent, nor could he recall how many years it was since they'd disappeared, leaving the space along the *riva* clear for other boats, no doubt boats more useful to the tourist industry.

What wonderful Latin names they'd had, floating there red and proud and ready at an instant to chug off to help the ships up the Canale della Giudecca. The boats that sailed into the city now were probably too big for those brave little tugs to be of any help: monsters taller than the Basilica, filled with thousands of ant-like forms crowded to the railings, they sailed in and docked, hurled down their gangplanks and set free their passengers to wander into the city.

Brunetti turned his mind from this and headed up to the Piazza, then cut through it and to the right, back into the centre of the city, toward Campo San Luca. Franca was there when he arrived, talking to a man Brunetti recognized but didn't know. As he approached, he saw them shake hands. The man turned toward Campo Manin, and Franca to look in the window of the bookstore.

'*Ciao*, Franca,' Brunetti said, coming to stand beside her. They'd been friends in high school, had for a time been more than friends, but then she had met her Mario, and Brunetti had gone off to university, where he met his Paola. She still had the same burnished blonde hair, a few shades lighter than Paola's, and Brunetti knew enough about such things now to know that she had had assistance in maintaining that colour. But the rest was the same: the full figure she had been so awkward about twenty years ago was now graced by her maturity; she had the unwrinkled skin common to robust women, though there was no evidence of assistance there. The soft brown eyes were the same; so was the warmth in them at the sound of his voice.

'*Ciao*, Guido,' she said, and put back her head to receive his two quick kisses.

'Let me offer you a drink,' he said, taking her arm out of decades-old habit and leading her toward the bar.

Inside, they decided to have *uno spritz* and watched the barman mix the wine and mineral water and then tip in the merest suggestion of Campari before sticking a slice of lemon on the rim and sliding the glasses across the counter toward them.

'*Cin cin,*' they said together and took their first sips.

The barman placed a small dish of potato chips in front of them, but they ignored it. The press at the bar gradually drove them back until they were crushed up against the front windows, through which they could see the city passing by.

Franca knew that this was a business meeting. Had Brunetti wanted to chat about her family, he would have done it on the phone, not asked her to meet him in a bar guaranteed to be so crowded that no one could overhear what they said.

'What is it, Guido?' she asked but smiled to take any sting from her words.

'Moneylenders,' he answered.

She looked up at him, then away, then just as quickly back.

'Who do you want to know it for?'

'Me, of course.'

She smiled, but just barely. 'I know it has to be for you, Guido, but is it for you as a policeman who is going to take a careful look at them or is it only the sort of question a friend asks?'

'Why do you want to know?'

'Because if it's the first, I don't think I have

anything to say to you.'

'And if it's the second?'

'Then I can talk.'

'Why the difference?' he asked, then stepped over to the bar and scooped up a few potato chips, more to give her time to think about her answer than because he actually wanted them.

She was ready when he returned. She shook her head at his offer of the chips, so he had to eat them. 'If it's the first, then anything I say to you I might have to repeat in court, or you might have to say where you got the information.' Before he could ask, she continued, 'If it's just casual talk between friends, then I'll tell you whatever I can, but I want you to know that I'll never remember having said it, should I ever be asked.' She didn't smile when she said this, though Franca was usually a woman whose joy in life flowed from her like music from a carousel.

'Are they that dangerous?' Brunetti asked, taking her empty glass and reaching over to place it beside his own on the bar.

'Let's go outside,' she said. Out in the *campo*, she moved over until she stood to the left of the flagpole, just in front of the windows of the bookstore. Whether by accident or design, Franca was at least two metres from the people nearest to her in the *campo*, two old women leaning toward one another, propped up by their canes.

Brunetti came up and stood beside her. The light rose over the tops of the buildings, making their reflections clearly visible in the window. Unclear and unfocused, the couple in the window could easily have been those teenagers who had, decades ago, often met here for a coffee with friends.

The question came unsummoned, 'Are you really that frightened?' Brunetti asked.

'My son's fifteen,' she said by way of explanation. Her level tone might just as easily have been used to comment on the weather or, indeed, upon her son's interest in soccer.

'Why did you want to meet here, Guido?' she asked.

He smiled, 'I know you're a busy woman, and I know where you live, so I thought this would be a convenient place: you're almost home.'

'That's the only reason?' she asked, looking away from the reflected Brunetti to the real one.

'Yes. Why do you ask?'

'You really don't know anything about them, do you?' was the only answer she gave.

'No. I know they exist, and I know they're here in the city. They'd have to be. But we've never had any official complaints about them.'

'And it's usually the Finanza that deals with them, isn't it?'

Brunetti shrugged. He had no idea just what the officers of the Guardia di Finanza did deal with: he often saw them, in their grey uniforms decorated with the bright flames of a presumed justice, but he saw little evidence that they did much other than encourage an oppressed people to new methods of tax evasion.

He nodded, not willing to commit his ignorance to words.

Franca looked away from him and around the small *campo*. Silently, she stood and looked around her. With her chin, she indicated the fast food restaurant that stood on the other side. 'What do you see?'

He looked across at the glass façade taking up most of that side of the small square. Young people went in and out; many of them sat at small tables, clearly visible through the immense windows.

'I see the destruction of two thousand years of culinary culture,' he said, with a laugh.

'And just outside, what do you see?' she asked soberly.

He looked again, disappointed that she had not laughed at his joke. He saw two men in dark suits, each with a briefcase in his hand, talking to one another. To the left of them, a young woman stood, handbag clutched awkwardly under her arm as she looked through her address book and tried to punch in a number on her *telefonino* at the same time. Behind her, a shabbily dressed man, perhaps in his late sixties, tall and very thin, was leaning down to speak to an older woman dressed all in black. She was bent forward with age, her tiny hands grasped tightly around the handle of a large black handbag. She had a narrow face and a long, pointed nose, a combination which, when added to her hunched posture, gave the general impression of one of the smaller marsupials.

'I see a number of people doing what people do in Campo San Luca.'

'Which is?' she asked, looking up at him, eyes sharp now.

'Meeting by chance or arrangement and talking, then going to have a drink, the way we did, and then going home to lunch, the way we will.'

'And those two?' she asked, tilting her chin toward the thin man and the old woman.

'She looks like she's on her way home to lunch, just back from a long mass at one of the smaller churches.'

'And he?'

Brunetti looked over toward them again. They were still deep in conversation. 'It looks like she's trying to save his soul and he doesn't want any part of it,' Brunetti said.

'He has none to save,' Franca said, surprising him that such a judgement should come from a woman he'd never heard speak badly of anyone. 'Nor does she,' she added in a cool, unforgiving voice.

She turned a half-step back toward the bookstore and looked into the window again. Keeping her back to Brunetti, she said, 'That's Angelina Volpato, and her husband, Massimo. They're two of the worst moneylenders in the city. No one has any idea when they started, but for the last ten years, they've been the ones most people have used.'

Brunetti sensed a presence at their side: a woman had come up to look into the window.

Franca said nothing. When she moved off, Franca continued, 'People know about them and know they're here most mornings. So they come and talk to them, and then Angelina invites them to their home.' She paused and then added, 'She's the real vampire,' then paused again. When she had grown calm, she went on. 'It's there that she calls in the notary and they make up the papers. She gives them the money, and they give her their houses or their businesses or their furniture.'

'And the sum?'

'That depends on how much they need and how long they need it for. If it's only a few million, then they agree to give her their furniture. But if it's a significant sum, fifty million or more, then she works out the interest – people have told me she can calculate interest in an instant, though the same people have told me she's illiterate; so's her husband.' She stopped here, lost in her own account, then resumed, 'If it's a large sum, then they agree to give her title to their house if they haven't paid her a certain sum by a certain date.'

'And if they don't pay?'

'Then her lawyer takes them to court, and she's got the paper, signed in front of a notary.'

As she spoke, always keeping her eyes on the covers of the books in the window, Brunetti examined his memory, and his conscience, and was forced to admit that none of this was news to him. The precise details were unknown, perhaps, but not the fact that this sort of thing went on. But it belonged to the Guardia di Finanza, or it had until now, until circumstance and dumb chance had called his attention to Angelina Volpato and her husband, still standing there, across from him, deep in conversation on a bright spring day in Venice.

'How much do they charge?'

'It depends on how desperate people are,' Franca answered.

'How do they know that?'

She took her eyes away from the little piggies driving fire engines and looked up at him. 'You know as well as I do: everyone knows everything. All you have to do is try to borrow money from a bank, and everyone in the bank knows it by the end of the day, their families by the morning, and the whole city by the afternoon.'

Brunetti had to admit the truth of this. Whether because people in Venice were all related to one another by blood or friendship, or simply because the city was in reality nothing more than a tiny town, no secret could survive long in this intense, incestuous world. It made perfect sense to him that financial need would quickly become public information.

'What sort of interest do they charge?' he asked again.

She started to answer, stopped herself, then continued, 'I've heard people talk of twenty per cent a month. But I've also heard them talk of fifty.'

The Venetian in Brunetti had it worked out in

an instant. 'That's six hundred per cent a year,' he said, unable to disguise his indignation.

'Much more if it's compound interest,' Franca corrected, demonstrating that her family's roots in the city extended deeper than Brunetti's.

Brunetti turned his attention back to the two people on the other side of the *campo*. As he watched, their conversation finished and the woman moved away, turning towards Rialto, while the man headed in their direction.

As he drew near, Brunetti saw the bulbous forehead, the skin rough and dangling in flakes as from some untreated disease, the full lips and heavy-lidded eyes. The man had a strange, bird-like walk and with each step lightly placed each foot down flat, as if concerned about wearing down the heels of his much-repaired shoes. His face bore the burdens of age and sickness, but the gangling walk, especially as Brunetti saw it from behind as the man turned into the *calle* that led toward the city hall, gave a strange sense of youthful awkwardness.

When he looked back, the old woman had disappeared, but the image of a marsupial, or some sort of upright rat, remained in Brunetti's memory. 'How do you know about all of this?' he asked Franca.

'I work in a bank, remember,' she answered.

'And those two are the court of last resort for the people who can't get anything from you?' She nodded. 'But how do people find out about them?' he asked.

She studied him, as if considering how much

she could trust him, then said, 'I've been told that sometimes people in the bank recommend them.'

'What?'

'That when people try to borrow money from a bank and are refused, occasionally one of the employees will suggest they try talking to the Volpatos. Or to whichever moneylender is paying them a percentage.'

'How much of a percentage?' Brunetti asked in a level voice.

She shrugged. 'I'm told that depends.'

'On what?'

'On how much they finally borrow. Or on the sort of deal the banker has with the usurers.' Before Brunetti could ask anything else, she added, 'If people need money, they'll get it somewhere. If not from friends or family, and if not from a bank, then from people like the Volpatos.'

The only way Brunetti could ask the next question was to be direct, and so he asked, 'Is this connected with the Mafia?'

'What isn't?' Franca asked in return, but when she saw his irritated response to this, she added, 'Sorry, that was just a wisecrack. I've no direct knowledge that they are. But if you think about it for a while, you'll realize how good a way it would be to launder money.'

Brunetti nodded. Only Mafia protection could allow something as profitable as this to go on unquestioned, unexamined by the authorities.

'Have I ruined your lunch?' she asked,

suddenly smiling, her mood changing in a way he remembered.

'No, not at all, Franca.'

'Why are you asking about this?' she finally asked.

'It might be connected with something else.'

'Most things are,' she added but asked him nothing, another quality he had always prized in her. 'I'll get home, then,' she said, and leaned up to kiss him on both cheeks.

'Thanks, Franca,' he answered, pulling her a bit closer to him, comforted by the feel of her strong body and even stronger will. 'It's always a joy to see you.' Even as she patted his arm and turned away, he realized that he had not asked her about the other moneylenders, but he couldn't call her back now and ask. All he could think of was to go home.

17

As he walked, Brunetti let his memory slip back to the time he had spent with Franca, more than two decades ago. He was conscious of how much he had enjoyed again putting his arms around that comfortable figure, once so familiar to him. He remembered a long walk they had taken on the beach of the Lido the night of Redentore; it must have been when he was seventeen. Fireworks long finished, they'd walked along, hand in hand, waiting for dawn, reluctant to let the night end.

But it had, as had many things between them, and now she had her Mario, and he had his Paola. He stopped at Biancat and bought a dozen irises for his Paola, happy to be able to do so, happy at the thought that she would be upstairs, waiting for him.

She was in the kitchen when he came in, seated at the table, shelling peas.

'Risi e bisi,' he said by way of greeting when he saw the peas, the irises held out in front of him.

Smiling at the sight of the flowers, she said, 'It's the best thing to do with new peas, isn't it, make risotto?' and raised her cheek to receive his kiss.

Kiss given, he answered, for no real reason, 'Unless you're a princess and you need them to put under your mattress.'

'I think the risotto's a better idea,' she answered. 'Would you put them in a vase while I finish these?' she asked, gesturing with one hand to the full paper bag on the table beside her.

He pulled a chair over to the cabinets, took a piece of newspaper from the table and spread it on the seat, then stepped up to reach for one of the tall vases that stood on top of one of the cabinets.

'The blue one, I think,' she said, looking up and watching him.

He stepped down, put the chair back in place, and took the vase over to the sink. 'How full?' he asked.

'About halfway. What would you like after?'

'What is there?' he asked.

'I've got that roast beef from Sunday. If you sliced it very thin, we could have that and then maybe a salad.'

'Is Chiara eating meat this week?' Spurred to

it by an article about the treatment of calves, Chiara had a week ago declared that she would be a vegetarian for the rest of her life.

'You saw her eat the roast beef on Sunday, didn't you?' Paola asked.

'Ah, yes, of course,' he answered, turning to the flowers and tearing the paper from them.

'What's wrong?' she asked.

'The usual things,' he answered, holding the vase under the tap and turning on the cold water. 'We live in a fallen universe.'

She returned to her peas. 'Anyone who does either of our jobs should know that,' she answered.

Curious, he asked, 'How does it come from yours?' A policeman for twenty years, he needed no one to tell him that mankind had fallen from grace.

'You deal with moral decline. I deal with that of the mind.' She spoke in the elevated, self-mocking tone she often used when she caught herself taking her work seriously. Then she asked, 'Specifically, what's done this to you?'

'I had a drink with Franca this afternoon.'

'How is she?'

'Fine. Her son's growing up, and I don't think she much likes working in a bank.'

'Who could?' Paola asked, but it was more a ritual response than a serious question. She returned to his original unexplained statement and asked, 'How does seeing Franca suggest it's a post-lapsarian universe? It usually has the opposite effect, on all of us.'

Slowly slipping the flowers one by one into the vase, Brunetti played back her comment a few times, searching for some hidden and possibly rancorous meaning and finding none at all. She observed his pleasure in meeting this old, dear friend, and she shared the joy he took in her company. At that realization, his heart gripped tight for an instant, and he felt a sudden flush of heat in his face. One of the irises fell to the counter. He picked it up, put it in with the others, and set the vase carefully aside, safely back from the edge.

'She said something about being afraid for Pietro if she talked to me about moneylenders.'

Paola stopped what she was doing and turned to look at him. 'Moneylenders?' she asked. 'What have they got to do with anything?'

'Rossi, that man from the Ufficio Catasto who died, he had the phone number of a lawyer in his wallet, a lawyer who had taken on a number of cases against them.'

'A lawyer where?'

'In Ferrara.'

'Not that one they murdered?' she asked, looking up at him.

Brunetti nodded, interested that Paola would so casually assume that Cappelli had been murdered by 'them', and then added, 'The magistrate in charge of the investigation excluded moneylenders and seemed very interested in persuading me that the killer actually got the wrong man.'

After a long pause, during which Brunetti watched the play of thought reflect itself in her face, she asked, 'Is that why he had his number, because of moneylenders?'

'I've no proof. But it's coincidental.'

'Life's coincidental.'

'Murder's not.'

She folded her hands on top of the pile of discarded pea pods. 'Since when is this murder? Rossi, I mean.'

'Since I don't know when. Maybe since never. I just want to find out about this and see why Rossi called him, if I can.'

'And Franca?'

'I thought, because she works in a bank, she might know about moneylenders.'

'I thought that's what banks are supposed to do, lend money.'

'They often don't, at least not on short notice and not to people who might not pay it back.'

'Then why ask her?' From the immobility of her posture, Paola might have been an examining magistrate.

'I thought she might know something.'

'You said that. But why Franca?'

He had no reason, save that she was the first person whose name had occurred to him. Besides, it had been some time since he'd seen her and he'd wanted to do so, nothing more than that. He stuffed his hands into his pockets and shifted his weight to his other foot. 'No real reason,' he finally said.

She unlatched her fingers and went back to

shelling the peas. 'What did she tell you, and why is she afraid for Pietro?'

'She mentioned, even showed me, two people.' Before Paola could interrupt, he said, 'We met in San Luca, and there was this couple there. They're in their sixties, I'd say. She said they lent money.'

'And Pietro?'

'She said there might be a connection to the Mafia and money laundering, but she didn't want to say anything more than that.' He saw from Paola's brief nod that she shared his opinion that the mere mention of the Mafia would be enough to make any parent fear for any child.

'Not even to you?' she asked.

He shook his head. She glanced up at him, and he repeated the gesture.

'Serious, then,' Paola said.

'I'd say so.'

'Who are the people?'

'Angelina and Massimo Volpato.'

'You ever heard of them?' she asked.

'No.'

'Who have you asked about them?'

'No one. I just saw them twenty minutes ago, before I came home.'

'What are you going to do?'

'Find out whatever I can about them.'

'And then?'

'That depends on what I learn.'

There was silence then Paola said, 'I was thinking about you today, about your work.' He waited. 'It was when I was washing the windows, and that's what made me think of you,' she added, surprising him.

'Why the windows?'

'I was washing them, and then I did the mirror in the bathroom, and that's when I thought of what you do.'

He knew she'd continue, even if he said nothing, but he also knew she liked to be encouraged, so he asked, 'And?'

'When you clean a window,' she said, eyes on his, 'you have to open it and pull it toward you, and when you do that, the angle of the light that's coming through it changes.' She saw that he was following, so she continued, 'So you get it clean. Or you think you do. But when you close the window, the light comes through from the original angle, and then you see that the outside's still dirty, or that you missed a patch on the inside. That means you have to open it and clean it again. But you can never be sure it's really clean until you close it again or until you move so that you see it from a different angle.'

'And the mirror?' he asked.

She looked up at him and smiled. 'You see a mirror only from one side. No light comes from behind, so when you clean it, it's clean. There's no trick of perception.' She looked back down at her work.

'And?'

Still looking at the peas, perhaps to hide her disappointment in him, she explained, 'That's what your work's like, or how you want it to be.

You want to clean mirrors, want everything to be two-dimensional and easy to take care of. But every time you begin to take a look at something, it turns out to be like the windows: if you change perspective or you look at things from a new angle, everything changes.'

Brunetti considered this for a long time and then added, hoping to lighten the mood, 'But in both cases, I've always got to clean up the dirt.'

Paola said, 'You said that; I didn't.' When Brunetti made no response, she dropped the last peas into the bowl, and got to her feet. She walked to the counter and set the bowl down. 'Whichever it is you do, I suppose you'd prefer to do it on a full stomach,' she said.

Stomach indeed full, he started to do it that afternoon, as soon as he got back to the Questura. He began, a better place than most, with Signorina Elettra.

Smiling, she greeted his arrival, today dressed in something that looked tantalizingly nautical: navy blue skirt, a square-yoked silk blouse. He caught himself thinking that all she lacked was a little sailor hat until he saw a stiff white cylindrical cap sitting on the desk beside her computer.

'Volpato,' he said before she could ask him how he was. 'Angelina and Massimo. They're in their sixties.'

She pulled forward a sheet of paper and began to write.

'Living here?'

'I think so, yes.'

'Any idea where?'

'No,' he answered.

'That's easy enough to check,' she said, making a note. 'What else?'

'I'd like financial records most of all: bank accounts, any investments they might have, property registered in their names, anything you can find.' He paused while she wrote and then added, 'And see if we have anything on them.'

'Phone records?' she asked.

'No, not yet. Just the financial stuff.'

'For when?'

He looked down at her and smiled. 'When do I always want everything?'

She pushed back her cuff and glanced down at the heavy diver's watch on her left wrist. 'I should be able to get the information from the city offices this afternoon.'

'The banks have closed already, so that can wait until tomorrow,' he said.

She smiled up at him. 'The records never close,' she said. 'I should have everything in a few hours.'

She reached down and pulled open a drawer, from which she took a pile of papers. 'I've got these,' she began but suddenly stopped and looked to her left, toward the door of her office.

He sensed, rather than saw, a motion and turned to see Vice-Questore Patta, just now returned from lunch. 'Signorina Elettra,' he began, making no acknowledgement that he was aware of Brunetti standing in front of her desk.

'Yes, Dottore?' she asked.

'I'd like you to come into my office to take a letter.'

'Of course, Dottore,' she said, placing the papers she had just taken from the drawer on the centre of her desk and tapping at them with the first finger of her left hand, a gesture which Brunetti's body prevented Patta from seeing. She pulled open her front drawer and removed an old-fashioned stenographer's pad. Did people still dictate letters, and did secretaries still sit, legs crossed like Joan Crawford's, quickly taking words down in little squiggles and crosses? As Brunetti wondered about this, he realized that he had always left it to Signorina Elettra to decide how to phrase a letter, had relied on her to choose the correct rhetorical elaboration with which to disguise simple things or to smooth the way for requests which went beyond the strict limits of police power.

Patta walked past him and opened the door to his office, and Brunetti had the distinct feeling that he was himself behaving in the manner of one of those timid forest animals, a lemur perhaps, which froze at the slightest sound, declaring itself invisible by virtue of its immobility and thus believing itself safe from any roving predator. Before he could speak to Signorina Elettra, he saw her get to her feet and follow Patta into his office, but not before glancing back at the papers on her desk. As she closed the door behind her, Brunetti observed no suggestion of timidity in her bearing.

He leaned over her desk, pulled the papers toward him, and then quickly wrote a note, asking her to find the name of the owner of the building in front of which Rossi had been found.

18

On the way up to his office, he looked at the papers he'd taken from Signorina Elettra's desk: a long print-out of all the numbers called from both Rossi's home and from his office. In the margin, she had noted that Rossi's name did not appear as a customer for any of the mobile telephone companies, which suggested that he had been calling on a phone issued by the Ufficio Catasto. Four of the calls made from his office were to the same number, one that had the Ferrara prefix and that Brunetti thought was the number of Gavini and Cappelli's office. When he got to his desk, he checked it and proved his memory right. The calls had all been made in a period of less than two weeks, the last one the day before Cappelli was murdered. Nothing after that.

Brunetti sat for a long time, wondering at the connection between the two dead men. He realized that he was now considering them the two murdered men.

While he waited for Signorina Elettra, he considered many things: the location of Rossi's office at the Ufficio Catasto and how much privacy it would have afforded him; the appointment of Magistrato Righetto to the investigation of Cappelli's murder; the likelihood that a professional killer would mistake another man for his victim and why, after that crime, no further attempt was made on the supposed real victim. He thought about these and other things, and then he returned to the list of the people who might be able to provide him with information, but stopped when he realized he wasn't at all sure what sort of information he wanted. Certainly he needed to know about the Volpatos, but he also needed to know more about financial trafficking in the city and the secret processes by which money flowed into and out of the hands of its citizens.

Like most citizens, he knew that the records of sales and transfers of property titles were kept at the Ufficio Catasto. Beyond that, his understanding of just what it was they did was vague. He remembered Rossi's enthusiasm that several offices were uniting their files in an attempt to save time and make information more simple to recover. He wished now that he had taken the trouble to ask Rossi more about this.

He grabbed the phone book from his bottom drawer, flipped it open to the Bs, and hunted for a number. When he found it, he dialled and waited until a female voice answered, 'Bucintoro Real Estate, good afternoon.'

'*Ciao*, Stefania,' he said.

'What's the matter, Guido?' she asked, startling him with the question and making him wonder what had been audible in his voice.

'I need some information,' he answered just as directly.

'Why else would you call me?' she said without the flirtatiousness that usually filled her voice when she spoke to him.

He chose to ignore both the silent criticism of her tone and the overt criticism of her question. 'I need to know about the Ufficio Catasto.'

'The what?' she said in a loud, artificially confused voice.

'Ufficio Catasto. I need to know what it is exactly they do, who works there, and who is to be trusted among them.'

'That's a big order,' she said.

'That's why I called you.'

Suddenly the flirtatiousness was back. 'And I, sitting here every day, hoping you'll call wanting something else.'

'What, my treasure? Just name it,' he offered in his Rodolfo Valentino voice. Stefania was joyously married and the mother of twins.

'An apartment to buy, of course.'

'I might have to do that,' he said, voice suddenly serious.

'Why?'

'I've been told that our home is going to be condemned.'

'What does that mean, condemned?'

'That we might have to pull it down.'

A second after he said this, he heard Stefania's sharp peal of laughter, but he wasn't sure if the target was the patent absurdity of the situation or her surprise that he might find this in any way unusual. After a few more small noises of mirth, she said, 'You can't be serious.'

'That's exactly how I feel about it. But I had someone from the Ufficio Catasto tell me exactly that. They couldn't find any record either that it had been built or that permits to do so had ever been given, so they might decide it has to be pulled down.'

'You must have misunderstood,' she said.

'He sounded serious.'

'When did this happen?'

'A few months ago.'

'Have you heard anything else?'

'No. That's why I'm calling you.'

'Why don't you call them?'

'I wanted to talk to you first, before I did.'

'Why?'

'To know what my rights are. And to know who they are, the people who make the decisions in the office.'

Stefania didn't respond, and so he asked, 'Do you know them, the people who are in charge there?'

'No more than anyone else in the business does.'

'Who are they?'

'The important one is Fabrizio dal Carlo; he's the boss of the entire Ufficio.' With dismissive scorn, she added, 'An arrogant shit. He has an assistant, Esposito, but he's a nonentity because dal Carlo keeps all the power in his own hands. And then there's Signorina Dolfin, Loredana, whose existence, or at least so I've been told, is entirely based on two pillars: the first is not letting anyone forget that, even though she might be no more than a secretary in the Ufficio Catasto, she is a descendant of Doge Giovanni Dolfin,' she said, then added, as if it mattered, 'I forget his dates.'

'He was Doge from 1356 to 1361, when he died of the plague,' Brunetti supplied seamlessly. To prompt her back into speech, he asked, 'And the second?'

'Disguising her adoration of Fabrizio dal Carlo.' She let that register and then added, 'I'm told she's much better at the first than the second. Dal Carlo makes her work like a dog, but that's probably what she wants, though how anyone could feel anything toward him except contempt is a mystery to me.'

'Is there anything there?'

Stefania's laugh exploded down the line. 'God, no, she's old enough to be his mother. Besides, he's got a wife and at least one other woman, so there'd be little enough time for her anyway, even if she weren't as ugly as sin.' Steffi considered all of this for a moment and then added, 'It's pathetic, really. She's given up years of her life being the loyal servant to this third-rate Romeo, probably hoping that he'll some day realize how much she loves him and fall into a dead faint at the thought that it is a Dolfin who's in love with him. God, what a waste: if it weren't so sad, it would be funny.'

'You make it sound as if all of this were common knowledge.'

'It is. At least to anyone who works with them.'

'Even that he has other women?'

'Well, that's meant to be a secret, I suppose.'

'But isn't?'

'No. Nothing ever is, is it? Here, I mean.'

'No, I suppose not,' Brunetti admitted, giving silent thanks that this was so.

'Anything else?' he asked.

'No, nothing that springs to mind. No more gossip. But I think you should call them and ask about this business with your apartment. From what I've heard, the whole idea of putting all the records together was just a smokescreen, anyway. It'll never happen.'

'A smokescreen for what?'

'What I heard was that someone in the city administration decided that so much of the restoration done in the last couple of years was illegal – well, that a large part of the actual work done was so much at variance with the designs submitted in the original plans – that it would be better if the permits and the requests for them were made to disappear. That way, no one could ever check the plans against what was actually done. So they set up this project to join everything together.'

'I'm not sure I follow you, Stefania.'

'It's simple, Guido,' Stefania chided him. 'With all these papers being shifted from one office to another, being sent from one side of the city to another, it's inevitable that some of them will be lost.'

Brunetti found this both inventive and efficient. He stored it away as an explanation he might try to use for the non-existence of the plans for his own house, should notice ever be given that he had to produce them. 'And so,' he continued for her, 'if questions were ever asked about the placement of a wall or the presence of a window, the owner would just have to produce their own plans and . . .'

Stefania cut him off: 'Which would of course correspond perfectly with the actual structure of the house.'

'And in the absence of the official plans, conveniently lost during the reorganization of the files,' Brunetti began, to an accompanying murmur of approval from Stefania, pleased that he had begun to understand, 'there would be no way for any city inspector or future buyer ever to be sure that the restorations that had in fact been made were different from the ones that had been requested and approved on the missing plans.' He finished saying this and, as it were, stepped silently back in order to admire what he had discovered. Ever since he was a child, he'd often heard people say of Venice, '*Tutto crolla, ma nulla crolla.*' And it certainly seemed true: more than a thousand years had passed since the first buildings rose on the swampy land, so surely many of them must be in danger of falling down, but nothing ever did fall down. They leaned, tilted, buckled, and curved, but he could not remember ever having heard of a building that had actually collapsed. Surely, he had seen abandoned buildings with roofs that had caved in, boarded-up houses with walls that had fallen in, but he'd never heard of a real collapse, of a building falling in on its inhabitants.

'Whose idea was this?'

'I don't know,' Stefania said. 'You never find out things like that.'

'Do the people in the various offices know about this?'

Instead of giving him a direct answer, she said, 'Think about it, Guido. Somebody has to see that some of these papers disappear, that files are lost, for you can be sure that a lot of others will be lost just because of the usual incompetence. But someone would have to see that specific papers ceased to exist.'

'Who would want that?' he asked.

'It would most likely be the people who own the houses where the illegal work was done, or it could be the people who were supposed to check the restorations and didn't bother.' She paused and then added, 'Or who did check and were persuaded,' she began, giving that last word ironic emphasis, 'to approve what they saw, regardless of what was drawn on the plans.'

'So who are they?'

'The Building Commissions.'

'How many are there?'

'One for every *sestiere*, six of them.'

Brunetti imagined the scope and breadth of such an undertaking, the number of people who would have to be involved. He asked, 'Wouldn't it just be easier for people to go ahead with the work and then pay a fine when it's discovered that something doesn't conform to the plans they submitted, rather than go to the trouble of bribing someone to see that the plans are destroyed? Or lost,' he amended.

'That's the way people did it in the past, Guido. Now that we're involved in all this Europe stuff, they make you pay the fine, but they also make you undo the work and do it again the right way. And the fines are terrible: I had a client who put up an illegal *altana*, not even a big one, about two metres by three. But his neighbour reported him. Forty million lire, Guido. And he had to take it down, as well. In the old days, at least he'd have been able to leave it there. I tell you, this business of being involved in Europe is going to ruin us. Soon you won't be able to find anyone brave enough to take a bribe.'

Though he could hear the moral indignation in her voice, Brunetti was not sure he shared it. 'Steffi, you've named a lot of people, but who do you think would be most likely to be able to arrange this?'

'The people there, in the Ufficio Catasto,' she answered instantly. 'And if anything's going on, dal Carlo would have to know about it, and I'd guess he'd have his snout in the trough. After all, the plans have to pass through his office at one time or another, and it would be child's play for him to destroy specific papers.' Stefania thought for a moment and then asked, 'Are you thinking of doing something like this, Guido, getting rid of the plans?'

'I told you, there are no plans. That's what put them on to me in the first place.'

'But if there are no plans, then you can claim they were lost along with the others that are going to be lost.'

'But how do I prove that my home exists, that it was really built?' Even as he asked the question, he was overcome with the absurdity of all of this: how did one prove the existence of reality?

Her response was immediate. 'All you've got to do is find an architect who will make the plans for you,' and before Brunetti could interrupt to ask the obvious question, she answered it for him, 'and have him put a false date on them.'

'Stefania, we're talking about fifty years ago.'

'Not really. All you've got to do is claim you made restorations a few years ago and then have plans drawn up to conform to the way the apartment is now, and put that date on them.'

Brunetti could think of no response to make to this, so she went on, 'It's simple, really. If you want, I can give you the name of an architect who will do it for you. Nothing easier, Guido.'

She'd been so helpful that he didn't want to offend her, so he said, 'I'll have to ask Paola about it.'

'Of course,' Stefania said. 'What a fool I am. That's the answer, isn't it? I'm sure her father knows the people who could get this taken care of. Then you wouldn't have to bother with getting an architect.' She stopped: for her, the problem was solved.

Brunetti was just getting ready to answer this, when Stefania broke in and said, 'I've got a call coming in on the other line. Pray it's a buyer. *Ciao*, Guido,' and she was gone.

He thought about their conversation for a while. Reality was there, malleable and obedient: all one had to do was wrest it this way, push it a bit that way, and make it conform to whatever vision one might have. Or if reality proved intractable, then one simply pulled up the big guns of power and money and opened fire. How simple, how easy.

Brunetti realized that this line of thought led to places he would prefer not to go, and so he flipped open the phone book again and dialled the number of the Ufficio Catasto. The phone rang repeatedly but no one picked it up. He glanced at his watch, saw that it was almost four, and put the phone down, muttering to himself that he was a fool to expect to find anyone at work there in the afternoon.

He hunched down in his chair and propped his feet on the open bottom drawer. Arms folded across his chest, he gave himself over to the reconsideration of Rossi's visit. He'd seemed an honest man, but that appearance was common enough, especially among the dishonest. Why had he followed up on the official letter by going in person to Brunetti's house? By the time he'd phoned, later, he'd learned Brunetti's rank. For a moment, Brunetti considered the possibility that Rossi had originally come in search of the offer of a bribe, but he dismissed that: the man had been too patently honest.

When he'd found out that the Signor Brunetti who couldn't find the plans of his apartment was a high-placed policeman, had Rossi flicked his line into the moving current of gossip to see what he could pull up about Brunetti? No one would dare to move ahead in any delicate dealing without doing this; the secret was knowing whom to ask, just where to drop the hook so as to catch the necessary information. And had he, subsequent to whatever his sources had reported about Brunetti, decided to approach him with what he had discovered at the Ufficio Catasto?

Illegal building permits and whatever could be earned in bribes from granting them seemed a cheap item on the vast menu of corruption offered by public offices: Brunetti found it impossible to believe that anyone would risk much, certainly not his life, by threatening to expose some ingenious scheme to loot the public purse. The implementation of the computer project to centralize documents and thus lose those which time had made inconvenient would raise the stakes, but Brunetti doubted this would be enough to have cost Rossi his life.

His reflections were interrupted by the arrival of Signorina Elettra, who came into his office without bothering to knock. 'Am I interrupting you, sir?' she asked.

'No, not at all. I was just sitting here thinking about corruption.'

'Public or private?' she asked.

'Public,' he said, putting his feet under his desk and sitting up straight.

'Like reading Proust,' she said, deadpan. 'You think you're finished with it, but then you discover there's another volume. Then another one after that.'

He looked up, waiting for more, but all she said, laying some papers on his desk, was, 'I've learned to share your suspicion of coincidence, sir, so I'd like you to take a look at the names of the owners of that building.'

'The Volpatos?' he asked, knowing somehow that it could be nothing else.

'Exactly.'

'For how long?'

She leaned over and pulled out the third page. 'Four years. They bought it from a certain Mathilde Ponzi. The declared price is here,' she said, pointing to a figure typed at the right side of the page.

'Two hundred and fifty million lire?' Brunetti said, his astonishment audible. 'It's four floors, must be at least a hundred and fifty square metres to the floor.'

'That's only the declared price, sir,' Signorina Elettra said.

Everyone knew that, to avoid taxes, the price of a house declared on the bill of sale never reflected the actual price paid or, if it did, it did so unclearly, through a glass darkly: the real price would be anywhere from two to three times as much. Everyone, in fact, referred as a matter of course to the 'real' price and the 'declared' price, and only a fool, or a foreigner, would think they were the same.

'I know that,' Brunetti said. 'But even if what they actually paid was three times as much, it's still a bargain.'

'If you look at their other real estate acquisitions,' Signorina Elettra began, pronouncing that noun with a certain measure of asperity, 'you'll see that they have enjoyed similar good fortune in most of their dealings.'

He turned back to the first page and read down through the information. Indeed, it did appear that the Volpatos had often managed to find houses that cost very little. Thoughtfully, Signorina Elettra had provided the number of square metres in each 'acquisition', and a quick calculation suggested to Brunetti that they had managed to pay an average declared price of less than a million lire a square metre. Even allowing for the variables created by inflation and factoring in the disparity between the declared price and the real price, they still ended up consistently paying far less than a third of the average price for real estate in the city.

He glanced up at her. 'Am I to assume that the other pages tell the same story?' he asked.

She nodded.

'How many properties are there?'

'More than forty, and I haven't even begun to examine the other properties listed under the names of Volpatos who might turn out to be relatives.'

'I see,' he said, turning his attention back to the papers. On the last pages she had attached current bank statements for their individual accounts as well as a number of joint accounts. 'How do you manage to do this,' he began, but seeing the sudden change that came over her face at these words, he added, 'so quickly?'

'Friends,' she answered, then added, 'Shall I see what sort of information Telecom has to give us about the phone calls they've made?'

Brunetti nodded, certain that she had already begun this process. She smiled and left the room; Brunetti returned his attention to the papers and the numbers. They were nothing short of staggering. He recalled the impression the Volpatos had made on him: that they were without education or social position or money. And yet they were people, from what these papers told him, of enormous wealth. If even only half the properties were rented – and people did not accumulate apartments in Venice to let them sit empty – then they must be receiving twenty or thirty million lire a month, as much as many people made in a year. Much of this wealth was safely deposited in four different banks, and even more was invested in government bonds. Brunetti understood little of the workings of the stock market in Milan, but he knew enough to recognize the names of the safest stocks, and the Volpatos had hundreds of millions invested in them.

Those shabby people: he summoned them from memory and recalled the worn handle on her plastic handbag, the stitching on her husband's left shoe that showed how often it had been repaired. Was this camouflage to protect them from the jealous eyes of the city or was it a form of avarice run mad? And where, in all of this, was he meant to fit the battered body of Franco Rossi, found fatally injured in front of a building owned by the Volpatos?

19

Brunetti spent the next hour contemplating greed, a vice for which Venetians had always had a natural propensity. La Serenissima was, from the beginning, a commercial enterprise, so the acquisition of wealth had ever been among the highest goals toward which a Venetian was trained to aspire. Unlike those profligate southerners, Romans and Florentines, who made money in order to toss it away, who delighted in hurling golden cups and plates into their rivers in order to make public display of their wealth, the Venetians had early on learned to acquire and maintain, to keep, to amass, and to hoard; they had also learned to keep their wealth hidden. Surely, the grand *palazzi* that lined the Canal Grande did not speak of hidden wealth; quite the contrary. But these were the Mocenigos, the Barbaros, families so lavishly blessed by the gods of lucre that any attempt to disguise their wealth would have been in vain. Their fame protected them from the disease of greed.

Its symptoms were far more manifest in the minor families, the fat merchants who built their more modest *palazzi* on the back canals, built them over their warehouses so that they could, like nesting birds, live in close physical contact with their wealth. There, they could warm their bosoms in the reflected glow of the spices and cloth brought back from the East, warm them in secret, with never an indication to their neighbours of just what lay behind the grilled barriers of their water doors.

Through the centuries, this tendency to accumulate had filtered down and taken firm root in the general population. It was called many things – thrift, economy, prudence – Brunetti himself had been raised to value all of these. In its more exaggerated form, however, it became nothing more than relentless, pitiless avarice, a disease which ravaged not only the person who suffered from it, but all those who came in contact with the infected person.

He remembered, as a young detective, being called to serve as a witness at the opening of the house of an old woman who had died one winter in the common ward of the hospital, her condition much aggravated by malnutrition and the sort of physical battering that came only from prolonged exposure to cold. Three of them had gone to the address given on her identity card, had broken the locks on the front door, all of them, and entered. There they found an apartment of more than two hundred square metres, squalid and stinking of cat, the rooms filled with boxes full of old newspapers, on top of which were piled plastic bags filled with rags and discarded clothing. One room contained nothing but bags of glass bottles of all types: wine bottles, milk bottles, small medicine bottles. Another contained a fifteenth-century Florentine wardrobe that was later valued at one hundred and twenty million lire.

Though it was February, there was no heat: not that the heat was not turned on but that no heating system existed in the house. Two of them were detailed to search for papers that might help find the old woman's relatives. Brunetti, opening a drawer in her bedroom, found a bundle of fifty-thousand-lire notes tied with a piece of dirty string, while his colleague, searching in the living room, found a stack of postal bank books, each with more than fifty million lire on deposit.

At that point, they'd left the house and sealed it, notified the Guardia di Finanza to come and sort it out. Later, Brunetti had learned that the old woman, who died without relatives or testament, had left more than four billion lire, left it, in lieu of surviving relatives, to the Italian state.

Brunetti's best friend had often said that he wanted death to take him just at the moment he laid his last lira down on a bar and said, 'Prosecco for everyone.' It had happened pretty much like that, and fate had given him forty years less than that old woman, but Brunetti knew that his had been the better life, and the better death.

He shook himself free of these memories and pulled the current duty roster out of his drawer, relieved to see that Vianello was on the night shift that week. The sergeant was at home, busy painting the kitchen, and very glad to be asked to meet Brunetti at the Ufficio Catasto at eleven the next morning.

Brunetti, like almost every citizen of the country, had no friends at the Guardia di Finanza, nor did he want any. He did, however, need access to the information they might have about the Volpatos, for only the Finanza, which busied itself burrowing into the intimate fiscal secrets of citizens, would have any clear idea of just how much of the Volpatos' enormous wealth was declared and thus taxed. Instead of bothering himself with considering the correct bureaucratic process by which a request for information could be made, he dialled Signorina Elettra and asked her if she could get into their files.

'Ah, the Guardia di Finanza,' she breathed, making no attempt to disguise the rapture with which she greeted this request, 'I've longed to be asked to do this.'

'You wouldn't do it on your own, Signorina?' he asked.

'Why no, sir,' she answered, surprised that he would ask. 'That would be, well, that would be poaching, wouldn't it?'

'And this, if I ask you to do it?'

'Big game hunting, sir,' she sighed and was gone.

He called down to the crime squad and asked when he was going to get the report on the building where Rossi's body had been found. After a few minutes' delay, he was told that the team had gone over to the site but, finding that workers were again busy with the building, had decided it was too contaminated for them to be able to get any accurate data and so had returned to the Questura without entering the building.

He was about to write it off as another failure resulting from a general lack of interest and initiative, when he thought to ask, 'How many workers were there?'

He was told to hold the line; after a short time, one of the crime team picked up the phone. 'Yes, Commissario?'

'When you went over to that building, how many workers were there?'

'I saw two, sir, up on the third floor.'

'Were there men on the scaffolding?'

'I didn't see any, sir.'

'Just the two?'

'Yes.'

'Where were they?'

'At the window, sir.'

'Where were they when you arrived?'

The man had to think about this for a moment, and then he answered, 'They came to the window when we banged on the door.'

'Please tell me exactly what happened,' Brunetti said.

'We tried the lock, then we banged on the door, and one of them stuck his head out the window and asked what we wanted. Pedone told them who we were and why we were there, and the guy said they'd been working in the place for two days, moving things around, so there was a lot of dust and dirt and nothing was the way it had been a few days before. Then another guy came and stood next to him. He didn't say anything, but he had a lot of dust all over him, so it was obvious they were working there.'

There was a long silence. At last Brunetti asked, 'And?'

'So Pedone asked about the windows, well, in front of the windows, because that's where we would have to look, isn't it, sir?'

'Yes,' Brunetti assented.

'The guy said they'd been hauling bags of cement through the windows all day, so Pedone decided it would be a waste of time.'

Brunetti let another silence elapse and then asked, 'How were they dressed?'

'What, sir?'

'How were they dressed? Like workers?'

'I don't know, sir. They were up at the window on the third floor, and we were looking up at them, so all we could see was their heads

226

and shoulders.' He thought about this and then said, 'I think the one we talked to might have been wearing a jacket.'

'Then why did you think he was a worker?'

'Because he said he was, sir. Besides, why else would he be in the building?'

Brunetti had a good idea of why the men would have been in the building, but there was nothing to be served by mentioning it. He started to order the man to get his partner and go over and do a proper scene of crime exam but thought better of it. Instead he thanked the man for his information and hung up.

A decade ago, a conversation like this would have launched Brunetti into incandescent rage; now, however, it did nothing more than gently confirm his grim assessment of his fellow officers. In his blackest moments, he wondered if most of them were in the pay of the Mafia, but he knew this incident was nothing more than another example of endemic incompetence and lack of interest. Or perhaps it was a manifestation of what he felt himself: a growing sense that any attempt to obstruct, prevent, or punish crime was doomed to failure.

Rather than remain here, on his private Dunkirk, he locked the papers about the Volpatos in his drawer and left the office. The day attempted to lure him with the wiles of its beauty: birds sang brightly, the wisteria sent a special thread of sweetness across the canal toward him, and a stray cat came and wound itself around his legs. Brunetti bent and scratched the cat behind the ears, deciding what to do.

Out on the *riva*, he boarded the vaporetto that was heading toward the station and got off at San Basilio, then cut back toward Angelo Raffaele and the narrow *calle* where Rossi had lain. As he turned into the narrow street, he saw the building up ahead, but no sign of activity of any sort. No workers climbed on the scaffolding, and the shutters on the windows were pulled closed. He approached the building and had a closer look at the door. The padlock still held the metal chain in place, but the screws that fixed the metal flange to the frame of the door were loose, and the whole thing could easily be pulled out. He did this, and the door swung back on its hinges.

He stepped inside. Curious, he turned to see if he could do it, and yes, the screws holding the flange could be stuck back into the holes: the chain was long enough to allow the door to remain open a hand's breadth while he did this. That done, he pulled the door closed and was safely inside: from outside, the house appeared securely locked.

He turned and found himself in a corridor. Stairs stood at the end, and he walked quickly toward them. Stone, they made no sound under his footsteps as he climbed up to the third floor.

He stopped for a moment at the top to orient himself, confused by having turned so many times on the stairs. Light filtered in from his left, so he assumed that must be the front of the house and turned toward it.

A sound came from above him, muffled and soft, but definitely a sound. He froze and wondered where he'd left his pistol this time: locked in the metal box at home, in his locker at the shooting range, or in the pocket of the jacket he'd left hanging in the closet of his office. Futile to think about where it might be when he was certain about where it was not.

He waited, breathing through his mouth, and had the distinct sensation that there was some sort of presence above him. Stepping over an empty plastic bottle, he moved into a doorway on his right and stood just inside. He glanced at his watch: six twenty. Soon it would begin to grow dark outside: it was already dark inside, save for the light that filtered through from the front of the house.

He waited: Brunetti was good at waiting. When he looked at his watch again, it was six thirty-five. Again, the sound from above, somewhat closer and more distinct. A long pause, and then the soft sound came down the stairs towards him, this time the unmistakable noise of a footfall on the wooden steps coming down from the attic.

He waited. The little light that filtered in turned the staircase into a hazy mist where Brunetti could perceive only the absence of being. He shifted his eyes to the left of the sound and perceived the grey ghost of a descending presence. He closed his eyes and slowed his breathing. At the next sound, which seemed to come from the landing just in front of him, he opened his eyes, perceived the vaguest of forms, and stepped suddenly forward, shouting as loudly as he could, 'Stop! Police!'

There was a scream of pure, animal terror, and then whatever it was fell to the floor at Brunetti's feet and continued to emit a piercing, high-pitched noise that caused the short hair on the back of Brunetti's neck to bristle.

He stumbled toward the front of the house and pulled open a window, then pushed open the wooden shutters to let the failing light of the day enter the room. Momentarily blinded, he turned and made his way back toward the doorway, from which the noise still came, lower now, less terrified, and more identifiably human.

The instant Brunetti saw him there, cowering full length on the ground, his arms wrapped around his thin body to protect it from the expected kicks or blows and his neck pulled down into his shoulders, he recognized the young man. He was one of a trio of drug addicts, all in their early twenties, who had for years spent their days near or in Campo San Bortolo, going from bar to bar, growing more out of touch with reality as day passed into night and year into year. This was the tallest of them, Gino Zecchino, frequently arrested for drug dealing and often for assault or making threats to strangers. Brunetti hadn't seen him in almost a year and was struck by his physical deterioration. His dark hair was long and greasy, no doubt disgusting to the touch, and his front teeth were long gone. Deep hollows were visible above and below his jawbone, and he looked as though he hadn't eaten for days. From Treviso, he had no family in the city and lived with his two friends in an apartment behind Campo San Polo with which the police were long familiar.

'You've done it this time, Gino,' Brunetti shouted at him. 'Get up, get on your feet.'

Zecchino recognized his name but not the voice. He stopped whimpering and turned his face toward the sound. But he didn't move.

'I said get up!' Brunetti shouted, in Veneziano, forcing as much anger as he could into his voice. He looked down at Zecchino; even this dim light showed the scabs on the back of his hands where he'd tried to find the veins. 'Get up before I kick your ass down the stairs.' Brunetti was using language he'd spent his life listening to in bars and police cells, anything to keep the adrenalin of fear pumping in Zecchino's veins.

The young man rolled on to his back and, body still protected by his arms, turned his head, eyes shut, toward the voice.

'Look at me when I talk to you,' Brunetti ordered.

Zecchino pushed himself back against the wall and looked up through slitted eyes at Brunetti, who towered in the shadows above him. With a single, fluid gesture, Brunetti leaned down over the young man, grabbed two handfuls of the front of his jacket, and pulled him to his feet, surprised at how easy it was.

When he got close enough to Brunetti to recognize him, Zecchino's eyes opened wide in terror and he began to chant, 'I didn't see anything. I didn't see anything. I didn't see anything.'

Roughly, Brunetti pulled the young man toward him, all the time shouting into his face, 'What happened?'

The words came bubbling out of Zecchino, pumped out by fear. 'I heard voices downstairs. It was an argument. They were inside. Then they stopped for a while, then they started again, but I didn't see them. I was up there,' he said, waving a hand toward the stairs that led to the attic.

'What happened?'

'I don't know. I heard them come up here and I heard them shouting. But then my girlfriend offered me some more stuff, and I don't know what happened after that.' He looked up at Brunetti, curious to see how much of his story Brunetti believed.

'I want more, Zecchino,' Brunetti said, putting his face directly in front of Zecchino's and breathing in the foul breath that spoke of dead teeth and years of bad food. 'I want to know who they were.'

Zecchino started to speak and then stopped himself and looked down at the floor. When he finally looked up at Brunetti, the fear had gone and his eyes had a different expression. Some secret calculation had filled them with feral cunning.

'He was outside when I left, on the ground,' he said at last.

'Was he moving?'

'Yes, he was pushing himself with his feet. But he didn't have a . . .' Zecchino began but the new cunning made him stop.

He had said enough. 'Didn't have what?' Brunetti demanded. When Zecchino didn't answer, he shook him again, and Zecchino gave a quick, broken sob. His nose began to run on to the sleeve of Brunetti's jacket. He whipped his hands free, and Zecchino fell back against the wall.

'Who was with you?' he demanded.

'My girlfriend.'

'Why were you here?'

'To fuck,' Zecchino said. 'This is where we always come.' The thought filled Brunetti with revulsion.

'Who were they?' Brunetti asked, moving a half-step towards him.

The instinct of survival had overcome Zecchino's panic, and Brunetti's advantage was gone, evaporated as quickly as a drug-induced phantom. He was left standing in front of this human wreck, only a few years older than his son, and he knew that any chance of getting the truth from Zecchino was gone. Brunetti found the idea of breathing the same air or being in the same space as Zecchino insupportable, but he forced himself to go back to the window. He looked down, and saw below him the pavement where Rossi had been thrown and across which he had tried to propel himself. The area for at least two metres in circumference around the window had been swept clean. There were no bags of cement, nor were there any in the room. Like the supposed workmen seen at this window, they had disappeared, leaving no trace.

20

Leaving Zecchino in front of the house, Brunetti started toward home, but he found no consolation in the soft spring evening, nor in the long walk along the water he permitted himself. His route would take him far out of his way, but he wanted the long views, the smell of the water, and the comfort of a glass of wine at a small place he knew near the Accademia to cleanse him of the memory of Zecchino, especially of the way he had grown furtive and feral at the end of their meeting. He thought of what Paola had said, that she was glad never to have found drugs attractive for fear of what might have happened; he lacked her openness of mind and had never tried them, not even as a student when everyone around him was smoking something or other and assuring him that it was the perfect way to liberate his mind from his choking middle-class prejudices. Little did they imagine how he, then, aspired to middle-class prejudice; middle-class anything, for that matter.

The memory of Zecchino kept breaking into his reflections, blotting out thought. At the foot of the Accademia Bridge he hesitated for a moment but decided to make a wide circle and pass through Campo San Luca. He started over the bridge, eyes on his feet, and noticed how many of the strips of white facing were broken or torn off the front edge of the steps. When had it been rebuilt, the bridge? Three years ago? Two? And already many of the steps were in need of repair. His mind veered away from contemplation of how that contract must have been awarded and returned to what Zecchino had told him before he began to lie. An argument. Rossi injured and trying to escape. And a girl willing to go up into the lair Zecchino had in that attic, there to engage in whatever it was the combination of drugs and Gino Zecchino would lead her to.

At the sight of the broad horror of the Cassa di Risparmio, he veered to the left, past the bookstore, and then into Campo San Luca. He went into Bar Torino and ordered a *spritz*, then took it and stood at the window, studying the figures who still congregated in the *campo*.

There was no sign of either Signora Volpato or her husband. He finished his drink, put the glass on the counter, and offered some bills to the barman.

'I don't see Signora Volpato,' he said casually, tilting his head toward the *campo*.

Handing him his receipt and change, the barman said, 'No, they're usually here in the morning. After ten.'

'I have to see her about something,' Brunetti said, sounding nervous but smiling awkwardly at the barman, as if in search of his understanding of human need.

'I'm sorry,' the barman said and turned to another customer.

Outside, Brunetti turned left, and left again, and went into the pharmacy, just closing now.

'*Ciao*, Guido,' his friend Danilo the pharmacist said, locking the door behind them. 'Let me finish and we'll go have a drink.' Quickly, with the ease of long practice, the bearded man emptied the cash register, counted the money, and took it into the back of the pharmacy, where Brunetti could hear him moving around. A few minutes later he came out, wearing his leather jacket.

Brunetti felt the scrutiny of those soft brown eyes, saw the beginning of a smile. 'You look like you're in search of information,' Danilo said.

'Is it that obvious?'

Danilo shrugged. 'Sometimes you stop for medicine, and you look worried; sometimes you stop for a drink, and you look relaxed; but when you come looking for information, you look like this,' he said, beetling his brows together and staring at Brunetti with what appeared to be the first signs of incipient madness.

'*Va là*,' Brunetti said, smiling in spite of himself.

'What is it?' Danilo asked. 'Or who is it?'

Brunetti made no move toward the door, thinking it might be better to have this conversation inside the closed pharmacy than in one of the three bars in the *campo*. 'Angelina and Massimo Volpato,' he said.

'*Madre di Dio*,' Danilo exclaimed. 'You'd be better taking the money from me. Come on,' he said, grabbing Brunetti's arm and pulling him toward the back room of the pharmacy, 'I'll open the safe and then say the thief wore a ski mask, I promise.' Brunetti thought it was a joke until Danilo continued, 'You aren't thinking of going to them, are you, Guido? Really, I've got money in the bank you can have, and I'm sure Mauro could let you have more,' he said, including his boss in his offer.

'No, no,' Brunetti said, laying a quieting hand on Danilo's arm. 'I just need to know about them.'

'Don't tell me they've finally made a mistake, and someone's filed a complaint against them?' Danilo said with the beginnings of a smile. 'Ah, what joy.'

'You know them that well?' Brunetti asked.

'I've known them for years,' he said, almost spitting out his disgust. 'Especially her. She's in here once a week, with her little pictures of her saints, and her rosary in her hands.' He hunched over and brought his hands together under his chin. He tilted his head to one side and looked up at Brunetti, his mouth pulled together in a purse-lipped smile. Turning his usual Trentino dialect into purest Veneziano and pitching his voice into a high squeal, he said, 'Oh, Dottor Danilo, you don't know how much good I've done to the people in this city. You don't know how many people are grateful to me for what I've done for them and how they should pray for me. No, you have no idea.' Though Brunetti had never heard Signora Volpato speak, he heard in Danilo's savage parody the echo of every hypocrite he'd ever known.

Suddenly Danilo stood upright, and the old woman he had become disappeared. 'How does she do it?' Brunetti asked.

'People know her. And him. They're always in the *campo*, one of them, in the morning, and people know where to find them.'

'How do they know?'

'How do people ever know anything?' Danilo asked by way of response. 'Word gets around. People who need enough to pay their taxes, or who gamble, or who can't meet the expenses for their business until the end of the month. They sign a paper saying they'll pay them back in a month, and the interest has always been added to the sum. But these are people who will have to borrow more money to pay that money back. Gamblers don't win; people never get any better at running their businesses.'

'What amazes me,' Brunetti said after a moment's reflection, 'is that all of this is legal.'

'If they've got the paper, drawn up by a notary and signed by both parties, nothing is more legal.'

'Who are the notaries?'

Danilo named three of them, respectable men with wide practices in the city. One of them worked for Brunetti's father-in-law.

'All three?' Brunetti asked, unable to hide his astonishment.

'You think the Volpatos declare what they pay them? You think they pay taxes on what they earn from the Volpatos?'

Brunetti was not in the least surprised that notaries would sink to being part of something as squalid as this; his surprise was only at the names of the three men involved, one of them a member of the Knights of Malta and another a former city councillor.

'Come on,' Danilo encouraged him, 'let's have a drink, and you can tell me why you want to know all this.' Seeing Brunetti's expression, he amended this to, 'Or don't tell me.'

Across the *calle* at Rosa Salva, Brunetti told him no more than that he was interested in the moneylenders in the city and their twilight existence between the legal and the criminal. Many of Danilo's clients were old women, and most of them were in love with him, so he was often the recipient of their endless streams of gossip. Amiable and patient, always willing to listen to them as they talked, he had over the years accumulated an Eldorado of gossip and innuendo and in the past had proven an invaluable source of information for Brunetti. Danilo named a few of the most famous moneylenders to Brunetti, describing them and cataloguing the wealth they had managed to accumulate.

Sensitive to both Brunetti's mood and his sense of professional discretion, Danilo kept up his stream of gossip, aware that Brunetti would ask him no more questions. Then, with a quick glance at his watch, Danilo said, 'I've got to go. Dinner's at eight.'

Together they left the bar and walked as far as Rialto, chatting idly about ordinary things. At the bridge they separated, both hurrying home for dinner.

The scattered pieces of information had been rattling about in Brunetti's mind for days now, and he'd been prodding them and toying with them, trying to work them into some sort of coherent pattern. People at the Ufficio Catasto, he realized, would know who was going to have to do restorations or would have to pay fines for work done illegally in the past. They'd know how much the fines were. They might even have had some say in deciding how much the fines should be. Then all they'd have to do would be find out what sort of financial shape the owners were in – there was never any trouble in finding that out. Surely, he reflected, Signorina Elettra was not the only genius in the city. Then to anyone who complained that they didn't have enough money to pay the fine, all they had to do was suggest they go and have a talk with the Volpatos.

It was high time to visit the Ufficio.

When he arrived at the Questura the next morning, a bit after eight thirty, the guard at the door told him a young woman had come in earlier, asking to speak to him. No, she hadn't explained what it was she wanted and, when the guard told her Commissario Brunetti had not arrived yet, had said she'd go and have a coffee and come back. Brunetti told the young man to bring her up when she did.

In his office, he read the first section of the *Gazzettino* and was thinking about going out to get a coffee when the guard appeared at his door and said that the young woman had returned. He stepped aside and a woman who seemed little more than a girl slipped into the room. Brunetti thanked the guard and told him he could return to duty. The officer saluted and closed the door as he left. Brunetti gestured to the young woman, who still stood by the door as if fearful of the consequences of coming any farther into the room.

'Please, Signorina, make yourself comfortable.'

Leaving it to her to decide what to do, he walked slowly around his desk and took his normal place.

Slowly she crossed the room and sat on the edge of the chair, her hands in her lap. Brunetti gave her a quick glance then bent to move a paper from one side of his desk to the other to give her some time to relax into a more comfortable position.

When he looked back at her, he smiled in what he thought might be a welcoming way. She had dark brown hair cut as short as a boy's and wore jeans and a light blue sweater. Her eyes, he noticed, were as dark as her hair, surrounded by lashes so thick that at first he thought they were false until he noticed that she wore no make-up at all and dismissed the idea. She was a pretty girl in the way most young girls are pretty: delicate bones, short straight nose, smooth skin, and a small mouth. Had he seen her in a bar having a coffee, he wouldn't have looked twice at her, but seeing her here, the thought came to him of how lucky he was to live in a country where pretty girls were so thick upon the ground and far more beautiful ones a normal enough event.

She cleared her throat once, twice, and then said, 'I'm Marco's friend.' Her voice was extraordinarily beautiful, low and musical and rich with sensuality, the sound one would expect from a woman who had lived a long life filled with pleasure.

Brunetti waited for her to explain, but when she said nothing further, Brunetti asked, 'And why have you come to speak to me, Signorina?'

'Because I want to help you find the people who killed him.'

Brunetti kept his face expressionless while he processed the information that this must be the girl who had called Marco from Venice. 'Are you the other rabbit, then?' he asked kindly.

His question startled her. She pulled her closed hands up toward her chest and automatically pursed her lips into a narrow circle, making herself look, indeed, very like a rabbit.

'How do you know about that?' she asked.

'I saw his drawings,' Brunetti explained, then added, 'and I was struck both by his talent and by the obvious affection he had for the rabbits.'

She bowed her head and at first he thought she had begun to cry. But she did not; instead, she raised her head again and looked at him. 'I had a pet rabbit when I was a little girl. When I told Marco about that, he told me how much he hated the way his father used to shoot and poison them on their farm.' She stopped here, then added, 'They're pests when they're outside. That's what his father said.'

Brunetti said, 'I see.'

Silence fell but he waited. Then she said, as if no mention had been made of the rabbits, 'I know who they are.' Her hands tortured one another in her lap, but her voice remained calm, almost seductive. It occurred to him that she had no idea of its power or its beauty.

Brunetti nodded to encourage her, and she continued, 'Well, that is, I know the name of one of them, the one who sold it to Marco. I don't know the name of the people he gets it from, but I think he'd tell you if you frightened him enough.'

'I'm afraid we're not in the business of

frightening people,' Brunetti said, smiling, wishing it were true.

'I mean frightening him so that he'd come and tell you what he knows. He'd do that if he thought you knew who he is and were going to get him.'

'If you give me his name, Signorina, we can bring him in and question him.'

'But wouldn't it be better if he came in by himself and told you what he knows, told you voluntarily?'

'Yes, it certainly would . . .'

She interrupted him. 'I don't have any proof, you know. It's not like I can testify that I saw him sell it to Marco or Marco told me that he did.' She moved around uneasily in her chair, then put her folded hands back in her lap. 'But I know he'd come in if he didn't have any other choice, and then it wouldn't be so bad for him, would it?'

This intense concern could be directed only at family, Brunetti realized. 'I'm afraid you haven't told me your name, Signorina.'

'I don't want to tell you my name,' she answered, some of the sweetness gone from her voice.

Brunetti opened his hands, spreading his fingers wide in symbol of the liberty he extended, 'That's entirely your right, Signorina. In that case, the only thing I suggest to you is that you tell this person that he should come in.'

'He won't listen to me. He never has,' she said, adamant.

Brunetti considered his options. He studied

245

his wedding band, saw that it was thinner than it was when he had studied it last, worn away by the years. He looked up and across at her. 'Does he read the newspaper?'

Surprised, her answer was instant, 'Yes.'

'The *Gazzettino*?'

'Yes.'

'Can you see that he reads it tomorrow?' he asked.

She nodded.

'Good. I hope it will be enough to make him talk to us. Will you encourage him to come?'

She looked down after he said this, and again he thought she was going to begin to cry. Instead, she said, 'I've been trying to do that since Marco died.' Her voice broke, and her hands balled themselves into tight fists again. She shook her head. 'He's afraid.' Again, a long pause. 'I can't do anything to make him. My par . . .' she broke off before finishing the word, confirming what he already knew. She shifted her weight forward, and he saw that, message delivered, she was ready to escape.

Brunetti got slowly to his feet and came around the desk. She stood and turned toward the door.

Brunetti opened it for her. He thanked her for having come to talk to him. As she started down the stairs, he closed the door, ran back to the phone, and dialled the number of the guard desk at the front door. He recognized the voice of the young man who had brought her up.

'Masi, say nothing. When that girl comes

down, take her into your office and see that she stays there at least a few minutes. Tell her you have to record in your ledger what time she left, make up some sort of story, but keep her there. Then let her leave.'

Giving him no chance to answer, Brunetti replaced the phone and walked to the large wooden closet that stood against the wall by the door. He yanked the door open, letting it slam back against the wall. Inside, he saw an old tweed jacket he had left there more than a year ago and ripped it from the hanger. Clutching it in one hand, he moved to the door of his office, opened it, looked down the stairs and took them two at a time down to the officers' room on the floor below.

Panting at the effort, he ran into the room and gave a sigh of silent thanks when he saw Pucetti at his desk. 'Pucetti,' he said, 'get up and take off your jacket.'

Instantly, the young officer was on his feet and his jacket flung on the desk in front of him. Brunetti handed him the woollen jacket, saying, 'There's a girl downstairs near the entrance. Masi's holding her for a few minutes in his office. When she leaves, I want you to follow her. Follow her all day if you have to, but I want to know where she goes, and I want to know who she is.'

Pucetti was already moving toward the door. The jacket hung loosely on him, so he flipped over the cuffs then pushed them up his forearms; he ripped off his tie and tossed it in the general direction of his desk. When he left the office, asking Brunetti for no explanation, he looked like a casually dressed young man who had chosen to wear a white shirt and dark blue trousers that day but had offset the military cut of the trousers by wearing an overlarge Harris tweed jacket with the sleeves pushed up in quite a dashing manner.

Brunetti went back to his office, dialled the news office of *Il Gazzettino* and identified himself. The story he gave them explained how the police investigating the drug-related death of a young student had discovered the identity of the young man believed to have been responsible for selling the drugs that had caused his death. An arrest was imminent, and it was hoped that this would lead to the arrest of even more people involved in the drug traffic in the Veneto area. When he put the phone down, he hoped only that this would be enough to force the young girl's relative, whoever he was, to find the courage to come into the Questura so that something positive could come of the stupid waste of Marco Landi's life.

He and Vianello presented themselves at the Ufficio Catasto at eleven. Brunetti gave his name and rank to the secretary on the first floor, and she told him that Ingeniere dal Carlo's office was on the third floor and she'd be glad to call ahead and tell him that Commissario Brunetti was on the way up. Brunetti, a uniformed Vianello silent in his wake, walked up to the third floor, amazed at the number of people, almost all of them men, who flowed up and down the stairs in two opposing streams. On each landing, they milled outside the doors of offices, rolls of blueprints and heavy folders of papers held to their chests.

Ingeniere dal Carlo's was the last office on the left. The door was open, so they went in. A small woman who looked old enough to be Vianello's mother sat at a desk facing them, next to the immense screen of a computer. She glanced at them over the thick lenses of her half-frame reading glasses. Her hair, heavily streaked with grey, was pulled back in a tight bun that forced Brunetti to think of Signora Landi, and her narrow shoulders were hunched forward as if with the beginning of osteoporosis. She wore no make-up, as if she'd long ago abandoned the idea of its possible utility.

'Commissario Brunetti?' she asked, remaining in her seat.

'Yes. I'd like to speak to Ingeniere dal Carlo.'

'May I ask what this is in aid of?' she asked, speaking precise Italian and using a phrase he hadn't heard in decades.

'I'd like to ask some questions about a former employee.'

'Former?'

'Yes. Franco Rossi,' he said.

'Ah yes,' she said, raising a hand to her forehead and shielding her eyes. She lowered her hand and removed her glasses, then looked up. 'The poor young man. He'd worked here for years. It was terrible. Nothing like this has ever happened before.' There was a crucifix on the wall above her desk, and she turned her eyes to it, her lips moving in a prayer for the dead young man.

'Did you know Signor Rossi?' Brunetti asked, then continued, as if he hadn't quite caught her name, 'Signora . . . ?'

'Dolfin, Signorina,' she answered briefly and paused, almost as if waiting to see how he responded to the name. She continued, 'His office was just across the hall. He was always a polite young man, always very respectful to Dottor dal Carlo.' From the sound of it, Signorina Dolfin could think of no higher praise.

'I see,' Brunetti said, tired of listening to the sort of empty compliments which death demanded be paid. 'Would it be possible for me to speak to the Ingeniere?'

'Of course,' she said, getting to her feet. 'You must excuse me for talking so much. It's just that one doesn't know what to do in the face of a tragic death like that.'

Brunetti nodded, the most efficient way he'd ever found to acknowledge cliché.

She led them the few steps that separated her desk from the door to the inner office. She raised her hand and tapped twice, paused a moment, and then added a third small tap, as though she had, over the years, devised a code which would tell the man inside just what sort of visitor to expect. When the man's voice from inside called out *'Avanti'*, Brunetti saw an unmistakable gleam in her eyes, noticed the way the corners of her mouth tilted up.

She opened the door, stepped inside and to one side to allow both men to enter, then said, 'This is Commissario Brunetti, Dottore.' Brunetti had glanced in as they entered and seen a large, dark-haired man behind the desk, but he kept his eyes on Signorina Dolfin as she spoke, intrigued by the change in her manner, even in the tone of her voice, far warmer and richer than when she had spoken to him.

'Thank you, Signorina,' dal Carlo said, barely glancing at her. 'That will be all.'

'Thank you, sir,' she said and, very slowly, turned away from dal Carlo and left the office, closing the door quietly behind her.

Dal Carlo got to his feet, smiling. He was in his late fifties, but had the taut skin and erect carriage of a younger man. His smile revealed teeth capped in the Italian manner: one size larger than necessary. 'How pleased I am to meet you, Commissario,' he said, extending his hand to Brunetti and, when he returned the gesture, giving it a firm, manly shake. Dal Carlo nodded to Vianello and led them to some chairs at one side of the room. 'How may I help you?'

Taking his seat, Brunetti said, 'I'd like to know something about Franco Rossi.'

'Ah, yes,' dal Carlo said, shaking his head a few times. 'Terrible thing, tragic. He was a wonderful young man, an excellent worker. He would have had a very successful career.' He sighed and repeated, 'Tragic, tragic.'

'How long had he worked here, Ingeniere?' Brunetti asked. Vianello took a small notebook from his pocket, opened it, and started to take notes.

'Let me see,' dal Carlo began. 'About five years, I'd say.' Smiling, he said, 'I can ask Signorina Dolfin. She'd be able to give you a more precise answer.'

'No, that's fine, Dottore,' Brunetti said with a casual wave of his hand and went on: 'What, exactly, were Signor Rossi's duties?'

Dal Carlo put his hand to his chin, a thinking gesture, and looked down at the floor. After a suitable time, he said, 'He had to examine plans to see that they conformed to restorations that were performed.'

'And how did he do that, Dottore?' Brunetti asked.

'He looked at the blueprints here in the office and then inspected the actual place where the work had been done to see that it had been done properly.'

'Properly?' Brunetti asked, his voice filled with layman's confusion.

'That it was the same as shown on the plans.'

'And if it wasn't?'

'Then Signor Rossi would report the discrepancies, and our office would initiate proceedings.'

'Such as?'

Dal Carlo looked across at Brunetti and appeared to weigh not only the question but the reason Brunetti was asking it.

'Usually a fine and an order that the work performed be redone to conform to the specifications on the blueprints,' dal Carlo answered.

'I see,' Brunetti said, nodding to Vianello to make a special point of that last answer. 'That could be a very expensive inspection.'

Dal Carlo looked puzzled. 'I'm afraid I don't understand what you mean, Commissario.'

'I mean that it could cost a great deal, first to do the work and then to do it again. To make no mention of the fines.'

'Of course,' dal Carlo said. 'The code is quite precise about that.'

'Doubly expensive, then,' Brunetti said.

'Yes, I suppose so. But few people are so rash as to attempt such a thing.'

Brunetti allowed himself a start of surprise here and looked over at dal Carlo with the small smile one conspirator gives another. 'If you say so, Ingeniere,' he said. Quickly, he changed topic and the tone of his voice and asked, 'Had Signor Rossi ever received any threats?'

Again, dal Carlo seemed confused. 'I'm afraid I don't understand that, either, Commissario.'

'Let me be clear with you, then, Dottore. Signor Rossi had the authority to cost people a great deal of money. If he reported that illegal work had been done on a building, the owners would be liable both for fines and for the cost of further work to correct the original restorations.' He smiled here and added, 'We both know what building costs are in this city, so I doubt that anyone would be pleased if Signor Rossi's inspection discovered discrepancies.'

'Certainly not,' dal Carlo agreed. 'But I doubt very much that anyone would dare to threaten a city official who was doing no more than his duty.'

Suddenly Brunetti asked, 'Would Signor Rossi have taken a bribe?' He was careful to watch dal Carlo's face as he asked his question and saw that he was taken aback, one might even say shocked.

Instead of answering, however, dal Carlo gave the question considerable attention. 'I'd never thought of that before,' he said, and Brunetti had no doubt he was telling the truth. Dal Carlo did everything but close his eyes and put his head back to give proof of further concentration. Finally he said, lying, 'I don't like to speak ill of him, not now, but that might be possible. Well,' with an awkward hesitation, 'might have been possible.'

'Why do you say that?' Brunetti asked, though he was fairly certain it was nothing more than a rather obvious attempt to use Rossi as a means to cover the tracks of his own probable dishonesty.

For the first time, dal Carlo looked steadily into Brunetti's eyes. Had he needed it, Brunetti could have found no surer proof that he was lying. 'You must understand it was nothing specific I can name or describe. His behaviour had changed in the last few months. He'd become furtive, nervous. It is only now, that you ask this question, that the possibility occurs to me.'

'Would it be easy to do?' Brunetti asked, and when dal Carlo seemed not to understand, he prompted: 'Take a bribe?'

He all but expected dal Carlo to say he had never thought of such a thing, in which case Brunetti didn't know if he could stop himself from laughing. They were, after all, in a city office. But the engineer restrained himself and said, eventually, 'I suppose it would be possible.'

Brunetti was silent for a long time, so long that dal Carlo was finally forced to ask, 'Why are you asking these questions, Commissario?'

At last Brunetti said, 'We're not completely satisfied,' having found it always far more effective to speak in the plural, 'that Rossi's death was an accident.'

This time, dal Carlo could not hide his surprise, though there was no way of knowing if it was surprise at the possibility or surprise that the police had discovered it. As various ideas played through his mind, he gave Brunetti a sly glance that reminded him of the look Zecchino had given him.

With the idea of the young drug addict in his mind, Brunetti said, 'We might have a witness that it was something else.'

'A witness?' Dal Carlo repeated in a loud, disbelieving voice, as though he had never heard the word.

'Yes, someone there at the building.' Brunetti

got to his feet suddenly. 'Thank you for your help, Dottore,' he said, extending his hand. Dal Carlo, obviously disconcerted by the strange turn the conversation had taken, pushed himself to his feet and shot out his hand. His grip was less hearty than when they had come in.

After opening the door he finally gave voice to his surprise. 'I find it incredible,' he said. 'No one would have killed him. There's no reason for such a thing. And that building's empty. How could anyone have seen what happened?'

When neither Brunetti nor Vianello spoke, dal Carlo walked through the door, ignoring Signorina Dolfin, busy at her computer, and saw the two policemen to the outer door of the office. None of them bothered with farewells.

21

Brunetti slept badly that night, waking himself repeatedly with memories of the day. He realized that Zecchino had probably lied about Rossi's murder and had seen or heard far more than he admitted; why else had he become so evasive? The endless night dragged in other things: Patta's refusal to see his son's behaviour as criminal; his friend Luca's lack of sympathy for his wife; the general incompetence that handicapped his every working day. Yet it was the thought of the two young girls that most troubled him, one so reduced by life that she would consent to sex with Zecchino in that squalid place and the other trapped between grief for Marco's death and the guilty knowledge of what had caused it. Experience had beaten any trace of the cavalier out of Brunetti, but still he could not rid himself of a grinding pity for these girls.

Had the first one been upstairs when he found Zecchino? He had been so intent on fleeing the house that he had not gone up to the attic to see if anyone else was there. The fact that Zecchino was coming down the stairs did not mean he was going out; he could just as easily have been on his way to investigate the noise made by Brunetti's arrival, leaving the girl behind him in the attic. At least Pucetti had provided a name for the second one: Anna Maria Ratti, who lived with her parents and brother in Castello and was an architectural student at the university.

It was some time after he heard the four o'clock bells ring that he decided to go back to the house that morning and try to talk to Zecchino again; soon after, he fell into a peaceful sleep, waking only after Paola had left for the university and the children had gone to school.

After he dressed, he called the Questura to tell them he would be late in arriving and went back to the bedroom to try to find his pistol. He pulled a chair over to the *armadio*, climbed up, and saw on the top shelf the box his father had brought back from Russia at the end of the war. The padlock was in place on the hasp on the front of the box, but he had no idea where he had put the key. He pulled the box down from the shelf, carried it over and set it down on the bed. A piece of paper was taped to the top, on it a message printed in Chiara's clear hand: '*Papà* – Raffi and I are not supposed to know that the key is taped to the back of the painting in *Mamma*'s study. *Baci.*'

He went and got the key, wondering if he should add something to her note; no, better not to encourage her. He unlocked the box and removed the pistol, loaded it, and slipped it into the leather holster he had clipped to his belt earlier. He put the box back in the closet and left the house.

The *calle*, as had been the case both times he had come here before, was empty, and there was still no sign of activity on the scaffolding. He pulled the metal hasp free from the wood and went into the building, this time leaving the door open behind him. He made no attempt to soften his footsteps or disguise in any way the sound of his arrival. He stopped at the bottom of the steps and called up, 'Zecchino, it's the police. I'm coming up.'

He waited for a moment, but no answering sound or shout came from above. Regretting that he had forgotten to bring a flashlight and glad of what little light came in from the open door behind him, he walked up to the first floor. There was still no sound from above. He went up to the second floor, then the third, and paused on the landing. He opened the shutters of two windows, providing enough light for him to see his way back to the staircase and up to the attic.

Brunetti paused at the top. There were doors

on either side of the landing and a third one at the end of a short corridor. A good deal of light filtered in from a broken shutter on his left. He waited, called out Zecchino's name again, and then, strangely comforted by the silence, went to the first door on the right.

The room was empty; that is, no one was inside, though there were some boxes of tools, a pair of sawhorses, and a discarded pair of lime-covered painter's pants. The door opposite led to the same sort of cluttered emptiness. That left only the door at the end of the corridor.

Inside, as he had hoped, he found Zecchino, and he also found the girl. In the light that sneaked down from a dirty skylight in the roof, he saw her for the first time, lying on top of Zecchino. They must have killed him first, or else he had given up and fallen under the rain of blows, and she had fought on, quite vainly, only to fall in the end on top of him.

'Gesù bambino,' Brunetti said softly as he saw them and resisted the urge to make the sign of the cross. There they were, a pair of limp figures, already shrunken in that special way death makes people look smaller. A dark halo of dried blood extended around their heads, which lay close together like puppies or young lovers.

He could see the back of Zecchino's head and the girl's face, or, more accurately, what was left of her face. Both of them appeared to have been battered to death: Zecchino's skull had lost all rotundity; her nose was gone, destroyed by a blow so violent that all that remained was a shard of cartilege lying across her left cheek.

Brunetti turned away from them and looked around the room. A pile of stained mattresses was heaped against one wall. Beside it lay the pieces of clothing – he realized only when he looked back at the dead couple that they were half naked – which they had discarded in their haste to do whatever it was they did on those mattresses. He saw a bloody syringe and the memory rushed at him of a poem Paola had read to him once in which the poet tried to seduce a woman by telling her that their blood was mingled inside the flea that had drunk blood from both of them. At the time, he'd thought it an insane way to view the union of man and woman, but it was no more insane than the needle that lay on the floor. Beside it lay a few discarded plastic envelopes, probably not much bigger than the ones that had been found in the pocket of Roberto Patta's jacket.

Downstairs, he pulled out the *telefonino* he had thought to carry that day and called the Questura, telling them what he had found and where to come to find him. The voice of professionalism told him to return to the room where the two young people lay and see what else he could discover. He chose to remain deaf to it and, instead, stood idly in a patch of sun in front of the building opposite while he waited for the others to come.

They eventually did, and he dispatched them upstairs, though he resisted the temptation to tell them that, as there were no workers in the building that day, they could get on with their investigation of the scene. There was nothing to be gained from a cheap gibe, and it would make no difference to them to learn that they had been duped the last time.

He asked who they'd called to examine the bodies and was glad to learn it was Rizzardi. He didn't move when the men went into the building and was still standing there twenty minutes later when the pathologist arrived. They nodded at one another by way of greeting.

'Another one?' Rizzardi asked.

'Two,' Brunetti said, turning toward the building and leading the way.

The two men made their way upstairs with little difficulty, the shutters all open now and light flooding in. At the top of the stairs they were drawn, moth-like, to the bright lights of the technicians that spilled out of the room and down the corridor, beckoning them to come and see this new proof of the fragility of the body, the vanity of hope.

Inside, Rizzardi went over and examined the bodies from above. Then he slipped on a pair of rubber gloves and bent down to touch the girl's, and then the boy's, throat. He set his leather bag on the floor and squatted down beside the girl, then reached across her body and slowly rolled her away from the boy and on to her back. She lay, staring up at the ceiling, and one shattered hand came drifting across her body and slapped down on to the floor, startling Brunetti, who had chosen to avert his eyes.

He came closer and stood above Rizzardi, looking down. Her short hair was hennaed a dark red and lay close to her head, greasy and dirty. He noticed that her teeth, which showed through the slit of her bloody mouth, were glistening and perfect. Blood had hardened around her mouth, though the flow from her savaged nose had apparently run into her eyes as she lay on the floor. Had she been pretty? Had she been plain?

Rizzardi placed a hand on Zecchino's chin and tilted his head toward the light. 'They were both killed by blows to the head,' he said, pointing to a place on the left of Zecchino's forehead. 'It's not easy to do and requires a lot of strength. Or a lot of blows. And the dying isn't quick. But at least they don't feel much, not after the first few blows.' He looked at the girl again, turned her face to the side to examine a darkening concavity at the back of her head. He looked down at two marks on her upper arms. 'I'd say she was held while she was hit, possibly with a piece of wood, or maybe a pipe.'

Neither of them thought it necessary to comment on this or to add, 'Like Rossi.'

Rizzardi got to his feet, slipped off the gloves, and put them in the pocket of his jacket.

'When can you do it?' was all Brunetti could think of to say.

'This afternoon, I think.' Rizzardi knew better than to ask Brunetti if he wanted to attend. 'If you call me after five, I should know something.' Before Brunetti could respond, Rizzardi added,

'But it won't be much, not much more than what we see here.'

After Rizzardi had left, the crime team began their deadly parody of domesticity: sweeping, dusting, picking up small things that had fallen to the floor and seeing that they were put in safe places. Brunetti forced himself to go through the pockets of the young people, first the discarded clothing that lay beside and atop the mattresses, then, after he'd accepted a pair of lab gloves from Del Vecchio, the clothing that they still wore. In the breast pocket of Zecchino's shirt, he found three more plastic envelopes, each containing white powder. He passed them to Del Vecchio, who carefully labelled them and placed them inside his evidence kit.

Rizzardi, he was glad to see, had closed their eyes. Zecchino's naked legs reminded him of the legs he'd seen in photos of those stick figures standing at the front gates of concentration camps: there was only skin and sinew, little sign of muscle. And how knobby his knees were. One pelvic bone was exposed, cutting sharp. Red pustules covered both of his thighs, though Brunetti couldn't tell if they were suppurating scars from old injections or symptoms of skin disease. The girl, though alarmingly thin and almost breastless, was not as cadaverous as Zecchino. At the realization that both were now, and for ever, cadaverous, Brunetti turned away from them and went downstairs.

Because he was in charge of this part of the investigation, the least he could do for the dead was remain until the bodies had been removed and the lab teams were satisfied that they had found, sampled, and examined everything that might be of future use to the police in finding the killers. He walked to the end of the *calle* and looked across at the garden on the other side, glad that forsythia always succeeded in looking so happy, however hastily dressed.

They would have to ask, of course, canvass the area and see who could remember seeing anyone going into the *calle* or into the building. When he turned around, he saw that a small group of people had already gathered at the other end of the *calle*, where it opened out on a larger street, and he started toward them, the first questions already forming in his mind.

As he expected, no one had seen anything, neither that day nor at any time in the last few weeks. No one had any idea that it was possible to get into the building. No one had ever seen Zecchino, nor could they remember ever having seen a girl. Since there was no way to force them to speak, Brunetti didn't make the effort to disbelieve them, but he knew from long experience that, when dealing with the police, few Italians could remember much beyond their own names.

The other questioning could wait until after lunch or the evening, when the people in the buildings in the area could be expected to be at home. But no one, he knew, would admit having seen anything. The word would quickly spread that two drug addicts had died in the building, and it would be the rare person who would see their deaths as anything special, certainly not as something worth the trouble of being questioned by the police. Why put up with endless hours of being treated as a suspect? Why run the risk of having to take the time off from work to be asked further questions or to attend a trial?

He knew the police were not viewed with anything even approaching sympathy by the general public; he knew how badly the police treated them, no matter how they fell into the orbit of an investigation, either as suspect or witness. For years he had tried to train the men under him to treat witnesses as people who were willing to be of help, as, in a sense, colleagues, only to walk past questioning rooms where they were being hectored, threatened, verbally abused. No wonder people fled in fear from the very idea of providing information to the police: he'd do the same.

The thought of lunch was intolerable: so was the idea of taking the memory of what he had just seen into the company of his family. He called Paola then went back to the Questura and sat there, doing whatever he could to dull his mind with routine, waiting for Rizzardi to call. It would not be news, the cause of their deaths, but it would at least be information, and he could put that in a file and perhaps take comfort from having imposed this small bit of order upon the chaos of sudden death.

For the next four hours, he sorted through

two months' backlog of papers and reports, neatly writing his initials at the bottom of folders he'd examined without understanding. It took him all afternoon, but he cleared his desk of papers, even went so far as to take them down to Signorina Elettra's office and, in her absence, leave her a note, asking that she see to their filing or consignment to whoever was due to read them next.

When this was done, he went down to the bar at the bridge and had a glass of mineral water and a toasted cheese sandwich. He picked up that day's *Gazzettino* from the counter and saw, in the second section, the article he had planted. As he expected, it said far more than he had, suggesting that arrest was imminent, conviction inescapable, and the drug trade in the Veneto effectively destroyed. He dropped the paper and went back to the Questura, noticing on the way that the sparse yellow tops of forsythia were pushing their way over the top of the wall on the other side of the canal.

At his desk, he checked his watch and saw that it was late enough to call Rizzardi. He was just reaching for the phone when it rang.

'Guido,' the pathologist began with no introduction, 'when you looked at those kids this morning, after I left, did you remember to wear gloves?'

It took a moment for Brunetti to overcome his surprise, and he had to think for a moment before he remembered. 'Yes. Del Vecchio gave me a pair.'

Rizzardi asked a second question. 'Did you see her teeth?'

Again, Brunetti had to put himself back in the room. 'I noticed only that it looked as if they were all there, not like with most drug addicts. Why do you want to know?'

'There was blood on her teeth and in her mouth,' Rizzardi explained.

The words took Brunetti back to that squalid room and the two figures draped across one another. 'I know. It was all over her face.'

'That was her blood,' Rizzardi said, putting heavy emphasis on the pronoun. Before Brunetti could question him, he went on, 'The blood in her mouth was someone else's.'

'Zecchino's?'

'No.'

'Oh, my God, she bit him,' Brunetti said, and then asked, 'Did you get enough to . . .' and stopped, uncertain about just what it was Rizzardi would be able to get. He'd read endless reports about DNA matching and blood and semen samples that could be used as evidence, but he lacked both the scientific knowledge to understand how it all worked as well as the intellectual curiosity to care about anything other than the fact that it could be done and that positive identifications could be made from the results.

'Yes,' Rizzardi answered. 'If you can find me the person, I have enough to match him to the blood in her mouth.' Rizzardi paused and Brunetti could tell from the tension on the line that he had much more to say.

'What is it?' he asked.

'They were positive.'

What did he mean? The results of his tests? The samples? 'I don't understand,' Brunetti admitted.

'Both of them, the boy and the girl. They were positive.'

'*Dio mio!*' Brunetti exclaimed, understanding at last.

'It's the first thing we check with addicts. He was much farther along than she was; the virus had really taken hold. He was already far gone, couldn't have lived another three months. Didn't you notice?'

Yes, Brunetti had noticed, but he hadn't understood, or perhaps he had been unwilling to look too closely or to understand what he saw. He had paid no real attention to how thin Zecchino was or to what that might mean.

Instead of answering Rizzardi's question, Brunetti asked, 'What about the girl?'

'She wasn't as bad; the infection wasn't as far advanced. That's probably why she was strong enough to try to fight them off.'

'But what about these new medicines? Why weren't they taking any?' Brunetti demanded, as if he thought Rizzardi would have an answer.

'I don't know why they weren't, Guido,' Rizzardi said patiently, remembering that he was speaking to a man with children little younger than the two victims. 'But I saw no sign in their blood, or anywhere inside them, that either one of them was taking anything. Drug addicts usually don't.'

Neither of them chose to say anything further about that. Instead, Brunetti asked, 'What about the bite? Tell me.'

'There was a lot of flesh caught between her teeth, so whoever it was she bit has a nasty wound.'

'Is it contagious like that?' Brunetti asked, amazed that, after years of information and talk and articles in the papers and magazines, he had no clear idea.

'Theoretically, yes,' Rizzardi answered. 'There are cases in the literature where it seems to have been spread that way, though I've never had first-hand knowledge of it. I suppose it could happen that way. But the disease isn't like it was years ago: the new medicines control it pretty well, especially if they start taking them in the early stages.'

Brunetti listened, wondering about the possible consequences of ignorance like his own. If he, a man who read widely and had a reasonably broad knowledge of what was happening in the world, had no idea of how contagious a bite could be and still had a sort of primitive, atavistic horror that the disease could be passed on in this manner, then it would not surprise him in the least if the fear were widespread.

He pulled his attention back to Rizzardi. 'But how bad is the bite?'

'I'd say he's got a chunk missing from his

arm.' And before Brunetti could ask, he said, 'There were hairs in her mouth. Probably from the forearm.'

'How big was it?'

After a moment's thought Rizzardi said, 'About the size of a dog's bite, perhaps a cocker spaniel.' Neither of them commented on the bizarre comparison.

'Enough to go to a doctor about?' Brunetti asked.

'Maybe, maybe not. If it becomes infected, then yes.'

'Or if they knew she was positive,' Brunetti continued. 'Or came to realize it after.' Anyone aware that he'd been bitten by an infected person would flee, terrified, to anyone who could tell him whether the disease had been passed on to him, Brunetti was sure. He considered the consequences: doctors would have to be called, hospital emergency rooms notified, contact made even with pharmacies where the killer might go in search of antiseptics or dressings.

'Is there anything else?' Brunetti asked.

'He would have been dead before the end of the summer. She might have lasted another year, but not much longer.' Rizzardi stopped for a moment and then added, in an entirely different voice, 'Do you think they leave scars on us, Guido, the things we have to say or do?'

'Sweet Jesus, I hope not,' Brunetti answered in a soft voice, said he'd be in touch with Rizzardi when he had an identification of the girl, and hung up.

22

He called down to the officers' squad room and told them to be alert for any new reports of a girl gone missing, about seventeen, and to start checking back through the records to see if any had been reported in the last few weeks. Even as he spoke to them, however, he knew it was entirely possible that no one would report her: many kids had become disposable, their parents not at all concerned at prolonged absences. He wasn't sure about her age, but seventeen would be his guess. He hoped she wasn't any younger. If she was, Rizzardi would probably know, but he didn't want to.

He went down to the men's room and washed his hands, dried them, and washed them again. Back at his desk, he took a piece of paper from his drawer and wrote in bold capital letters the headline he wanted to see in tomorrow's papers: 'Killer's Victim Takes Vengeance With Fatal Bite'. He looked down at it, wondering, like Rizzardi, what sort of scars these things would leave on him, drew an insert mark between 'Vengeance' and 'With' and added, 'From Beyond the Grave' on the line above. He studied this for a moment but decided the additional phrase made the line too long to fit in one column and so crossed it out. He pulled out the dog-eared notebook in which he kept names and phone numbers and again dialled the office number of the crime reporter of *Il Gazzettino*. His friend, flattered that Brunetti had liked the other story, agreed to see that this one got into next morning's edition. He said he loved Brunetti's headline and would make sure it appeared as written.

'I don't want you to get in any trouble,' Brunetti said in response to the man's eager compliance. 'There's no risk, is there, if you print it?'

The man laughed outright. 'Trouble for printing something that's not true? Me?' Still laughing, he started to say goodbye, when Brunetti stopped him.

'Is there any way you could get this into *La Nuova*, as well?' he asked. 'I want it in both papers.'

'Probably. There's someone over there who's been hacking into our computer for years. It saves them the cost of a reporter. So I'll just type this in, and they'll use it, especially if I make it sound really lurid. They can't resist blood. But they won't use your headline, I'm afraid,' he said with real regret. 'They always change them, at least one word.'

Content with what he had got, Brunetti resigned himself to this, thanked his friend, and hung up.

In order to give himself something to do, or perhaps just to keep himself moving and away from his desk, he walked downstairs to Signorina Elettra's office, where he found her, head bent over a magazine.

She looked up at the sound of his footsteps, 'Ah, you're back, Commissario,' she said, beginning to smile. When she saw the expression he brought into the office with him, her smile dissolved. She closed the magazine, opened a drawer, and pulled a folder from it. Leaning forward, she passed it up to him. 'I heard about the two young people,' she said. 'I'm sorry.'

He didn't know if he was meant to thank her for her condolences or not. Instead, he nodded as he accepted the folder, then pulled open the cover. 'The Volpatos?' he asked.

'Uh huh,' she answered. 'You'll see from what's in there that they've got to be very well protected.'

'By whom?' he asked, glancing down at the first page.

'Someone in the Guardia di Finanza, I'd say.'

'Why?'

She stood and leaned over her desk. 'On the

second page,' she prompted. When he turned to it, she pointed to a row of numbers. 'The first number's the year. Then comes the total of their declared wealth: bank accounts, apartments, stocks. And the third column is what they declared as income for those same years.'

'So,' he said, commenting on the obvious, 'each subsequent year, they should earn more, as they certainly own more.' That much was evident from the expanding list of properties.

He continued to study the lists. Instead of growing larger each year, the third number decreased, even though the Volpatos acquired more apartments, businesses, and houses. Relentlessly, they continued to acquire more and pay less.

'Have they ever been audited by the Finanza?' he asked, holding in his hands a fiscal red flag so large and incarnadine as to be easily visible as far away as the central offices of the Guardia di Finanza in Rome.

'Never,' she said, shaking her head and sitting back down. 'That's why I say they've got to be protected by someone.'

'Did you get copies of their tax returns?'

'Of course,' she answered simply, making no attempt to disguise her pride. 'Those numbers for what they earn every year are repeated on all of them, but they manage to prove that they've spent a fortune on capital improvements to their properties, year after year, and they seem incapable of selling a single piece of property at a profit.'

275

'Who do they sell them to?' Brunetti asked, though years of similar experiences had made him familiar with this particular script.

'So far, among other sales, they've sold two apartments to city councillors and two to officers of the Guardia di Finanza. Always at a loss, especially the one that got sold to the colonel.

'And,' she continued, flipping over a page and pointing to the top line, 'it seems they've also sold two apartments to a Dottor Fabrizio dal Carlo.'

'Ah,' Brunetti sighed. He looked up from the paper and asked, 'Did you by any chance . . . ?'

Her smile was a benediction. 'It's all there: his tax records, a list of the houses he owns, his bank accounts, his wife's, everything.'

'And?' he asked, resisting the impulse to look down at the paper and wanting her to have the pleasure of telling him.

'Only a miracle could protect him from an audit,' she said, tapping the papers with the fingers of her left hand.

'Yet no one's noticed,' Brunetti said calmly, 'all these years: not dal Carlo and not the Volpatos.'

'That's not likely to happen, not while prices like these,' she said, turning back to the front page, 'are available to city councillors.' After a pause, she added, 'And to colonels.'

'Yes,' he agreed, closing the file with a tired sigh, 'and to colonels.' He tucked the folder under his arm. 'What about their phone?'

She came close to smiling. 'They don't have one.'

'What?' Brunetti asked.

'Not that I can discover. Not in either of their names and not at the address where they live.' Before Brunetti could ask, she supplied possible explanations. 'Either it's because they're too cheap to pay a phone bill, or else they've got a *telefonino* listed in someone else's name.'

It was hard for Brunetti to imagine that anyone could, today, exist without a telephone, especially people who were involved in the purchase and sale of properties, the lending of money and all the contacts with lawyers, municipal offices, and notaries those things would entail. Besides, no one could be so pathologically frugal as not to have a phone.

Seeing one avenue of possible investigation eliminated, Brunetti turned his attention back to the murdered couple. 'If you can,' he said, 'see what there is to find out about Gino Zecchino, would you?'

She nodded. She already knew the name.

'We don't know who the girl is yet,' he began, and the possibility struck him that they might never know. He refused to give voice to this thought, however, and said only, 'Let me know if you find anything.'

'Yes, sir,' she said, watching as he left the office.

Upstairs, he decided to add to the scope of the disinformation that was to appear in the newspapers the next morning and spent the next hour and a half on the phone, often consulting the pages of his notebook or occasionally calling a friend for the phone numbers of men and women scattered on both sides of the law. With cajolery, the promise of some future favour, and sometimes with open menace, he convinced a number of people to speak loudly and speak widely of this strange case of the killer who had been doomed to a slow and horrible death by the bite of his victim. Generally there was no hope, usually no therapy, but sometimes, just sometimes, if the bite was treated in time by an experimental technique that was being perfected in the Immunology Laboratory of the Ospedale Civile and dispensed at the Emergency Room, then there was a chance that the infection could be stopped. Otherwise, there was no escape from death, the headline would quickly be proven true, and the victim would indeed Take Vengeance With a Fatal Bite.

He had no idea if this would work, knew only that this was Venice, city of rumour, where an uncritical populace read and believed, listened and believed.

He dialled the central number for the hospital and was about to ask for the office of the Director when he thought better of it and, instead, asked to speak to Dottor Carraro in Pronto Soccorso.

The call was finally put through and Carraro all but barked his name into the receiver; a man too busy to be disturbed, the lives of his patients at risk if he lingered on the phone, kept there by whatever stupidity he was about to be asked.

'Ah, Dottore,' Brunetti began, 'how nice to speak to you again.'

'Who is this?' asked the same rude, impulsive voice.

'Commissario Brunetti,' he said and waited for the name to register.

'Ah, yes. Good afternoon, Commissario,' the doctor said, a sea change audible.

When the doctor seemed disposed to say no more, Brunetti said, 'Dottore, it seems I might be able to be of some help to you.' He stopped, giving Carraro the opportunity to enquire. When he failed to, Brunetti went on, 'It seems we've got to decide whether to pass the results of our investigation on to the examining magistrate. Well, that is,' he corrected himself with an officious little laugh, 'we've got to give our recommendation, whether to continue and begin a criminal investigation. For culpable negligence.'

He heard no more than Carraro's breathing at the other end. 'Of course, I'm persuaded that there's no need of that. Accidents happen. The man would have died anyway. I don't think there's any need to cause you any trouble about this, to waste police time in investigating a situation where we're going to find nothing.'

Still silence. 'Are you there, Dottore?' he asked in a hearty voice.

'Yes, yes, I am,' Carraro said in his new, softer voice.

'Good. I knew you'd be happy to hear my news.'

'Yes, I am.'

'While I have you on the line,' Brunetti said, managing to make it clear he had not just thought of it, 'I wonder if I could ask you a favour.'

'Of course, Commissario.'

'In the next day or so, a man might come into the Emergency Room with a bite on his hand or his arm. He'll probably say it's a dog bite, or he might try to say his girlfriend did it to him.' Carraro remained silent. 'Are you listening, Dottore?' Brunetti asked, voice suddenly much louder.

'Yes.'

'Good. The instant this man comes in, I want you to call the Questura, Dottore. The instant,' he repeated, and gave Carraro the number. 'If you're not there, I expect you to leave word for whoever takes your place that he is to do the same thing.'

'And what are we supposed to do with him while we wait for you to get here?' Carraro asked with a return to his normal tone.

'You are to keep him there, Dottore, lying to him and inventing some form of treatment that will take long enough for us to get to the hospital. And you are not to allow him to leave the hospital.'

'And if we can't stop him?' Carraro demanded.

Brunetti had little doubt that Carraro would

obey him, but he thought it best to lie. 'We've still got power to examine the hospital records, Dottore, and our investigation of the circumstances surrounding Rossi's death isn't over until I say so.' He allowed steel to penetrate his voice with the last phrase, that hollow lie, paused a moment, and then said, 'Good, then, I look forward to your cooperation.'

After that, there was nothing for the men to do except exchange pleasantries and say goodbye.

That left Brunetti at a loose end until the papers came out the next morning. But it also left him restless, something he always dreaded because the feeling spurred him to rashness. It was difficult for him to resist the urge to, as it were, put the cat among the pigeons and stir things up. He went downstairs, to Signorina Elettra's office.

The sight of her, elbows on her desk, chin propped up on her fists, head bent over a book, led him to ask as he came in, 'Am I interrupting anything?' She looked up, smiling, and shook away the very idea with a sideways motion of her head.

'Do you own your apartment, Signorina?'

Accustomed as she was to Brunetti's sometimes odd behaviour, she displayed no curiosity and answered 'Yes,' leaving it to him, if he pleased, to explain the question.

He'd had time to think about it, and so he added, 'I suppose it doesn't matter, though.'

'It does to me, sir, quite a bit,' she remarked.

'Ah, yes, I'm sure it does,' he said, realizing the confusion that would result from his remark. 'Signorina, if you're not busy, I'd like you to do something for me.'

She reached for a pad and pencil, but he stopped her.

'No,' he said, when he saw what she was doing, 'I want you to go and talk to someone.'

He had to wait more than two hours for her to come back, and when she did, she came directly up to his office. She entered without knocking and approached his desk.

'Ah, Signorina,' he said, inviting her to take a seat. He sat next to her, eager, but silent.

'You're not in the habit of giving me a Christmas present, are you, Commissario?' she asked.

'No,' he answered. 'Am I about to begin to do so?'

'Yes, sir,' she said emphatically. 'I'll expect a dozen, no, two dozen white roses from Biancat and, I think, a case of prosecco.'

'And when would you like this present to arrive, Signorina, if I might ask?'

'To avoid the Christmas rush, sir, I think you might send them around next week.'

'By all means. Consider it done.'

'Too kind, Signore,' she said with a gracious nod of acceptance.

'No more than my pleasure,' he answered. He allowed six beats to pass and then asked, 'And?'

'And I asked in the bookstore in the *campo*,

and the owner told me where they lived, and I went and talked to them.'

'And?' he prodded.

'They may be the most loathsome people I've ever met,' she said in an uninterested, aloof tone. 'Let's see, I've worked here for more than four years, and I've come in contact with quite a few criminals, though the people in the bank where I used to work were probably worse, but these two were in a class by themselves,' she said with what seemed like a real shudder of disgust.

'Why?'

'Because of the combination of greed and piety, I think.'

'In what way?'

'When I told them that I needed money to pay my brother's gambling bills, they asked me what I had to put up as security, and I told them I had an apartment. I tried to sound a bit nervous about saying that, the way you told me. He asked me the address, and I gave it to him, then he went into the other room, and I heard him talking to someone.'

She stopped here for a moment and then added, 'It must have been a *telefonino*. There were no phone jacks in the two rooms I was in.'

'What happened then?' Brunetti asked.

She tilted her chin and raised her eyes to the top of the *armadio* on the other side of the room. 'When he came back, he smiled at his wife, and that's when they began to talk about the possibility of their being able to help me. They asked how much I needed, and I said fifty million.'

It was the sum they had agreed on: not too much and not too little, just the sort of sum a gambler might rack up in a night's rash gambling and just the sort of sum he would believe he could easily win back, if only he could find the person to pay off the debt and thus get him back at the tables.

She turned her eyes to Brunetti. 'Do you know these people?'

'No. All I know is what a friend told me.'

'They're terrible,' she said, voice low.

'What else?'

She shrugged. 'I suppose they did what they usually do. They told me that they needed to see the papers for the house, though I'm sure he was calling someone to make sure I really did own it or that it was listed in my name.'

'Who could that be?' he asked.

She looked down at her watch before answering, 'It's not likely there was still anyone at the Ufficio Catasto, so it must be someone who has instant access to their records.'

'You do, don't you?' he asked.

'No, it takes me a while to break . . . to get into their system. Whoever could give him that information immediately had to have direct access to the files.'

'How were things left?' Brunetti asked.

'I'm to go back tomorrow with the papers. They'll have the notary come to the house at five.' She stopped and smiled across at him. 'Imagine that: you can die before a doctor will make a house call, but they've got a notary on twenty-four-hour call.' She raised her eyebrows at the very notion. 'So I'm supposed to go back at five tomorrow, and we'll sign all the papers, and they'll give me the cash.'

Even before she stopped speaking, Brunetti had raised one finger and was waving it back and forth in silent negation. There was no way he'd permit Signorina Elettra to get that close to these people again. She smiled in silent acknowledgement of his command and, he thought, relief.

'And the interest? Did they say how much it would be?'

'They said we'd talk about that tomorrow, that it would be on the papers.' She crossed her legs and folded her hands on her lap. 'So I guess that means we don't get to talk about it,' she said with finality.

Brunetti waited a moment and then asked, 'And piety?'

She reached into the pocket of her jacket and pulled out a narrow rectangle of paper, slightly smaller than a playing card. She passed it to Brunetti, who looked at it. Stiff, a sort of fake parchment, it had a painting of a woman dressed as a nun with her hands and, it seemed, her eyes crossed in matching piety. Brunetti read the first few lines printed below – a prayer, the first letter an illuminated 'O'.

'Santa Rita,' she said after he had studied the picture for a while. 'It seems she's another patron saint of Lost Causes, and Signora Volpato feels especially close to her because she believes she also helps people when all other help is closed to them. That's the reason for her special devotion to Santa Rita.' Signorina Elettra paused to reflect momentarily upon this wonder and then saw fit to add, 'More than to the Madonna, she confided to me.'

'How fortunate, the Madonna,' Brunetti said, handing the small card back to Signorina Elettra.

'Ah, keep it, sir,' she said, waving it away with a dismissive hand.

'Did they ask why you didn't go to a bank, if you owned the house?'

'Yes. I told them my father originally gave me the house, and I couldn't risk his learning what I was doing. If I went to our bank, where they know us all, he'd find out about my brother. I tried to cry then, when I told her that.' Signorina Elettra gave a small smile and went on: 'Signora Volpato said she was very sorry about my brother; she said gambling is a terrible vice.'

'And usury isn't?' Brunetti asked, but it wasn't really a question.

'Apparently not. She asked me how old he was.'

'What did you tell her?' Brunetti asked, knowing she had no brother.

'Thirty-seven, and that he's been gambling for years.' She stopped, reflected upon the events of the afternoon, and said, 'Signora Volpato was very kind.'

'Really? What did she do?'

'She gave me another card of Santa Rita and said she'd pray for my brother.'

23

The only thing Brunetti did before going home that afternoon was sign the papers that would release the body of Marco Landi so that it could be sent to his parents. After he had done this, he called downstairs and asked Vianello if he would be willing to accompany the body back to the Trentino. Vianello agreed instantly, saying only that, as the next day was his day off, he didn't know if he could wear his uniform.

Brunetti had no idea if he had the authority to do so, but he said, 'I'll change the roster,' opening a drawer to start to look for it, buried among the papers that came to him every week to be ignored and eventually discarded unread. 'Consider yourself on duty and wear your uniform.'

'And if they ask about what's happening here, if we've made any progress?' Vianello asked.

'They won't ask, not yet,' Brunetti answered, not at all sure why he knew, but sure he was right.

When he got home, he found Paola on the terrace, her feet stretched out before her, resting on one of the cane chairs that had weathered yet another winter exposed to the elements. She smiled up at him and pulled her feet off the chair; he accepted her invitation and sat opposite her.

'Should I ask how your day was?' she asked.

He sat lower in the chair, shook his head, but still managed to smile. 'No. Just another day.'

'Filled with?'

'Usury, corruption, and human greed.'

'Just another day.' She took an envelope from the book in her lap and leaned forward to hand it across to him. 'Maybe this will help,' she said.

He took it and looked at it. It came from the Ufficio Catasto; he was uncertain of how this could be of any help to him.

He pulled out the letter and read it. 'Is this a miracle?' he asked. Then, looking down at it, he read the last sentence aloud, ' "Sufficient documentation having been presented, all former correspondence from our office is superseded by this decree of *condono edilizio*." '

Brunetti's hand, still holding the letter, fell into his lap. 'Does this mean what I think it means?' he asked.

Paola nodded, without smiling or looking away.

He searched for both wording and tone and, finding them, asked, 'Could you perhaps be a bit more precise?'

Her explanation came quickly. 'From the way I read it, I'd say it means the matter's closed, that they've found the necessary papers, and we will not be driven mad by this.'

'Found?' he repeated.

'Found,' she said.

He looked down at the single page in his hand, the paper on which the word 'presented' appeared, folded it, and slipped it inside the envelope, considering as he did so how to ask, whether to ask.

He handed the envelope back to her. He asked, still in command of his tone but not of his words, 'Does your father have anything to do with this?'

He watched her and experience told him just how long she thought about lying to him; the same experience saw her abandon the idea. 'Probably.'

'How?'

'We were talking about you,' she began, and he disguised his surprise that Paola would discuss him with her father. 'He asked me how you were, how your work was, and I told him you had more than the usual problems at the moment.' Before he could accuse her of betraying the secrets of his work, she added, 'You know I never tell him, or anyone, specific things, but I did tell him you were more burdened than usual.'

'Burdened?'

'Yes.' Then, by way of explanation, she went on, 'With Patta's son and the way he's going to get away with this,' she said. 'And those poor dead young people.' When she saw his expression, she said, 'No, I didn't mention any of this to him, just tried to tell him how hard it's been for you recently. Remember, I live and sleep with you, so you don't have to give me daily reports on how much these things trouble you.'

He saw her sit straighter in her chair, as if she thought the conversation finished and herself free to get up and get them a drink.

'What else did you tell him, Paola?' he asked before she could rise.

Her answer took a while to come, but when it did, it was the truth. 'I told him about this nonsense from the Ufficio Catasto, that though we hadn't heard anything further, it still loomed over us like a kind of bureaucratic sword of Damocles.' He knew the tactic: deflecting wit. He was not moved by it.

'And what was his response?'

'He asked if there was anything he could do.'

Had Brunetti been less tired, less burdened by a day filled with thoughts of human corruption, he probably would have let it go at that and allowed events to take their course above his head, behind his back. But something, either Paola's complacent duplicity or his own shame at it, drove him to say, 'I told you not to do that.' Quickly, he amended it to, 'I asked you.'

'I know you did. So I didn't ask him to help.'

'You didn't have to ask him, did you?' he said, voice beginning to rise.

Her voice matched his. 'I don't know what he did. I don't even know that he did anything.'

Brunetti pointed to the envelope in her hand. 'The answer's not far to seek, is it? I asked you not to have him help us, not to make him use his system of friends and connections.'

'But you saw nothing wrong in using ours,' she shot back.

'That's different,' he insisted.

'Why?'

'Because we're little people. We don't have his power. We can't be sure that we'll always get what we want, always be able to get around the laws.'

'You really believe that makes a difference?' she asked, in astonishment.

He nodded.

'Then which is Patta?' she asked. 'One of us or one of the powerful people?'

'Patta?'

'Yes, Patta. If you think it's all right for small people to try to get around the system, but it's wrong for big people to do it, which is Patta?' When Brunetti hesitated, she said, 'I ask because you certainly make no attempt to disguise your opinion of what he did to save his son.'

Anger, instant and fierce, flooded him. 'His son is a criminal.'

'He's still his son.'

'And that's why it's all right for your father to corrupt the system, because he's doing it for his daughter?' The instant the words were out of his mouth, he regretted them, and the regret overwhelmed his anger, snuffing it entirely. Paola looked across at him, mouth open in a tiny o, as if he had leaned across and slapped her.

At once he spoke: 'I'm sorry. I'm sorry. I shouldn't have said that.' He put his head back against the chair and shook it from side to side. He wanted to close his eyes and make all of this go away. Instead, he raised a hand, palm up, then let it fall to his lap. 'I'm really sorry. I shouldn't have said that.'

'No, you shouldn't have.'

'It's not true,' he said by way of apology.

'No,' she said, voice very calm. 'I think that's why you shouldn't have said it. Because it is true. He did it because I'm his daughter.'

Brunetti was about to say that the other part wasn't true: Conte Falier couldn't corrupt a system that was already corrupt, had probably been born corrupt. But all he said was, 'I don't want to do this, Paola.'

'Do what?'

'Fight about this.'

'It doesn't matter.' Her voice was distant, disinterested, faintly imperious.

'Oh, come on,' he said, angered again.

Neither of them said anything for a long time. Finally Paola asked, 'What do you want me to do?'

'I don't think there's anything you can do.' He waved a hand toward the letter. 'Not after we've got that.'

'I suppose not,' she agreed. She held it up. 'But beyond this?'

'I don't know.' Then, in a softer voice, he said, 'I suppose you can't be asked to return to the ideals of your youth?'

'Would you want me to?' At once she added, 'It's impossible; I have to tell you that. So my question is entirely rhetorical. Would you want me to?'

As he got to his feet, however, he realized that a return to the ideals of their youth was no guarantee of peace of mind.

He went back into the apartment, then emerged a few minutes later with two glasses of Chardonnay. They sat together for half an hour, neither saying much of anything, until Paola glanced at her watch, got up, and said she would begin dinner. As she took his empty glass, she bent down and kissed his right ear, missing his cheek.

After dinner, he lay on the sofa, caught up in the hope that he would somehow find the means to keep his family at peace and that the terrible events with which his days were filled would never lay siege to his home. He tried to continue with Xenophon, but even though the remaining Greeks were nearing home and safety, he found it difficult to concentrate on their story and impossible to concern himself with their two-thousand-year-old plight.

Chiara, who came in at about ten to kiss him goodnight, said nothing about boats, little realizing that, if she had, Brunetti would have agreed to buy her the *QE2*.

As he had hoped, when he bought the paper on his way to work the next morning he found his headline on the front page of the second section of *Il Gazzettino* and sat at his desk to read it through. It was all more horrible and more urgent than he had made it sound, and, like so many of the wild fancies that appeared in this particular publication, it sounded utterly convincing. Though the article stated clearly that this therapy functioned only against possible transmission by biting – how much nonsense would people believe? – he feared the hospital would be swamped with drug addicts and infected people, hoping for the magic cure said to be in the possession of the doctors of the Ospedale Civile and available on request at the Pronto Soccorso. On the way in, he had done something he seldom did, bought *La Nuova*, hoping that no one who knew him would see him with it. He found it on page twenty-seven: three columns, even a picture of Zecchino, apparently cropped from some larger group scene. If possible, the danger of the bite sounded infinitely graver, as did the hope offered by the cure to be had only at the Pronto Soccorso.

He had been in his office no more than ten minutes when the door was thrown open and Brunetti looked up, first startled and then astonished to observe Vice-Questore Giuseppe Patta standing in the doorway. But he didn't stand there long: within seconds, he was across the room and directly in front of Brunetti's desk. Brunetti started to get to his feet, but Patta raised a hand as if to push him back down, then clutched the hand into a fist and brought it crashing down on Brunetti's desk.

'Why have you done this?' he shouted. 'What have I ever done to you that you'd do this to us? They'll kill him. You know that. You must have known that when you did it.'

For a moment, Brunetti feared that his superior had gone mad or that the stresses of his job, perhaps the private stresses of his life, had driven him beyond the point where he could contain his feelings, and he had been forced across some invisible barrier into heedless rage. Brunetti placed his hands palm down on his desk and was very careful not to move or attempt to get up.

'Well? Well?' Patta shouted at him, placing his own palms flat on the desk and leaning across it until his face was very close to Brunetti's. 'I want to know why you did this to him. If anything happens to Roberto, I'll destroy you.' Patta stood upright, and Brunetti noticed that his hands were now clasped into tight fists at his side. The Vice-Questore swallowed and then demanded, 'I asked you a question, Brunetti,' in a voice filled with soft menace.

Brunetti moved backward in his chair and grasped its arms. 'I think you'd better sit down,

Vice-Questore,' he said, 'and tell me what this is all about.'

Any calm that might have settled on Patta's features vanished, and he shouted again, 'Don't lie to me, Brunetti. I want to know why you did it.'

'I don't know what you're talking about,' Brunetti said, letting some of his own anger slip into his voice.

From the pocket of his jacket, Patta pulled out yesterday's newspaper and smacked it down on Brunetti's desk. 'I'm talking about this,' he said, jamming an angry finger at the page. 'This story that says Roberto is about to be arrested and will surely testify against the people in control of the drug business in the Veneto.' Before Brunetti could respond, Patta said, 'I know how you work, you northerners, like a secret little club. All you have to do is call one of your friends on the paper, and he'll print any shit you give him.'

Suddenly exhausted, Patta sank down into a chair that stood in front of Brunetti's desk. His face, still red, was covered with perspiration, and when he tried to wipe it away, Brunetti saw that his hand was shaking. 'They'll kill him,' he said, almost inaudibly.

Realization overcame Brunetti's confusion and his sense of outrage at Patta's behaviour. He waited a few moments until Patta's breathing had grown more normal and said, 'It's not about Roberto,' striving to keep his voice calm. 'It's about that boy who died of an overdose last week. His girlfriend came in and told me she knew who had sold him the drugs, but she was afraid to tell me who it was. I thought this would encourage him to come in voluntarily to talk to us.'

He saw that Patta was listening; whether he was believing was entirely a different matter. Or, if he believed, whether it made any difference.

'It has nothing at all to do with Roberto,' he said, his voice level and as calm as he could make it. Brunetti pushed away the urge to say that, as Patta had insisted Roberto had nothing to do with selling drugs, it was impossible that this article could put him in any danger. Not even Patta was worth a victory as cheap as that. He stopped and waited for Patta to answer.

After a long time, the Vice-Questore said, 'I don't care who it's about,' which suggested that he believed what Brunetti had said. He looked across at Brunetti, eyes direct and honest. 'They called him last night. On his *telefonino*.'

'What did they say?' Brunetti asked, very much aware that Patta had just confessed that his son, the son of the Vice-Questore of Venice, was selling drugs.

'They said they better not hear any more about this, that they better not hear that he'd talked to anyone or gone to the Questura.' Patta stopped and closed his eyes, reluctant to continue.

'Or what?' Brunetti asked in a neutral voice.

After a long time, the answer came. 'They didn't say. They didn't have to.' Brunetti had no doubt that this was true.

He found himself suddenly overwhelmed with the desire to be anywhere but here. It would be better to be back in the room with Zecchino and the dead girl, for at least his emotion there had been a clean, profound pity; there had been none of this niggling sense of triumph at the sight of this man for whom he had so often felt such utter contempt reduced to this. He did not want to feel satisfaction at the sight of Patta's fear and anger, but he could not succeed in repressing it.

'Is he using anything or is he just selling?' he asked.

Patta sighed. 'I don't know. I have no idea.' Brunetti gave him a moment to stop lying, and after a while, Patta said, 'Yes. Cocaine, I think.'

Years ago, when he was less experienced in the art of questioning, Brunetti would have asked for confirmation that the boy was also selling, but now he took it as given and moved on to his next question. 'Have you talked to him?'

Patta nodded. After a while, he said, 'He's terrified. He wants to go and stay with his grandparents, but he wouldn't be safe there.' He looked up at Brunetti. 'These people have to believe he won't talk. It's the only way he'll be safe.'

Brunetti had already arrived at the same conclusion and was already calculating its cost. The only way to do it was to plant another story, this one saying that the police had begun to suspect they had been given false information and in fact had been unable to make a link between recent drug-related deaths and the person responsible for the sale of those drugs. This would most likely remove Roberto Patta from immediate danger, but it would also discourage Anna Maria Ratti's brother, or cousin, or whoever he was, from coming in to name the people who had sold him the drugs that had killed Marco Landi.

If he did nothing, Roberto's life would be in danger, but if the story appeared, then Anna Maria would have to live with her secret grief that she had, however remotely, been responsible for Marco's death.

'I'll take care of it,' he said, and Patta's head snapped up, his eyes staring across at Brunetti.

'What?' he demanded, then, 'How?'

'I said I'll take care of it,' he repeated, keeping his voice firm, hoping that Patta would believe him and take quickly from the room whatever show of gratitude he might be moved to. He went on, 'Try to get him into a clinic of some sort, if you can.'

He watched Patta's eyes widen in outrage at this inferior who dared to give advice.

Brunetti wanted it done quickly. 'I'll call them now,' he said, looking in the direction of the door.

Angered by this as well, Patta wheeled around, walked toward the door and let himself out.

Feeling not a little bit the fool, Brunetti called his friend at the paper again and did it quickly, all the time conscious of how enormous a debt he was running up. When it came time to pay it back, and he did not for an instant doubt that this time would come, he knew it would be at the cost of some principle or the flouting of some law. Neither thought made him hesitate for an instant.

He was about to leave for lunch when his phone rang. It was Carraro, saying that a man had phoned ten minutes before: he'd read the story in the paper that morning and wanted to know if it was really true. Carraro had assured him that, yes, it was: the therapy was absolutely revolutionary and the only hope for whoever it was that had been bitten.

'Do you think he's the one?' Brunetti asked.

'I don't know,' Carraro said. 'But he seemed very interested. He said he'd come in today. What are you going to do?'

'I'm coming over right now.'

'What do I do if he comes in?'

'Keep him there. Keep talking to him. Invent some sort of screening process and keep him there,' Brunetti said. On his way out, he put his head into the officers' room and shouted a quick command that they get two men and a boat over to the entrance to the Pronto Soccorso immediately.

It took him only ten minutes to walk to the hospital, and when he got there he told the *portiere* that he needed to be taken to the doctors' entrance to Pronto Soccorso so that he would not be seen by any patients who were waiting. His sense of urgency must have been contagious because the man left his glass-enclosed office and led Brunetti down the main corridor, past the patient entrance to the Emergency Room, and then through an unmarked door and down a narrow corridor. He emerged into the nurses' station at the Pronto Soccorso.

The nurse on duty looked up at him in surprise when he appeared on her left with no warning, but Carraro must have told her to expect someone, for she got to her feet, saying, 'He's with Dottore Carraro.' She pointed to the door to the main treatment room. 'In there.'

Without knocking, Brunetti opened the door and went in. A white-jacketed Carraro stood over a tall man lying on his back on the examining table. His shirt and sweater lay across the back of a chair, and Carraro was listening to his heart with his stethoscope. Because he had the earpieces in place, Carraro was not aware of Brunetti's arrival. But the man on the table was, and when his heart quickened at the sight of Brunetti, Carraro looked up to see what had caused his patient's reaction.

He saw Brunetti but said nothing.

The man on the table lay still, though Brunetti saw the stiffening of his body and the quick flush of emotion on his face. He also saw the inflamed mark on the outer edge of his right forearm: oval, its two edges stamped out with zipper-like precision.

He chose to say nothing. The man on the

examining table closed his eyes and lay back, letting his arms fall limply to his sides. Brunetti noticed that Carraro was wearing a pair of transparent rubber gloves. If he'd come in now and seen the man lying like that, he would have thought him asleep. His own heartbeat quieted. Carraro moved away from the table and went over to his desk, laid the stethoscope down, and then left the room without speaking.

Brunetti moved a step closer to the table but was careful to stay more than an arm's length away. He saw now just how strong the man must be: the muscles of his chest and shoulders were rounded and taut, the result of decades of heavy work. His hands were enormous; one hand lay palm up, and Brunetti was struck by the flatness of the tips of those broad, spatulate fingers.

In repose, the man's face had a quality about it that spoke of absence. Even when he had first seen Brunetti and perhaps realized who he was, little expression had been visible on his features. His ears were very small; indeed, his curiously cylindrical head seemed a size or two too small for the rest of that heavy body.

'Signore,' Brunetti finally said.

The man's eyes opened, and he looked up at Brunetti. His eyes were a deep brown and made Brunetti think of bears, but that might be because of his general thickness. 'She told me not to come,' he said. 'She said it was a trap.' He blinked, keeping his eyes closed for a long time, then opened them, and said, 'But I was afraid. I heard people talking about the story, and I was afraid.' Again, that long, timeless closing of the eyes, so long it seemed that during it the man went off to some other place while they were closed, like a diver beneath the waters of the sea, happier to remain amidst that greater beauty and reluctant to return.

His eyes opened. 'But she was right. She always is.' Saying that, he sat up. 'Don't worry,' he said to Brunetti. 'I won't hurt you. I need the doctor to give me the cure, and then I'll come with you. But first I have to have the cure.'

Brunetti nodded, understanding his need. 'I'll get the doctor,' he said, and went out to the nurses' station, where Carraro stood, talking on the phone. There was no sign of the nurse.

When he saw Brunetti, he hung up and turned to him. 'Well?' The anger was back, but Brunetti suspected it had nothing to do with any violation of the Hippocratic Oath.

'I'd like you to give him a tetanus shot, and then I'll take him to the Questura.'

'You leave me alone in a room with a murderer, and now you expect me to go back in there and give him a tetanus shot? You've got to be out of your mind,' Carraro said, crossing his arms in front of him as a visual sign of his refusal.

'I don't think there's any risk, Dottore. He could need one, anyway, for that bite. It looks infected to me.'

'Oh, so you're a doctor now, too, huh?'

'Dottore,' Brunetti said, looking down at his

shoes and taking a long breath, 'I'm asking you to put your rubber gloves back on and come into the next room and give your patient a tetanus shot.'

'And if I refuse?' Carraro asked with empty belligerence, wafting a breath in Brunetti's direction that smelled of mint and alcohol, the sort of thing real drinkers make their breakfast of.

'If you refuse, Dottore,' Brunetti said in a lethally calm voice and reaching toward him with one hand, 'I will pull you back into that room and tell him you refuse to give him the injection that will cure him. And then I'll leave you alone with him.'

He watched Carraro as he spoke, saw that the doctor believed him, which was enough for his purposes. Carraro's arms fell to his side, though he muttered something under his breath, something that Brunetti pretended not to hear.

He held the door for Carraro and went back into the room. The man sat now on the side of the examining table, long legs dangling toward the floor, buttoning his shirt over his barrel-shaped chest.

Silently, Carraro went to a glass-doored cabinet at the far side of the room, opened it, and pulled out a syringe. He stooped down and searched noisily through the boxes of medicine stored there until he found the box he wanted. He took a small, rubber-capped glass vial from it and went back to his desk. Carefully, he pulled on a new pair of rubber gloves, opened the plastic package and took out the syringe, and stuck its point through the rubber seal on the top of the small bottle. He sucked all of the liquid up into the needle, and turned back to the man on the table, who sat, his shirt now tucked into his trousers, one sleeve rolled up almost to his shoulder.

As Brunetti watched, he held his arm out toward the doctor, turned his face away, and squeezed his eyes closed much in the way children do when they receive inoculations. With unnecessary force, Carraro jabbed the needle into the man's muscle and plunged the liquid into his arm. He yanked the needle out, pushed the man's arm roughly upright so the pressure would stop the bleeding, and went back to the desk.

'Thank you, Dottore,' the man said. 'Is that the cure?'

Carraro refused to speak, so Brunetti said, 'Yes, that's it. You don't have anything to worry about now.'

'It didn't even hurt. Much,' the man said and looked toward Brunetti. 'Do we have to go now?'

Brunetti nodded. The man lowered his arm and looked down at the place where Carraro had stuck the needle. Blood welled up from it.

'I think your patient needs a bandage, Dottore,' Brunetti said, though he knew Carraro would do nothing. The doctor pulled the gloves from his hands and tossed them toward a table, not at all troubled to see them land on the floor far short of it. Brunetti stepped over to the cabinet and looked at the boxes on the top shelf. One of them held standard-sized plasters. He took one and went back to the man. He unwrapped the sterile paper covering and was about to put the plaster on the bleeding spot when the man raised his other hand and made a gesture telling Brunetti to stop.

'I might not be cured yet, Signore, so you better let me do that.' He took the plaster and, left hand clumsy, placed it over the wound, then smoothed the sticky sides to his skin. He rolled down his sleeve, got to his feet, and leaned down to get his sweater.

When they got to the door of the examining room, the man stopped and looked down at Brunetti from his greater height. 'It would be terrible if I got it, you see,' he said, 'terrible for the family.' He nodded in silent affirmation of his own truth and stepped back to allow Brunetti to go through the door first. Behind them, Carraro slammed the door of the medicine cabinet shut, but government issue furniture is durable, and the glass did not break.

In the main corridor stood the two uniformed officers Brunetti had ordered to be sent to the hospital, and at the dock waited the police launch, the ever-taciturn Montisi at the tiller. They emerged from the side entrance and walked the few metres to the tethered boat, the man keeping his head lowered and his shoulders hunched, a posture he had adopted from the instant he saw the uniforms.

His walk was heavy and rough, absolutely lacking the fluid motion of a normal pace, as though there were static on the line between his brain and his feet. When they stepped on to the boat, one of the officers on either side, the man turned to Brunetti and asked, 'Can I sit downstairs, Signore?'

Brunetti pointed to the four steps that led downwards and the man went and sat on one of the long padded seats that lined both sides of the cabin. He folded his hands between his knees and bent his head over them, staring at the floor.

When they pulled into the dock in front of the Questura, the officers jumped out and tied the boat to the dock, and Brunetti went to the stairs and called, 'We're there now.'

The man looked up and got to his feet.

On the trip back, Brunetti had considered taking the man to his office to question him, but he had decided against it, thinking that one of the windowless, ugly questioning rooms, with their scuffed walls and bright lighting, would be better suited to what he had to do.

With officers leading the way, they went to the first floor and down the corridor, stopping outside the third door on the right. Brunetti opened it and held it for the man, who walked silently inside and stopped, looking back at Brunetti, who indicated one of the chairs that stood around a scarred table.

The man sat down. Brunetti closed the door and came to sit on the opposite side of the table.

'My name is Guido Brunetti. I'm a

commissario of police,' he began, 'and there is a microphone in this room that is recording everything we say.' He gave the date and the time and then turned to the man.

'I've brought you here to ask questions about three deaths: the death of a young man called Franco Rossi, the death of another young man called Gino Zecchino, and the death of a young woman whose name we don't yet know. Two of them died in or near a building near Angelo Raffaele, and one died after a fall from the same building.' He stopped here, then continued, 'Before we go any further, I must ask you your name and ask you to give me some identification.' When the man did not respond, Brunetti said, 'Would you tell me your name, Signore?'

He looked up and asked with infinite sadness, 'Do I have to?'

Brunetti said with resignation, 'I'm afraid so.'

The man lowered his head and looked down at the table. 'She's going to be so angry,' he whispered. He looked up at Brunetti and in the same soft voice said, 'Giovanni Dolfin.'

24

Brunetti searched for some sort of familial resemblance between this awkward giant and the thin, hunched woman he had seen in dal Carlo's office. Seeing none, he did not dare to ask how they were related, knowing it was better to let the man talk on, while he himself played the role of one who already knew everything that could be said and was there to do no more than ask questions about minor points and details of chronology.

Silence spread. Brunetti let it do so until the room was filled with it, the only sound Dolfin's laboured breathing.

He finally turned toward Brunetti and gave him a pained look. 'I'm a count, you see. We're the last ones; there's no one after us because

Loredana, well, she never married, and . . .'
Again, he looked down at the surface of the
table, but it still refused to tell him how to
explain all of this. He sighed and started again,
'I won't marry. I'm not interested in all of, all of
that,' he said with a vague motion of his hand, as
though pushing 'all of that' away.

'So we're the last, and that makes it important
that nothing happens to the family name or to
our honour.' Keeping his eyes on Brunetti's, he
asked, 'Do you understand?'

'Of course,' Brunetti said. He had no idea of
what 'honour' meant, especially to a member of
a family that had carried a name for more than
eight hundred years. 'We have to live with
honour,' was all he could think of to say.

Dolfin nodded repeatedly. 'That's what
Loredana tells me. She's always told me that.
She says it doesn't matter that we're not rich, not
at all. We still have the name.' He spoke with the
emphasis people often give to the repetition of
phrases or ideas they don't really understand,
conviction taking the place of reason. Some sort
of mechanism seemed to have been triggered in
Dolfin's mind, for he lowered his head again
and started to recite the history of his famous
ancestor, Doge Giovanni Dolfin. Brunetti
listened, strangely comforted by the sound,
carried back by it to a period of time in his
childhood when the women of the
neighbourhood had come to their house to recite
the rosary together and he found himself caught
up in the murmured repetition of the same

310

prayers. He let himself be carried back to those other whisperings, and he stayed there until he heard Dolfin say, '. . . of the Plague in 1361'.

Dolfin looked up then, and Brunetti nodded his approval. 'It's important, a name like that,' he agreed, thinking that this would be the way to lead him on. 'A person would have to be very careful to protect it.'

'That's what Loredana told me, just the very same thing.' Dolfin gave Brunetti a look filled with dawning respect: here was another man who could understand the obligations under which the two of them lived. 'She told me, especially this time, that we had to do anything we could to maintain and protect it.' His tongue stumbled over the last words.

'Of course,' Brunetti prompted, ' "especially this time".'

Dolfin went on: 'She said that man at the office had always been jealous of her because of her position.' When he saw Brunetti's confusion, he explained, 'In society.'

Brunetti nodded.

'She never understood why he hated her so much. But then he did something with papers. She tried to explain it to me, but I didn't understand. But he made up false papers that said Loredana was doing bad things in the office, taking money to do things.' He put his palms flat on the desk and pushed himself half out of the chair. Voice raised to an alarming volume, he said, 'Dolfins do not do things for money. Money means nothing to the Dolfins.'

Brunetti raised a calming hand, and Dolfin lowered himself back into his chair. 'We do not do things for money,' he said forcefully. 'The whole city knows that. Not for money.'

He continued: 'She said everyone would believe the papers and there would be a scandal. The name would be ruined. She told me . . .' he began and then corrected himself, 'No, I knew that myself; no one had to tell me that. No one can lie about the Dolfins and not be punished.'

'I see,' Brunetti agreed. 'Does that mean you'd take him to the police?'

Dolfin flicked a hand to one side, with it flicking aside the idea of the police. 'No, it was our honour, and so we had the right to take our own justice.'

'I see.'

'I knew who he was. I'd been there sometimes, to help Loredana when she did the shopping in the morning and had things to carry home. I'd go and help her.' He said this last with unconscious pride, the man of the family announcing his prowess.

'She knew where he was going that day, and she told me that I should follow him there and try to talk to him. But when I did, he pretended not to understand what I was saying and said it had nothing to do with Loredana. He said it was that other man. She warned me that he'd lie and try to make me believe it was someone else in the office, but I was ready for him. I knew he was really out to get Loredana because he was jealous of her.' He put on his face the expression he'd seen people use when they said things he was later told had been clever, and Brunetti again had the impression he'd been taught to recite this lesson, as well.

'And?'

'He called me a liar and then he tried to push past me. He told me to get out of the way. We were in that building.' His eyes grew wide with what Brunetti thought was the memory of what had happened but which turned out to be the scandal of what he was about to say. 'And he used *tu* when he talked to me. He knew I was a count, and he still called me *tu*.' Dolfin glanced over at Brunetti, as if to ask if he had ever heard of such a thing.

Brunetti, who never had, shook his head as if in silent astonishment.

When Dolfin seemed disposed to say nothing more, Brunetti asked, his real curiosity audible in the question, 'What did you do?'

'I told him he was lying to me and wanted to hurt Loredana because he was jealous of her. He pushed me again. No one's ever done that to me.' From the way he spoke, Brunetti was convinced Dolfin thought the physical respect people must have shown him was a response to his title rather than to his size. 'When he pushed me, I stepped back and my foot hit a pipe that was there, on the floor. It twisted and I fell down. When I got up, the pipe was in my hand. I wanted to hit him, but a Dolfin would never hit a man from behind, so I called him, and he turned around. He raised his hand then, to hit me.' Dolfin stopped talking here, but his hands clenched and unclenched in his lap as though they'd suddenly taken on an existence independent of his own.

When he looked again at Brunetti, time had clearly passed in his memory, for he said, 'He tried to get up after that. We'd been by the window and the shutter was open. He'd opened it when he came in. He crawled over to it and pulled himself up. I wasn't angry any more,' he said, his voice dispassionate and calm. 'Our honour was saved. So I went over to see if I could help him. But he was afraid of me, and when I came toward him, he stepped backwards and he hit his legs on the sill and he fell backwards. I reached out and tried to grab him, really I did,' he said, repeating the gesture as he described it, his long, flat fingers closing repeatedly, hopelessly, on the empty air, 'but he was falling and falling and I couldn't hold him.' He pulled his hand back and covered his eyes with the other. 'I heard him hit the ground. It was a very loud noise. But then someone was at the door to the room and I became very afraid. I didn't know who it was. I ran down the steps.' He stopped.

'Where did you go?'

'I went home. It was after lunchtime, and Loredana always worries if I'm late.'

'Did you tell her?' Brunetti asked.

'Did I tell her what?'

'What had happened?'

'I didn't want to. But she could tell. She saw it

when I couldn't eat. So I had to tell her what happened.'

'And what did she say?'

'She said she was very proud of me,' he answered, his face radiant. 'She said I had defended our honour and what had happened was an accident. He pushed me. I swear by God that's the truth. He knocked me down.'

Giovanni cast a nervous look at the door and asked, 'Does she know I'm here?'

When he saw Brunetti shake his head in response, Dolfin put one immense hand to his mouth and tapped the side of his clenched fingers repeatedly against his lower lip. 'Oh, she's going to be so angry. She told me not to go to the hospital. She said it was a trap. And she was right. I should have listened to her. She's always right. She's always been right about everything.' He placed his hand gently on top of the place on his arm where he had received the injection but said nothing further. He ran his fingers lightly back and forth over the spot.

In the ensuing silence, Brunetti wondered how much truth there had been in what Loredana Dolfin had told her brother. Brunetti had no doubt now that Rossi had learned about the corruption in the Ufficio Catasto, but he doubted that it concerned the honour of the Dolfin family.

'And when you went back?' he asked. He was beginning to be concerned about the increasing restlessness of Dolfin's movements.

'That other one, the one who took drugs, he

was there when it happened. He followed me home and asked people who I was. They knew me because of my name.' Brunetti heard the pride with which he said that, and then the man went on. 'He came back to the apartment, and when I came out to go to work, he told me he'd seen everything. He said he was my friend and wanted to help me keep out of trouble. I believed him, and we went back there together and started to clean the room upstairs. He said he would help me do that, and I believed him. And when we were there, the policemen came, but he said something to them, and they went away. When they were gone, he told me that if I didn't give him money, he'd bring the policemen back and show them the room, and I'd be in a lot of trouble, and everyone would know what I did.' Dolfin stopped speaking here as he considered what the consequences of this would have been.

'And?'

'I told him I didn't have any money, that I always gave it to Loredana. She knew what to do with it.'

Dolfin pushed himself up to a half-standing position and turned his head from side to side, as if listening for some sound to emerge from the back of his neck.

'And?' Brunetti repeated in that same bland voice.

'I told Loredana, of course. And then we went back.'

'We?' Brunetti asked instantly and

immediately regretted both the question and the impulse that made him ask it.

Until Brunetti spoke, Dolfin had continued turning his head from side to side. Brunetti's question, or his tone, however, stopped him. As Brunetti watched, Dolfin's trust in him evaporated, and he saw the other man adjust to finding himself in the camp of the enemy.

After at least a minute had passed, Brunetti asked, 'Signor Conte?'

Dolfin shook his head firmly.

'Signor Conte, you said that you went back to the building with someone else. Will you tell me who that person was?'

Dolfin propped his elbows on the table and, lowering his head, covered his ears with the palms of his hands. As Brunetti began to speak to him again, Dolfin shook his head violently from side to side. Angry with himself for having pushed Dolfin into a place from which there was no retrieving him, Brunetti got to his feet and, knowing he had no choice, went to phone Conte Dolfin's sister.

25

She answered with the name, 'Cà Dolfin', nothing else, and Brunetti was so surprised by the sound, like a trumpet voluntary containing nothing but discordant notes, that it took him a moment to identify himself and explain the purpose of his call. If she was at all disturbed to hear what he had to say, she disguised it well and said only that she would call her lawyer and be at the Questura in a short time. She asked no questions and demonstrated no curiosity whatsoever at the announcement that her brother was being questioned in connection with murder. It could have been an ordinary business call, some confusion about a line on a blueprint, for all the response she made. Not being a descendant, at least as far as he knew, of a Doge,

Brunetti had no idea how such people dealt with murder in the family.

Brunetti never wasted an instant considering the possibility that Signorina Dolfin had had anything to do with something so vulgar as the enormous bribery system Rossi must have discovered washing in and out of the Ufficio Catasto: 'Dolfins do not do things for money.' Brunetti believed this absolutely. It had been dal Carlo, with his studied uncertainty about whether someone in the Ufficio Catasto would be able to take a bribe, who had set up the system of corruption Rossi had discovered.

What had poor, stupid, fatally honest Rossi done – confronted dal Carlo with his evidence, threatened to denounce him or report him to the police? And had he done it with the door left open to the office of that Cerberus in a twinset, both her hairstyle and her hopeless longing dating back twenty years? And Cappelli? Had his phone calls with Rossi hastened his own death?

He had no doubt that Loredana Dolfin had already coached her brother in what he was to say should he be questioned: after all, she had warned him against going to the hospital. She would not have called it a 'trap' unless she had known how he had got that telltale bite on his forearm. And he, poor creature, had been so driven by his fear of infection that he had ignored her warning and had fallen into Brunetti's trap.

Dolfin had stopped talking just at the time

when he began to use the plural. Brunetti was sure of the identity of the second part of that fatal 'we', but he knew that, once Loredana's lawyer got to speak to Giovanni, all chance of filling in that blank would disappear.

Less than an hour later, his phone rang, and he was told that Signorina Dolfin and Avvocato Contarini had arrived. He asked that they be shown up to his office.

She came first, led by one of the uniformed officers who stood guard at the front door of the Questura. Behind her trailed Contarini, overweight and always smiling, a man ever able to find the right loophole to ensure that his clients benefited from every technicality of the law.

Brunetti did not offer to shake hands with either of them but turned and led them back into the office. He retreated behind his desk.

Brunetti looked across at Signorina Dolfin, who sat, feet pressed together, back straight as an arrow but not touching the back of her chair, hands neatly folded on top of her purse. She returned his look but remained silent. She looked no different than when he had seen her in her office: efficient, ageing, interested in what was going on but not fully involved in whatever it might be.

'And what is it you think you've discovered about my client?' Contarini asked, smiling amiably.

'In a recorded session made here in the Questura this afternoon, he has admitted killing

Francesco Rossi, an employee of the Ufficio Catasto where,' Brunetti said with a bow of his head in her direction, 'Signorina Dolfin works as a secretary.'

Contarini seemed uninterested. 'Anything else?' he asked.

'He also said that he later went back to the same place in the company of a man called Gino Zecchino, and together they destroyed the evidence of his crime. Further, he said that Zecchino subsequently attempted to blackmail him.' So far nothing Brunetti said seemed to be of much interest to either of the two people across from him. 'Zecchino was later found murdered in that same building, as was a young woman who still remains unidentified.'

When he judged that Brunetti had finished, Contarini pulled his briefcase up on to his lap and opened it. He sorted through papers and Brunetti felt the hairs on his arms rise when he realized how similar his fussy actions were to those of Rossi. With a little snort of pleasure, Contarini found the paper he was looking for and pulled it out. He extended it across the desk toward Brunetti, 'As you can see, Commissario,' he said, pointing to the seal at the top of the paper but not letting go of it, 'this is a certificate from the Ministry of Health, dated more than ten years ago.' He pulled his chair closer to the desk. When he was sure that Brunetti's attention was directed at the paper, he continued, 'which declares that Giovanni Dolfin is . . .' and paused, gracing Brunetti with yet another smile, a shark preparing to get down to business. Though it was upside down, he began to read the text out slowly to Brunetti:' "a person with special needs who is to receive special preference in obtaining employment and is never to be discriminated against because of any inability to perform tasks beyond his powers." '

He moved a finger down the paper until it pointed to the last paragraph, which he read out, as well. " 'The person above named, Giovanni Dolfin, is declared not to be in complete possession of his intellectual faculties and hence is not to be subjected to the full rigour of the law." '

Contarini let go of the paper and watched it flutter quietly to the surface of Brunetti's desk. Smiling still, he said, 'That's a copy. For your files. I assume you're familiar with such documents, Commissario?'

Brunetti's family were passionate Monopoly players, and here it was to the life: a Get Out of Gaol Free card.

Contarini closed his briefcase and got to his feet. 'I'd like to see my client, if that's possible.'

'Of course,' Brunetti said, reaching for his phone.

The three of them sat in silence until Pucetti knocked at the door.

'Officer Pucetti,' Brunetti said, touched to see that the young man was out of breath, having run up the stairs in answer to Brunetti's summons, 'please take Avvocato Contarini down to room seven to see his client.'

Pucetti snapped a salute. Contarini got to his feet and looked enquiringly at Signorina Dolfin, but she shook her head and remained where she was. Contarini said polite things and left, smiling all the way.

When he was gone, Brunetti, who had stood up at Contarini's departure, sat down again and looked across at Signorina Dolfin. He said nothing.

Minutes passed until finally she said, in an entirely ordinary voice, 'There's nothing you can do to him, you know. He's protected by the state.'

Brunetti was determined to remain silent and curious to see how far this would drive her. He did nothing at all, didn't move objects around on his desk or put his hands together: he simply sat, looking across at her with a neutral expression.

A few more minutes passed, and then she asked, 'What are you going to do?'

'You've just told me, Signorina,' he conceded.

Like two sepulchral statues they sat, until at last she said, 'That's not what I mean.' She glanced away and out the window of his office, then back at Brunetti, 'Not to my brother. I want to know what you're going to do to him.' For the first time, he saw emotion on her face.

Brunetti had no interest in playing with her, so he did not feign misunderstanding. 'You mean dal Carlo?' he asked, not bothering with a title.

She nodded.

Brunetti weighed it all, and not a little part of it was the realization of what might happen to his home if the Ufficio Catasto were forced into honesty. 'I'm going to feed him to the wolves,' Brunetti said, glad to say it.

Her eyes shot wide in astonishment. 'What do you mean?'

'I'm going to give him to the Guardia di Finanza. They'll be delighted to get records of his bank accounts, the apartments he owns, the accounts where his wife . . .' he said that word with special relish, 'has money invested. And once they begin to ask around and offer immunity to anyone who has given him a bribe, they will let loose an avalanche, and he will be buried under it.'

'He'll lose his job,' she said.

'He'll lose everything,' Brunetti corrected her and forced himself to give a joyless little smile.

Stunned at the sight of his malice, she sat with mouth agape.

'Do you want more?' he asked, driven beyond himself by the realization that, no matter what happened to dal Carlo, he could never do anything to her or to her brother. The Volpatos would remain like vultures in Campo San Luca, and all chance of finding Marco's killer was lost by the printed lies that had removed Patta's son from danger.

Knowing she had no responsibility for the last but still wild with the desire that she be made to pay, he continued, 'The newspapers will put it all together: Rossi's death, a suspect with bite marks made by the murdered girl ruled out because he's been declared mentally incompetent by the court, and the possible involvement of dal Carlo's secretary, an older woman, *una zitella*,' he said, surprising himself with the force of the contempt he put into the word 'spinster'. '*Una zitella nobile*' – he all but spat that last word – 'who was pathetically besotted with her boss – a younger, married, man,' he thundered down on the shaming adjectives – 'and who just happens to have a brother who has been declared mentally incompetent by the courts and who hence might be the person suspected of killing Rossi.' He paused and watched as she shrank away from him in real horror. 'And they will assume that dal Carlo was neck-deep in these murders, and he will never be free of that suspicion. And you,' he said, pointing across the desk at her, 'you will have done that to him. It will be your last gift to Ingeniere dal Carlo.'

'You can't do that,' she said, voice rising up beyond her control.

'I'm not going to do a thing, Signorina,' he said, appalled at the pleasure he took in saying all of this. 'The papers will say it, or suggest it, but no matter where the words come from, you can be sure that the people who read it will put it all together and believe it. And the part they will like best is the spectacle of the ageing *zitella nobile* with her pathetic obsession with a younger man.' He leaned across the desk and all but shouted at her: 'And they will ask for more.'

She shook her head, mouth agape: if he had slapped her, she would have borne it better. 'But you can't. I'm a Dolfin.'

Brunetti was so stunned that all he could do was laugh. He put his head back against the top of his chair and allowed himself the sudden release of mad laughter. 'I know, I know,' he said, voice difficult to control as new waves of wild mirth swept through him. 'You're a Dolfin, and the Dolfins never do anything for money.'

She stood, her face so red and tormented it sobered him instantly. Clutching her purse in fingers that creaked with the strain, she said, 'I did it for love.'

'Then God help you,' Brunetti said and reached for the phone.